WENDY
after Peter

A Maiden Journey
by Sarah Durham Wilson
2014.

For Leanne and Danny; and Jeet.

1.

Wendy stepped off the ferry and laid down 15,000 cash for a Jeep Wrangler.

It was the end of summer season on the little island off the coast of Maine, and the Brazilian man at the car rental place couldn't believe his good luck. She pressed the clutch of the little green Wrangler into first gear.

Even though she hadn't driven a standard since her father taught her in her fifteenth summer on a hill behind the high school, she remembered. There was peace for a moment remembering who she was before she fucked everything up.

Then she made her way up island towards the rental home her former publicist had booked for her for the winter. Her hangover was raging and she was sweating Sauvignon Blanc through her pores and possibly crying it from her eyes, but she hid that behind dark glasses.

She hadn't taken those glasses off since he left her; they shielded her from the light, and from life itself.

She felt, how she had felt since she was 16, that if someone looked at her wrong, she might shatter into a thousand pieces. And while she couldn't remember who she was or what she was good at anymore, she knew she was good at that, protecting herself from life. Not participating in her very existence, but numbing herself to it.

She had been doing it for fifteen years, since her mother's funeral when someone handed her her first Xanax when she had started to do that convulsing, heaving "ugly cry." She remembered the first moment the tiny white specks of sedation swam into her bloodstream, the blanket of calm, like she had found a way out of the pain.

She remembered asking herself, dressed in all black, her mother's silk orange and white scarf tied around her neck, *"You mean feeling is actually an option?"* And thinking to herself, *"Well then, why doesn't everyone just opt out?"*

And from that moment, she did. She leaned way back out of her own life. And now life was demanding she lean back in, because there was no one left to do it for her. And there had always, until now, been someone to do it for her.

He was gone. Peter was no longer hers. And now, terrifyingly, all she had was herself. She wasn't someone she liked very much, was all she knew. Recently she'd taken to slapping her own face in the mirror, which at first startled her, of course. But then it became another shameful habit.

She did it partly out of self-loathing, and partly because it always seemed so glamorous to her when a tearful woman slapped a man and walked away; there was just so much, passion, and she wanted to feel passion, and she wanted, for once, to be the one who walked out. As much as she tried, she couldn't walk away from herself.

Sometimes she slapped herself just for the sting of being alive, to wake herself back up. Once when she was about eight years old, she sat on the big yellow bus to school next to a normal, shiny blond-haired little girl and she was running her tongue over a sore inside her mouth. She felt tingly in her flesh when the pain flared up.

She said to the blond girl, *"Do you ever play with something even though it hurts?"* And the girl looked at her with big horrified brown eyes and said, without hesitation, *"No."*

And that was Wendy's first clue she was different. She and Peter had played with each other's hearts until they broke — which she never really thought would actually happen — she had thought that was how you played Love's Game, breaking each other's hearts, putting them back together, then doing it all over again. But Peter had finally called an end to it, it turns out it wasn't a game to him, he had said something like, "I think for a long time I thought it was ok that we were like *Who's Afraid of Virginia Woolf*, that we'd drink and fight and make up in the morning and then do it all over again at night, but now I realize life doesn't have to be like that and I want out." And he got out and now here she was, alone on this island where she had vacationed as a child, but hadn't been back to in five years, since their wedding.

She thought back to that night in 2009; she wore a white silk slip dress, combat boots and red lips and purple hair, and a serious red wine and pills buzz. OK, buzz is polite. She was, as usual, wrecked.

But she had just signed the book contract, and Peter's second record had a glowing review in *Rolling Stone*, and all looked bright.

But there had never been any intimacy for them, everything was on a stage. Fuck, she didn't even know what intimacy was, and she was pretty sure she still didn't.

Their wedding had been a voyeuristic event; his whole hometown came and Peter had managed to turn it into a concert after the vows, with people crying his name like a God while she stood in her usual post, drinking heavily in the shadows of backstage.

While she had made some good friends in his hometown, she still always felt like the impostor who had stolen away their golden boy, and she felt eyed with suspicion and walking a tight rope till she fucked up, when she would fall into a waiting trap of hungry alligators like the ones in *Romancing the Stone*, one of the movies she watched on repeat to try to transport back to childhood.

And she did fuck up. And they did eat her alive.

And thanks to the booze and the show, the wedding almost didn't feel different from any other night on any tour, expect she had a conflict-free *love stone* on her fourth finger, and she was dressed in white, and he had just professed his love for her in front of hundreds, but he could scream it from the world's very rooftop and her heart still wouldn't hear it. She wouldn't believe him.

He used to say no one could fill the hole inside of her. Not ten thousand men. She had thought marriage would finally make her feel safe and claimed and loved, but it was true, apart from the vows they had just exchanged, which, really, were just words, everything else had felt the same. She was still terrified of losing him, and she was still standing in his shadow, and she was still slipping into substance oblivion to numb the fear of abandonment.

It's funny how people thought a ring on your finger meant security. *Nah*, thought Wendy, looking down at her bare hand. She knew better now.

She had grown so used to the feel of the heavy velvet of the curtains of backstage while Peter played, the feeling of leaning up against them like falling into a soft vertical couch. She could half pass out standing up and no one really noticed. Because no one was really looking at her.

If they couldn't find Peter, they would talk to her, but the conversation was about Peter and looking for Peter, how to find him. And that was the whole thing about being with someone famous — it was like secondhand smoke, it made you famous by proxy, and if everyone loved him and he loved you, well, that must make you sort of special, right?

That summed up their relationship — the light on him, her in the dark. Him front and center stage, her in the dark of backstage, so dark she could, and did, disappear.

She pulled into the dusty parking lot of the Old Al's general store she had worked in as a pudgy brace-faced teenager. She wondered where that wedding dress was, and if she could even fit a leg in it anymore.

She missed being able to throw on a slip, what others would consider for bedtime only, and go to dinner. She loved the shock value of her nipples raised through the thin material and the absence of an underwear line. She loved the lingering *HowDareShe* looks at her lingerie.

She hadn't realized what a full-blown attention addict she was. She had usually just risen an hour or so before it was time to party again. Getting wasted was her main motivation for getting up.

She had a glass of red wine in her hand five minutes after waking, and she lied to herself that it was glamorous, getting up as the sun was going down and drinking red wine in silk as you put your makeup on.

But it was unsustainable smeared-lipstick Courtney Love-ish glamor, and it lasted five fucked-up years. Courtney Love was partially to blame. She had worshiped her growing up. She had been obsessed with the whole grunge scene. Hole, Nirvana, Pearl Jam.

Eddie Vedder swinging from the rafters, and Angela Chase moaning about the meaning of life and kissing Jordan Catalano in the boiler room but being ignored by him in the hallways, and that's what love was to her — painful and dramatic and mostly unrequited, and plaid shirts and holey jeans and Doc Martens and teenage angst. Her parents had loved each other but split and thats how love was framed for her, dramatic and always about to end.

She cataloged every *Rolling Stone* and every *Spin* and every *Sassy* along the shelves of her childhood bedroom, and when other kids asked her why she didn't do her homework, she'd say, *"Because I'm going to become a rock journalist."* And she did and she was. Until she met Peter.

And now, ever since Peter had left her, she had only eaten frozen pizzas in the glow of bad *Lifetime* movies and drank wine like water. She had finally descended so deep into an underworld from which she had no hopes of returning. She was sure she had fallen too far to ever get back up.

It's like she had gone drunken spelunking into a cave and the rope had broken, and no one had known or cared that she was gone. There was no one on the other side waiting for her to rise. It was just her, at the bottom of the world, looking up at everyone carrying on with their lives on the surface. They had the handbook and the map to this life, she had never gotten it.

When Peter was leaving her so easily, like a sweater he had grown tired of, an old friend from her early days at *Rolling Stone* had said, *"I think, to be the kind of woman someone fights for, you have to be the kind of woman who fights for herself."*

And it was so true that it took the wind out of her, but she hadn't known how to do it. She had officially given up, let herself go. That was another thing Peter had said to her on his way out, "you don't even look like you anymore."

Her skin was gray and somehow, freakishly, both dry and broken out, at war with itself, and she was heavy in spirit, although she wasn't sure she had one — and she was dark and heavy as well in what was left of her mind and her bloated body. Her hair was ravaged from mistreatment of dye jobs and extensions, some days she felt like she had four dry strands left.

She wore sweats on most days, the same faded burgundy $19.99 set from Target, the ones that could make you feel homeless in your own home, and she was most certainly homeless, a beggar at the gates of her own life.

She felt — no, she knew — terrifyingly so, that she was waiting to die, like maybe that was all that was left to do. It was as if she had burned every bridge and there was nowhere left in the world to go.

She had this gnawing feeling that the last place to go was inside of her self, and that thought terrified her. She had tried to just go back, to go back home again, even though it's in every folk song that you can't.

But for three horrible months, she did try, to go back into her Before Peter Life, she found a shitty apartment under a bridge in Brooklyn, and thought maybe she could just start all over again. But she could only compare it to the roomy light-filled East Village two bedroom they'd shared, and at night, as she blacked out, she'd imagine she was banging on a brick wall until her fists bled, trying to find a door back to their old life. And the other nights, when she wasn't doing that, she was sleeping with some random guy she'd met at a bar, and in the morning, he was never Peter. And then she went back to *Rolling Stone* to interview for an Editor position, and the new guy interviewing her looked aghast, like he saw a ghost, like what a ghost looked like if it had been spit out of the wrong end of the rock n roll machine. And Wendy was on Klonopin but thought maybe she was pulling it off, and maybe if she named dropped a little bit more he'd hire her, but she started to realize she was losing him when the starstruck look in his eyes that he was sitting with Peter Jackson's ex wife faded, and then she heard herself pleading for a job, like in *Say Anything* when Ione Skye goes into the IRS to beg them to tell her what's happening to her father, and she says something like, "I thought if I came in here today to talk to you I'd feel better, but I look like shit and I feel like shit, will someone please talk to me?" But no one did.

2.

It had been in the middle of things, about two years in, when Wendy and Peter had started to fall apart.

It was after the glory glow of their new love had begun to fade, when their swept off their feet love story was no longer enough to sustain them.

Then the body of their love begun to decay. And the house their love built began to feel fragile and hollow and haunted, like it could blow away with one strong gust of wind. She began to overprotect it, didn't let it breathe, she was jealous and over bearing with Peter, and it was like the love itself stopped living.

And a pallor of doom set upon them, a death-like wind always at their backs, one they could only pretend not to feel for so long. Once such a warm passionate house, a chill took over, it was suddenly always sweater weather.

When the shiny surfaces of their projected images were worn down and seen through by time, they were faced with each other's internal dark seas, and they were in over their heads. It wasn't that she ever stopped loving him, she loved him so much, sometimes he said too much.

He was often asking for breath under the heavy blanket of her love. She focused everything on him, abandoned herself, and then, well, then her resentment seeped in and it poisoned their well, she grew needy and starved for validation and attention.

Only in hindsight had she started to realize that love was like a living thing itself, that maybe it needed to be watered and fed and given space and room to grow. That love itself needed love.

She had always thought it was curious the way the words live and love were separated by just one letter, and she was beginning to think there was no life without love, that nothing could live without love, that everything died without love.

Right after her parents divorced, her mother, alone with a broken heart, was diagnosed with lung cancer. She had stayed in bed after the heartbreak, and then came the cancer, and so Wendy had associated heartbreak with death. In her mind, her mother had died without love.

They had found the cancer in her lungs, that place in the body that stores the stories of grief; the death of our dreams, the agony of things unsaid and love *un-lived*, the pain of the people we can no longer touch. Wendy was so obsessed with the idea that she would die without Peter, she didn't realize she kind of already had.

Once on their apartment's balcony overlooking 2nd Avenue, on a beautiful summer night, with the yellow taxis streaming below, a flesh-tickling breeze on their skin and cool drinks in their hands, but death in her belly and throat, he had asked her, *"Where is the girl I fell in love with?"* And right then he vocalized every fear she had had, that she had lost herself, and in turn lost him, and she had crumbled and said, *"I don't know,"* and then hot tears, like lava, burned down her face, and she had ruined another night.

She had really really wanted to find herself, to retrieve herself, she really wanted to get to the bottom of herself, before she ruined everything for good, but she just couldn't break her own muddled surface. She didn't have the tools. So she watched them fall apart in slow motion.

She was completely disempowered and repressed, and everything she did made it worse. It felt like being in the quicksand like in *Princess Bride*, but as if Prince Wesley had abandoned her in the Fire Swamp's mud to save himself.

And she didn't know you aren't supposed to thrash around in quicksand. You're actually supposed to breathe and stay calm, and lay back like you're floating, stay open to something bigger than you to get you through. Some would call it surrendering.

But instead, when she was stuck and sinking in her own quicksand, Wendy thrashed around like a drowning woman, which is exactly what she was.

Peter had also hoped one day she would just wake up *fixed*, just *find herself*, and start writing again, and finally finish the book and turn her own light back on, instead of being a ravenous moth to his flame.

Having a depressed wife, as a touring rock star, was a major drag, a super buzz kill. Every time she called or texted from the road, she acted out for attention until one day he finally likened her to a rescue dog he should never have adopted, a mistake he wanted to send back to the pound.

She remembered that conversation viscerally; she was on the vintage green couch in their apartment, in between wine glass two and three, and he was on the bus, in between St. Paul and Minneapolis, and the guys were roughhousing in the background of their conversation. The music was blasting, and the beers were cracking open; it was the soundtrack of that never-ending party at which she wished she could always be.

"So I'm the dog?" she had asked.

"Well, you know," he had said, and she could feel his shrug, his apathy, like he was there, but not. She often had asked him, *"Where are you?"* when he was lying right there. And he would say, *"Here,"* like she was crazy, but with that far-off look in his eyes, making her only feel lonelier, because his body was there but his being was somewhere else. It was as if she could touch him, but not *touch* him, and she had no idea how to express that. And the more she pushed at him, the more he pulled away. That was the physics of love.

"I had the best intentions," he said. *"You were lost and adorable and I wanted to take care of you. But I'm just not up for the job. It's too much."*

She couldn't remember a time she felt less sexy or less empowered than her husband likening her to a rescue dog.

Every time he went on tour, her doctor was always upping her Klonopin dosage, which made her feel even more like a rescue with abandonment issues who needed to be treated for separation anxiety.

And because when he left the house for tour, she stopped leaving it too, she was even more like a dog who was too fearful to leave its crate. So yes, as usual his metaphor landed, but this one hurt like a bitch.

She had tried to suppress the truth of their doom, but it kept rising in her like the sun, that nagging way truth has of always refusing to be suppressed. Of eating you alive from the inside, like a wolf in a cage until you let it out. He finally ended it, like a mercy kill, when you kill something that is suffering and has no chances of survival. She would never forget that call from the road. *"I'm not coming home and I never loved you."*

Wendy brought the Wrangler to a four-cornered stop sign and looked around. The island was more beautiful than she remembered, with winding sand roads and green ragged cliffs that fell into the blue sea like the landscape of Scotland or Ireland. It was magical.

She had been on so many tours with the band, but they had never really left the hotel rooms or backstage areas. And now she wondered, *had she been to Scotland?* Maybe, but she had been that sleepy fuzzy pill drunk, her preferred lens on life, so tours were also a blur.

She loved the Neverland of tour, she never had to see herself clearly, she never had to take responsibility, she never had to face reality, she never had to be alone with herself, she never had to clean up, she never had to pay for anything, she never had to even feel her hangover, on tour she'd drink again as soon as she woke up, and whatever she did the night before vanished behind them on the horizon as they moved on to the next town. She never -had-to-land in one place long enough to face her consequences. She loved Ken the Tour Manager, he scheduled every meal, every hotel, every place they needed to show up. On tour all Wendy had to do was look hot and drink.

The bus would let the band out into the backdoor of venues, and Ken would lead Wendy and the boys like moles down dark tunnels to where the booze sat ready for them on catered tables. The boys in the band had become her brothers. Like Wendy, they were a bit lost, and eagerly followed their captivating fearless leader, Peter. She missed them too now. When she and Peter broke up, it was like everyone else had broken up with her as well. When their love ended she lost the whole world they shared together, and everyone in it. She had been cast out like an exile. But once he had loved her so much, before she lost her light.

Peter had written many songs about the loss of her light. Songs about her *never coming true*. They had hurt so stabbingly bad that she couldn't help wondering if they were the truth. That she had not only failed him, she had failed in life. She wished lives were like cars, that she could just trade this one in for a new one.

She had ruined this one past the point of repair. And she would feel the pain of that for a second, but then she would swallow a pill and open the second bottle of wine and think, the next day, tomorrow, she would get better, and she would start writing again. That she would get off the medicine that was killing her and she would finish something.

But that *someday* just kept slinking away. Peter had wanted her to get her act together in the here and now. She felt that if she had been something, and meant something to him, once, and didn't that count for something? But the past lost its currency with him.

She hadn't always been so small in soul. She had been pregnant with potential, bursting with promise. But all that pressure on her potential broke her into pieces. Which is how she never ended up writing that book.

There had been so much blinding promise about the book deal, that it landed her an agent and a publicist. She was, according to *Variety*, going to be the *Voice of a Generation*.

She would write her story, from an intern at *Rolling Stone* fresh out of her small southern high school to working her way up the New York magazine circuit, to the Kings of Leon hotel parties and car service on Bon Jovi's lap to marrying a rock star, and retiring at 26 to play housewife.

She used to live like she was always writing some story for the public, not actually living it for herself. She valued how it looked over how it felt. And she thought that started happening right after her mother's death, because that was the day she put that glass between herself and her life, and disengaged from it, and stopped being able to hear or feel herself, it was like her soul scrambled back up to heaven and she was an empty body wandering the earth looking to be saved.

She had thought living it was far too dangerous and painful, but now she realized it was the other way around. Not living your life is what will kill you.

On paper her life had been so cool. Great cocktail conversation, great fodder — once again, a great story. But as for a real life, for a real life it was a real fucking mess, so messy she lost herself in its fog.

Her agent had been kind about it for a while. *"I get it,"* she had said. *"There's too much smoke on the battlefield of your life. You need to wait until it clears to see."* Except that the smoke never did clear. And she never did write that book. And all that promise, well, all that promise disappeared in the smoke.

Wendy was looking at the directions the publicist had sent her for the winter rental, so she would get away from the *gogogo* distraction of the city into the peace of nature, where her therapist had begged her to rest until she felt better, and to avoid the tabloid glare.

Specifically her therapist had said, speaking from her chair with Wendy sprawled out across from her on the beige leather couch, *"The public just loves a downfall, and they'll gobble you up, looking like...,"* and then she snaked a finger through the air around Wendy's sweat-panted and dirty t-shirt clad form in pity, *"... this."*

When her mother had died in their small southern town, for weeks people brought by big deep glass dishes of frozen casseroles. Big deep creamy cheese and noodle dishes that bubbled in the stove and made the house smell like a real home and comforted her so deep Wendy soon walked around with a whole extra down layer on.

It was like in *Lars and the Real Girl*, when Lars is allowing his imaginary girlfriend to die so he might have a real relationship, and the women from the town come over with casseroles, and they say to him, *"We came over to sit. That's what people do when tragedy strikes, they come over to sit. "*

Wendy had never received so much attention as when her mother died. And she knew there was more than a little something there, about the way she had attracted tragedy since.

All that presence around her finally, after a childhood of sitting alone, now there were people sitting with her and feeding her those warm gooey casseroles that momentarily filled the hole in her soul.

She had all those feelings to eat, and the more she ate, the more she felt a layer of protection between herself and the new terrifying reality. But then her mother's sister, in town for the memorial, had pulled her aside into the dim hallway off the kitchen.

"I have a feeling that life has chosen to put a spotlight on you," she'd said. *"Your mother had the same thing. So you need to learn now that people are always going to talk about you. And it's best to not give them anything...,"* her eyes flickered up and down Wendy's body, *"extra... to talk about."*

And that was sort of what her therapist was saying, now, that people were already talking, don't give them even more to tear apart. Fall apart in private. Go into hiding. Like a big fat depressed bear for winter. See who she was in the spring.

3.

Wendy stepped onto the creaky wooden porch of the general store to gather the night's dinner of wine and cheese, which was every night's dinner of late. She called it *The Single Girl Special.*

The store was exactly how she remembered, with dusty warped wooden floors, heavy beneath rows of colorful boutique food marked up to spectacular tourist rates, racks of magnets and postcards of sandy beaches and sharks having cocktails next to stacks of mainland and local island newspapers shelved over bundles of firewood; the store's checkout counter sat somewhere beneath boxes of chocolate and toys.

It was still, as she remembered, a child's paradise, a tourist's haven, all very Willy-Wonka-meets-New-England nostalgia. But halfway to the wine rack, Wendy couldn't avoid, even on the island, the tabloids. She couldn't avoid, even on the island, her self. Her mess.

The news was still fresh, the magazines were still gossiping about the divorce, about Peter leaving her for the girl from his opening band.

This, this was the exact story Wendy had always worried about, which she had pestered him about with her dreadful insecurity, an unworthiness she had unconsciously expected everyone but herself to fix.

And now she wondered if she had willed this union of Peter and the girl; if, with her suspicion and dread, she had sent them into each other's arms with her gnawing belief that it would actually happen. Is it possible, she thought, your unyielding belief that something would happen could actually make it happen?

What she saw took the wind out of her, then she sighed, loud. The tears started to sting. She looked around about the store, but no one was watching her holding vigil over the ashes of her life.

She heard within her the Paul Simon lines from *Crazy Love*, *"Somebody could walk into this room and say your life is on fire. It's all over the evening news, all about the fire in your life on the evening news."*

And that's how she felt, exposed all over the news, but still it seemed that while her life was over, life just went on for everyone else.

There was an old man in black and red flannel thumbing through the newspapers. There was a middle-aged woman in tortoiseshell glasses and white cashmere, reaching for goat cheese. There was the hum from the speakers of a blues singer singing about drinking whiskey at dawn.

She turned back to the magazines, and tugged her sweatshirt around her body, then she pulled the hood further down over her face and adjusted her black sunglasses self-consciously, as if she was in the Witness Protection Program. She knew she shouldn't keep looking, but she couldn't help herself. She wasn't any good at that.

How had this happened to her? How had her heartbreak ended up on *In Touch* and *People*, at the general store she'd worked in as a dorky innocent kid?

Wendy remembered the moment they happened. Their moment.

She had always wanted to interview Peter Jackson. At the height of his career, her own was running up the ladders, and they had simply and inevitably, met and merged. Fused together.

He had made every music magazine cover with his Jim Morrison good looks and his torrential passion, he was full of such anger and pain and poetry that it seemed every hot-blooded woman in the world wanted him to take it out on her in bed, in sweaty shredded sheets.

Most men concealed their feelings. Not Peter. He screamed and cried them from the rafters, and you felt it — you felt them as your own, you felt it right where it mattered.

In your sex and your gut and your heart and your throat, as he released the things you'd always longed to say, he screamed your secrets and desires for you. Well, at least Wendy felt that way. Here was her very own Eddie Vedder, the man she'd longed for as a teenager in her lonely blue bedroom.

Peter did to her what Eddie had done to her then, which is to say, undid her.

Wendy could be walking in Times Square, rushing from a liquid lunch to an album-listening party, or from work to a dinner date with a publicist before a concert, and she would hear his music in her ears in the middle of thousands of people and feel totally naked, like every piece of clothing and everything she'd ever kept hidden was ripped from her, everything that ever stood between her and a big real true life just dropped off of her, and she was naked in body and in soul.

It was terrifying and thrilling and she was ravenous for it.

That was the gift of real artists, she thought, to be able to express their soul. She still had no idea how to express her own yet, or if she ever would, which was why being a music journalist, writing about others' art, was as close as she got to her own self expression.

It was a torturous feeling, not knowing how to express herself, feeling trapped in the wrong skin, on the outside looking in. But she was enormously attracted to those who could self-express, who knew how, in beautiful magnetic ways.

She was his the minute she first heard his soul spilled onto a record. People were always saying about love, *this person feels like home to me.* She finally got that with Peter. She finally got what all the love poetry and love songs in the world were about.

Before she met him in person, she would come back to her Lower East Side apartment from bad dates with men who made her feel nothing, who made her feel more alone and more dead by their company, whose jokes didn't land, and certainly hers didn't with them.

All too often they were musicians who were only dating her for publicity, for placement in one of the magazines she wrote for.

She was too dark and neurotic for most of them, not proper arm candy, and then she would come home, turn off the lights and turn Peter's albums on and lie in bed with his darkly beautiful thoughts filling the room.

And then she would pretend her own hands were his, the ones she'd watched throttle and finger his shiny black Gibson, and she'd explore her body the way he touched that guitar, and when she came she'd cry out his name.

Long before drugs and alcohol, music had been her portal out and into another plane, since she was ten years old and first heard Springsteen sing.

She had been lying in the way back of her parent's Volvo on the way to the island for vacation, looking up through the rear window at the stars shining in the black ink of night over the highway.

It was the song *The River*, the live version, where Springsteen tells a story about the tension with his father before the E Street Band launches into triumphant song, his deep voice moaning about Mary's body tan and wet down at the reservoir, and a shotgun wedding out of integrity, but not love.

That was the night music became her magic, she could escape into it, be carried away.

And then thirteen years later she had heard Peter's magic soul, and that was the beginning, and that was the end. She had not only met her match, he was *the* match that lit her aflame.

His fire was so bright, like he could burn your whole life up in one second, if you weren't careful, but maybe Wendy didn't feel like being careful. Maybe Wendy wanted to be set on fire.

And her bosses knew that, and they were always sending her to interview the bad boys. It was an easy recipe, for Wendy liked them and they liked Wendy, so some sort of transgression almost always happened that made for a salacious story to print.

Still, she could never have predicted how fast the rocket ride of them, their story, would take off.

Why had she liked bad boys so much? How come she hadn't outgrown them, like her friends from high school, who had all settled down with nice guys? There were those words, *settled* and *down*. Neither was very appealing to her.

Seven years ago she had walked into that East Village bar to interview the Peter Jackson Band, in tight black jeans and a silver sequined jacket, red lips and big hair, and Peter's eyes locked in on her like a jungle cat stalking its prey.

And while Wendy had felt his gaze in every cell, and her flesh rippled beneath her clothes, and her heart leapt from its cage like a bird at dawn after an endless night, she pretended not to notice him. She was very good at pretending, dangerously good, and it was a great trick with lead singers.

They got noticed enough. Not being noticed, even as a game, was at least somewhat of a challenge for them, and when you were a famous lead singer who got everything you wanted, you began to miss the challenge. Their job is to be stared at and wanted, they were stared at and wanted all night long.

If you at least wanted a chance with them, you had to let them think you didn't notice and you didn't care.

How many times had she been front row or backstage and felt a singer's eyes x-raying her, crawling all over her flesh like a sex spider, and she had just peered into her drink, or talked absently to a friend, meanwhile devouring the feeling of being devoured.

Pretending not to notice while being eye-fucked by a musician, that was some fine multitasking which she had mastered.

But that was then. God, but these days it seemed she could be run over by a truck and the driver would just keep going with a *"must have been nothing"* shrug.

Wendy still stood there, frozen in front of the tabloids, and while she was aware of the screen door of the general store creaking open and slamming closed, of people moving around her, she remained hovered in front of the stories of their decay, forgetting to breathe.

Her left hand clenched into a tight fist, her thumb felt for her wedding ring like a missing limb. But there was no ring on her finger anymore, just the ring in her ear of him screaming, *"I would rather be with anyone but you. I never loved you,"* in response to her question, *"What does she have that I don't?"*

"Everything," he had said. *"For one thing, Wendy, she's alive. She's actively creating a life for herself."*

She had said, *"But I gave my life up for you…"*

And he had said, *"I never ever ever asked you to do that."*

And that was true. He never had. She had thrown herself, like a sacrifice, on love's fire. But he had never asked her to do that.

"You know what it is about you, Wendy? Do you know what happened?"

Wendy had braced herself. *"It's that you didn't happen. You just never came true. You were going to be something. You were going to be someone. You promised you were going to write that book. And you just, you never came true."*

She reached out to the *People* magazine in front of her. Her hands shook as she picked it up. They had found a particularly dashing picture of Peter, a particularly pathetic picture of Wendy and a particularly sexy picture of Cassandra. Even that name was sexy. It was like Egyptian-Sex-Priestess sexy. Like her vagina unlocked ancient secrets. Like when you took her to bed a purple mist filled the air and hidden stone doors rumbled open and snakes rose from jewel-filled golden treasure chests.

Cassandra got to be new. Everything new was always shiny and exciting. Beginnings were thrilling. If only we could stay in the beginnings of things. Now she was the old movie he had seen a million times and he knew every scene and every line and couldn't bare to sit there and watch anymore. But

Cassandra was a new trailer. It was Cassandra who had the promise now. And Wendy had failed to meet her potential. Wendy had never come true.

She felt terribly old. She felt how she imagined one felt at 99 years old. Ready to go. Ready to pack it in and call it a life.

At thirty-three, she felt like the Crypt Keeper. At the end of the line, of her very rope.

The tabloids cried, *"Left For Lolita, Wendy Jackson gone into hiding. Drugs! Drinking! And... a Suicide Attempt?!"*

Suicide. Her breath quivered. It wasn't like she hadn't thought of that. She still kept a bottle of Klonopin buried in her tote bag, despite promising her therapist that she had none left. She kept it there like a fire extinguisher — *In Case of Emergency, Break Glass.* It would just take swallowing them all and drifting off to an eternal sleep. She would Marilyn Monroe it.

She wished she had never met him. Or, at the very least, not married him. Not given everything up for him. But when life itself picked up the pen and wrote furiously, there had been no way to stop it. And of course, she hadn't wanted to. They had been inevitable. Like death.

Sometimes she swore she could hear an invisible director's voice calling *Action*, when a moment in her life felt divinely scripted, deja-vu familiar. When something big was beginning, she could feel it. And she had felt it that night in the bar, that they had already been written.

She had sat down next to him, acting completely nonchalant while her heart sang and her mind kept playing scenes of their wedding. She she took off her jacket to reveal her tight black tank top and he had watched, as if in slow motion, his eyes sucking up every inch of her flesh.

And when her bare arm would brush his, they would pause there — skin to skin, just for for a second, but with enough electricity to light up the world.

They were peas in a pod, they said everything at the same time. So much so they eventually had to stop saying *Jinx*.

They made the same jokes. They liked jokes that were so bad they were good, and then they liked to beat a dead horse with the joke until the other cried through weary laughter *Okay, Stop*. And then they would slip it in one more time with a wink, just for the groan, and be done with it. They were childlike and mischievous and magnetic, and they loved a crowd.

She could feel him watching her out of the corner of his eye, she could feel him adjusting to the reality that he was falling in love.

She gave him the time to catch up to that truth, time she didn't need, for she felt as if she had been waiting for him since the moment she was born. His love, finally, made her feel real. *This is what makes people real,* she had thought — Love. For a moment there, it felt like together they had glimpsed heaven, like they had been given its very keys.

He had held her hand under the table after the first drink, and while she felt like she should be surprised, she wasn't. She had slowly felt her hand release in his, then relax, held, weightless, and let go. Held. She felt every bone and muscle settle, completely at ease in his strong muscled palm.

Home. Home. Home. She had a vision of herself taking her bags off like a weary traveler, when you get home after a long journey, and you put your heavy suitcases down one by one. *Home. Take your shoes off and rest. You're finally home.*

There could be no sweeter relief than finally, finally, coming home after all your seeking, and laying your tired head down.

Then the band had wanted to head to a second bar to play pool, so they migrated, with Wendy and Peter trailing behind the black-jeaned group of tussling boys, walking hand and hand on the sidewalk that glittered in the moonlight.

Wendy was thinking to herself that not only was it the best night of her life, it felt like her first. Their chemistry pulled their bodies together like a star-drawn contract, and he had grabbed her by the waist and pulled her into a dark alley to kiss her against a brick wall, kiss her so deep he mined her soul.

Wendy could still feel the bricks scratching her back where her shirt had been pushed up, and she was hoping the scratches would stay forever, scars from their first night out at the bars, and she felt his fingers pressing into the skin of her hips, down to the bone. She could still hear him whisper in her ear, *"I can't believe this is happening."*

And she had kissed the sweaty slope of his neck and had said, *"I can't but I can,"* and he had known exactly what she meant, like maybe he had felt her coming too, and she was one with that holy feeling of being *gotten*.

They were so similar then, both strange and dangerous, they were *strangerous*, they were wild and untamable with stars in their eyes. At least she had been, at first.

They were like lion cubs in love, reckless and roaring and rolling and playing, always pushing past the paradigms of what was possible, blind to life's rules and deaf to the heeds of those who told them to slow down, to be careful.

But it was like when Harry runs to Sally on New Year's Eve and says, *"When you realize you want to spend the rest of your life with somebody, you want the rest of your life to start as soon as possible."* They could find no reason to wait to drown in each other.

By midnight they were wrapped around each other in bed in his hotel room, planning their life together. They got down to the very marrow. They'd have two cats, a dog, three kids and a Subaru. She had always thought if she had a Subaru she would feel normal and stable.

She would leave her job, her career, go on tour with him, be his wife, the job suddenly felt like something she was just doing while waiting for him. Oh and yes, she would write that book.

And then without blinking an eye, or giving a thought to everything she had worked for to start out as a kid from a broken home in a small southern town to become the music editor of the biggest arts magazine in New York City, she said *Yes*. Because she had a habit of throwing things, of throwing herself, away.

She had walked in to her Editor's office on Broadway and she had given her two weeks. And she said No, she wasn't going to another magazine, she was going to Love, specifically with Peter Jackson, and he had seemed so very *unsurprised* and he had sighed and said, *"Good Luck Wendy, you're going to need it."*

The screen door of Al's store slammed again and Wendy put down the *People* gingerly and walked to the wine rack. With her hoodie on tight and wearing her sunglasses, she looked very Unabomber chic. Armed with two bottles of Cabernet and a block of Jarlsberg she walked up to the counter.

She felt so fragile and cellophane see-through, but the check-out girl barely looked at her, just banged away at the register keys and slid a pen across the counter for the credit card receipt. She had become the Invisible Woman. No one seemed to notice her. No one seemed to care.

The small part of her that once glittered like gold cried out in resistance for a second, but mostly Wendy, who now just hoped to retire from life at 33 with the pity money her husband had thrown at her in the divorce settlement, was relieved.

She could rest in peace, never have to try again, alone at the corner of the world.

Back in the Wrangler, she snaked down a road named South and turned right down three bumpy dirt roads until she came upon her little cabin on the cliff of the bright blue sea.

When she stepped out of the jeep and let the breeze whip her hair, she felt somewhere the voice of that unseen director calling *Action* again. She bristled.

Standing before the cabin, a new scene was starting, and she felt that someone, some other presence, was watching, and for the first again time in forever, she felt it — the feeling of not being alone. She looked around to see if anyone was there, but there was no one around for miles.

There was just the breeze, blowing through the trees, and the silver chimes that hung from the porch, singing as they danced.

4.

Wendy grabbed the paper bag of dinner from the passenger seat and pushed open the soft wood door of the cabin with a motorcycle-booted foot.

Light filled the quiet little space, it fell in from the windows and the french doors of the living room. It fell in glittering sheets like it was being poured from golden pitchers from heaven. Wendy stepped into it, and in the light remembered God. Or at least, a meeting with a presence that felt like God.

She had been in Paris at seventeen years old, on a trip with the money her mother had left her when she died, and she had trekked up Montmartre in hiking boots and khaki shorts and a thin coating of sweat to Sacré-Cœur, because it was what one did, when they were in Paris.

As much as she hated doing what one did just because it was what one did, she felt paralyzed by programming, and she didn't know another way. It felt like there was a way out she had yet to find, a secret door out of the mundane that beckoned yet stayed hidden.

She had entered the church on her tip toes and sat in a back pew alone; she had taken in its enormity, the marble, the stained glass, the flickering candles, the silence that felt anything but empty.

She had never felt very welcome or comfortable in church, always like a repenting daughter who could never quite please her father. But this church had felt different, she realized, even as she sat there, tapping her foot, like, *okay, check this off the list, how long do I have to sit here?*

But then, as if being moved by an invisible force, with an exhaustion that had been waiting in the wings for what felt like an eternity, she had closed her eyes and fell to her bare knees and she had started to cry. And then she started to speak — to whom, she had no idea.

"I know this is crazy," she said. "I don't know if you can hear me. If anyone is there. But I'm so scared. I'm alone and I'm so scared. Can you tell my mother I miss her? Can you tell my mother I love her? Mom, are you there? I miss you. Will you come back?"

And the Presence came — a calming energy that filled her heart, that raised flesh bumps on her skin, that slowed her tears, that made her feel she just might not die, that things just might be okay. And that was the meeting. But it wasn't the first meeting, it was the second.

The first had been the day her mother had left the earth. Wendy had come home from the hospital wearing her mother's clothes, her black silk pants and her blue and black striped sweater and in no underwear or bra, which, as a young girl, felt radically rebellious.

No one had done laundry in the house in weeks, in the final descent; none of the people who came by to help had remembered, when faced with the bigness of the end. Little things, the everyday details, shattered in the face of death. Who could think of laundry in a time like this?

Wendy thought maybe she'd been in that same emergency mode, ever since. She wanted only to wear her mother's clothes that still smelled like her, for the rest of her life.

She would sit in her mother's closet, surrounded by her shoes, smothered by all of her dresses still smelling of *Tresor*, and slide the door closed, till it got so dark she couldn't see her own hand in front of her face.

It was her personal tomb, or maybe, a womb, a dark safe place, where she could still be with her mother, and she wanted to stay there forever. Sometimes, when things got too much, Wendy still sat in closets and closed the door, like waiting out life in a war bunker.

That first night home from the hospital, after her mother's last breath, Wendy had walked up the stairs to her bedroom and fallen back on the bed and begun to wail.

And when the wailing stopped, when she had nothing left, she had just stared at the ceiling, in slack-jawed awe of the pain that was ripping her apart, like a soldier wounded on a battlefield, like a patient on an operating table.

And that was the first time she had felt a presence that she couldn't see. And it was something she hadn't told anyone about, because it was the kind of thing that made one seem crazy.

But she had been lifted up, the way you pick someone up off the ground — carefully, but sturdily, one hand under the knees, one hand on the upper back, in that place where it feels like our wings once were.

And she had laid there, suspended between the bed and the ceiling, suspended between this world and some other one. And it had only been for a moment, but she had remembered it ever since.

And for some reason she couldn't understand, she was reminded of it by the light that fell in this rented cabin on the cliff.

She stood in the living room, where a driftwood coffee table and a white cotton couch sat on a peach and blue Turkish rug. To the right was the kitchen, with a small silver island on a dark wood floor, and a big porcelain white sink sat under a window over looking the sea.

She walked up to the sink and opened the window, and she could hear the sea sighing in and out like someone breathing.

She set the brown bag of dinner on the white marble kitchen counter, and walked to the sliding door at the back of the living room. She looked out onto a porch with two soft beige recliners, and past the porch, just that endless horizon of possibility.

The sun was sinking across the water like a peachy egg yolk. Her therapist was right. It was all anyone could ever need. She flicked on the kitchen radio to the local station, where John Hiatt was singing *Lipstick Sunset.*

The best radio stations had an uncanny, *Truman Show* way of soundtracking the moment.

She uncorked the wine from Al's, and found a brown and blue pottery mug in the cupboard. She poured the light pink rosé in the dusty mug. Dirt never bothered her. It was cleanliness, where you could see everything down to the bone, where you could see your own reflection, that scared her.

She took the mug and the bottle to the couch in the living room, and she lay down on a recliner. Recently, when she went to sleep, she half hoped she could sleep forever; that would be the way to go, just sail off to sleep and never wake up.

When she closed her eyes, she had visions of her own burial. Of herself inside a coffin, lifeless and stiff, all her chances gone. She saw a handful of people standing around her grave, throwing dirt on her coffin the way they had on her mother's — a traditional but terribly cruel thing for a child to watch.

And it didn't even seem strange, to see that, to see her funeral. That felt like exactly like what was happening.

The Next Day.

Wendy opened her eyes to the morning. She was in fetal position on the white couch, with a gray chenille blanket over her shoulders; her bare feet had burrowed under the cushions.

She needed coffee, and something to eat to soak up the alcohol. But there was nothing in the fridge, there had never been a full fridge in any house she was ever in.

She groaned. She had to go into town, she had to, as Joni Mitchell sang, *Belong to the living.* She pulled a black fedora over the rat motel of her hair and she wore what she had slept in — Peter's band hoodie and tight black jeans.

She didn't wash her face, black makeup was smeared around her eyes like waking up from last night's party. She used to think it was so cool to always look like she was not so fresh from a party. But if her current life was a party, it was the worst party she had ever been to. And she had been to a lot of parties.

Her friend, Monica, a celebrity stylist and fashion writer, was always saying things to her no one else would dare say. Because when people did tell Wendy the truth, she had a way of bringing the pain. She pulled that card that made people afraid to tell her the truth, she flipped hysterical and burned the bridge. Even though beneath her anger was only fear — fear of abandonment, fear of not being loved. But that was a dangerous card to play, because eventually they stopped telling you the truth. And then you were all alone with your lies.

But Monica was a tough Jewish girl from the city, and she wasn't scared of Wendy. They'd been in the trenches at *Rolling Stone* together, and they knew who each other were beneath the masks of designer clothes and fancy magazines and famous acquaintances and handsome actors and musicians pretending to romance them to work their way up the ladder.

And truly, as much as her ego hated it, Wendy longed for the truth, for someone to love her enough to tell her the truth. "Sometimes I feel like I'm the last person you haven't scared away," Monica had said. "Do I get a prize?"

Monica and Wendy had spoken on the ferry over to the island; Wendy was on the top deck halfway across the sea, and all she could see was blue. She had the phone tucked into her neck and she was drinking an airplane bottle of cheap chardonnay she had bought at the ship's snack counter.

She was watching families and lovers cuddle together for windswept vacation photos when Monica had said, "Don't get mad, but…"

Wendy inhaled, Monica continued.

"I would be super bummed to be headed to an empty New England island for the winter. I mean, our chances in the real world of finding a man are hard enough, let alone in a Narnic frozen tundra."

"But I don't want love right now," Wendy had said, slugging from the little plastic bottle. "Love almost killed me." Besides, wasn't it obvious she was still in love with Peter?

"Well, I do, and everyone does, so I think you're lying, but I wasn't finished. I was going to say, in your case I actually think it's good. It's like the Universe has grounded you. You've been sent to your proverbial room. I mean, think about your life. Your first job was *Rolling Stone*, your first interview was Mick Jagger and your first boyfriend was a Smashing Pumpkin. And then you were married to a rock star, and you have literally been at a party for the last ten years of your life. Not just A party, the after-party, and then, normally, the after-after party, where you weren't not having sex in bathrooms with a substance up your nose."

"What's your point?" Wendy asked.

"That maybe this is good. Maybe you need a time out." Monica had said matter-of-factly.

Wendy sighed. "Well, it feels anything but good right now."

"Give it time," Monica said.

"I don't know how much of that I have."

She heard Monica sigh. She'd been a good friend, to hang in through Wendy's armageddon. As the benefits of being Wendy's friend had died down to nothing — no great parties, no guest list access, very little laughter — her phone rang less and less. Yet Monica had hung in there, without the perks.

But now, nudging her to save her life was pushing it.

"I have to go fit Lana Del Rey for her *Nylon* cover," Monica said. "You've got this."
"If 'this' is the cover of *People* on my divorce, then yes, I've got this."
"I'll call you as soon as I can. I'll check up on you."
"If I don't answer, I'm dead," Wendy had said.

"Ugh, I can't," said Monica. Wendy could feel her roll her eyes. "Look. This morning, there was a man on the *Today* show, he said something and I totes thought of you. His family had survived a hurricane and lost everything. Even their dog. He said, like, 'in the darkest of times, you can either let it destroy you or let it create you.' So maybe, maybe try to let this create you instead of destroy you. Think of your life as a blank slate."

"How?" Wendy had asked, desperate, scrounging for hope outside of herself, the tears coming again, and she didn't know if she was crying for herself or the lost dog in the storm.

"Well," Monica paused. "Maybe write that book…"
"Don't mention the book."
"Well, my therapist would say, if you can't talk about it maybe there's something there."
"Thank you, Monica. And Monica's therapist. And the Hurricane Survivor Guy on the *Today* Show."
"You're welcome," she had said. "From all of us. Shit, I seriously gotta go. Love you."

Wendy fumbled for the keys to the jeep and swung open the door. The Band's *The Weight*, which just happened to be her mother's favorite song, was playing on the radio, and she cried. Again.

She wondered if most people cried when they realized the stark difference between what they had dreamed their life would be like as a child and what it had actually become.

Something was happening — life had cornered her here at the edge of the world so she might finally face everything she had been running from.
Her whole body shuddered from the tears. Well, this is getting old, she thought to herself, wiping the inky black deluge away with the back of her hand.
She hadn't cried so much since she was a baby, but back then someone would stick a pacifier in her mouth and rock her. Now there was no one around to

touch her at all. This is why, she thought, she took all those pills. To suppress the river of tears that was always pushing at the dam within her.

Well, now that dam was officially broken.

"Fuck," she whispered. "This hurts." She could see her mother in white jeans dancing to The Band in the glow of the living room lamp. She could see Peter at the grill on their honeymoon here on the island, smiling at her like they had found the answer, unlocked life's secret. She could see that there was no victim and there was no villain. Just a tragic love story. It had been so much easier to play victim.

She chugged along the dirt road until she got to Al's, where she stood in the icy freeze of the dairy cooler for a good five minutes. *Did she want eggs? Did she like eggs? Were they cage-free? Had the chickens been happy?*

Decisions were never her strong point. They took knowing what she wanted, knowing where she wanted to go. For years, she had left them up to Peter. Now she was stranded at sea, no one to captain her ship.

A voice croaked behind her.

"You going to pick something, or wait till something just picks you?"

Wendy jumped and turned to see an older woman glaring at her.

"We've got about one ice cap left for those poor polar bears to stand on," the woman said, her long white hair flowing over ample breasts that pushed up beneath a worn grey cashmere sweater.

"Sorry," Wendy said.

"Don't apologize, that's wasting more time. Just do something."

Suddenly Wendy grabbed a carton of eggs, shredded cheddar cheese and some Half and Half for coffee. It felt good — no, mildly triumphant. Like progress had been made. Like she had moved her own boat. Or at least, stuck a hand in the water outside of her stalled boat and begun to row.

She turned around, but the woman was gone.

5.

At home she made an omelet, that thing she could make on a dime.

Growing up with a mother so often in the hospital or in bed recovering, there was takeout and delivery, there were all those donated casseroles, and there were a lot of omelets.

Breakfast for dinner wasn't some fun novelty thing like in houses with safety and structure; no, it was pretty much omelets on the reg. Omelets, or, what one of her mother's friends once called *Prison Pasta*.

One night during Wendy's freshman year, she had been sitting alone at the empty kitchen table, stabbing a plate of spiral noodles dusted in Kroger's parmesan cheese, and her mother's friend, a writer visiting from New York, as most of them were — writers from New York — had walked up to her and peered down into her dinner. Before she had Wendy, her mother had lived this romantic New York City writer's life, and Wendy felt she was the reason her mother had to give it all up and grow up, why they had to move to a small town and get realistic. Wendy likened growing up with dream deaths, with resentment and disappointment, so by all accounts, she hadn't.

From that night in the kitchen, she only remembered the khaki pants of her mother's writer friend, but not his face, and not his name. She mostly just remembered the lower halves of the adults in the house back then, a parade of faceless pants and skirts patting her on the head. Mr. Khaki Pants had said, in a sort of snitty, apathetic way, "Oh you poor thing, sitting there alone eating your Prison Pasta." Wendy had looked down at the fare she so often ate, and suddenly realized she was supposed to feel sorry for herself.

Before that remark, she had felt sort of bachelorette-cool, at fourteen years old, making her own rules and schedule and meals. The term had stuck. She thought about it now, how apt it was. If prison was something that kept you from living your life, she had actually existed in a sort of prison of fear, of if and when her mother would die.

There was something terrible that happened to you when your worst fear came true. Something changed in you; you lived with baited breath, bracing for all the walls to fall down again. But she'd heard it made others fearless, to survive their worst fear. But Wendy hadn't felt as if she had survived it, and she was left just feeling her more fearful.

Once Monica had said, "Don't take this the wrong way" (which, Wendy thought, was one of the worst ways to start a sentence, right up there with *I hate to be the one to tell you this* or *You're not going to like this*).

"But," she said, "it's like, when your mother died, you did too."

Wendy felt the presence of the ghosts that lived within her, she felt like a walking ghost motel. Her mother, her abandoned career, her unwritten book and now her marriage haunting her, there was no more room at the inn within. She was stirring the wet yolk in the pan with a wooden spatula, thinking about wearing a t-shirt that said No Vacancy. She looked down at her small freckled hand, it looked exactly like her mother's. She dropped the spatula and she held her left hand with her right.

When she held her own hand, she held her mother's hand. It felt so nice. It felt, whole. She was wishing she had held her mother's hand during her descent a whole lot more when she heard the woman in grey, "Don't apologize, that's wasting more time. Just do something."

Do something. But what?

Peter had been the do-er. She loved to watch him do, before the resentment grew. He was a phenomenal creator. A prolific artist. He would slip out of bed in the middle of the night into the guest room, like an entranced creature that felt called to walk off into the woods and die or give birth, and she'd hear him whispering and plucking at a new song in his chair where the moonlight fell through the window. She would smile and roll over, listening to him whisper out seeds of lyrics, toying with chords. At breakfast they'd play with the new lyrics together, her heart bursting with pride.

She marveled at his creativity; it was like a mysteriously granted gift. Where did it all come from? Why did some have it, and some didn't?

While Wendy was still working as a journalist, it could take her days of labor pains to find the right sentence that sang even mildly, that had any resonance at all, that didn't land with a thud and slide down the wall like a piece of rubbery spaghetti.

While her writing could sometimes make her feel like a clumsy sculptor stabbing at marble with a butter knife, Peter was like the most skilled of miners, his lines slicing right down to the gold.

She ate her sad omelet in five forkfuls standing over the stove, and thought about Diane Lane eating her chicken breast over the sink at her rock bottom in *Must Love Dogs*, and then she turned to look in the mirror on the kitchen wall.

Her tired sad eyes, her frizzy brown hair, her broken out skin, her extra weight, the cushion she kept between herself and The Experience. She was no Diane Lane. It was just three in the afternoon but she took a bottle of general store red wine into bed and clutched the remote for the television that hung on the opposite wall, despite the crashing and the calling of the waves outside. She wasn't ready for the ocean yet.

She wasn't ready for the feel of its cool waking air on her skin and the crunch of a million perfect seashells, each a tiny little masterpiece, beneath her bare feet. The cries of children and the naps of lovers. She had once loved the ocean. All her favorite memories had been at its shore, this shore, specifically. But she wasn't ready to feel all that it asked her to feel again. Everything she tried to bury seemed to rise with the waves. She pressed the remote. On television, *Baby Boom,* starring Diane Keaton, was on.

Not only was this the movie she and her mother shared as a favorite, it was what she had watched for weeks after her mother had died, and the film itself became like a time capsule, she could crawl in it and stop time and still be in bed with her mother, watching the neat, safe storyline tie up with a golden, giddy bow, a happily ever after.

The familiar opening credits began to roll, there was the swarm of white-sneakered power-walkers, the introductory voice-over, and she felt a smile creep on her lips. Those muscles had almost forgotten how, they were stiff from underuse.

80's movies penned by Norah Ephron and Nancy Meyers were home to her. They were the middle where she and her mother met. *Baby Boom, Private Benjamin, When Harry Met Sally, Heartburn.* If she were to believe in signs, *Baby Boom* playing on the television sure felt like one.

Here, the Universe seemed to say, chucking a bone in her direction. She took it in, hungrily, starved for comfort.

Diane's character, J.C. Wiatt, newly single and newly a mother, was at the edge of her old life and falling into the ocean of their new one. She was just making her way out of New York in a wooden Winnebago for the red and gold country of Vermont when Wendy passed out beneath the home sewn comforter and thick hushing of the waves.

The Next Day.

Wendy was in sweatpants and her mother's green cotton sweater, pumping hot coffee into a white paper cup at Al's, when she saw the white-haired woman again.

Her heart raced; she realized she was hungry for more of the woman's wisdom, even just another one-liner from her — she would take whatever she could get.

And despite her fear of intimacy, of being seen, she was beginning to long for human contact.

So Wendy just sort of lingered around the woman, like a shadow, like a hungry cat in an alley nearly weaving in between her feet until the woman almost tripped over her, until the woman had no choice but to acknowledge her.

"Oh," she said to Wendy.

Wendy smiled limply, she was getting used to people's half hearted reactions to her.

"How are those decisions coming?" the woman asked Wendy while she examined a carton of coconut water in her strong wrinkled hand.

"Um," said Wendy. "Not so great."

Then the woman muttered something to the coconut water about a racket, and put it back on the shelf. "Well, you sure can pick a bottle of wine fast."

Wendy looked down at her combat boots. *Touché*, she thought.

She looked at Wendy now, peering at her pores. "You drinking any real wata?" Her accent was so tough it could crack an oyster. "I mean the shit without the sugah?" She pressed. "Most people never do. Looks like you haven't had any in about 14 years." Wendy winced.

"I should, more," she agreed. She both hated this woman and loved her at once for her authenticity. She was entranced by her. This woman could see her. Wendy was longing to be seen, beneath the story of who she was now, to who she was before, and to maybe who she could become.

"Mmmhmm," said the woman. "Yep," she nodded. She was so sure of herself. She was so... confident. It seemed to come from deep within. From a place that needed no external validation.

"What kind of shipwreck are you crawling out of?" she asked Wendy.

"What do you mean?"

"That's how people end up here," she said, fumbling with her change purse, counting dollar bills. "They're crawling out of some fucking disaster. They call you wash-ashores. By the time you get here from the mainland, you're barely breathing. Ask most of the women here. They came here to heal and stayed. It might as well be called Heartbreak Island."

"I...," Wendy was startled by the accuracy. This woman sliced right through the bullshit. Wendy felt starved for something real. She was hungry for what this woman had to say. Her words fed Wendy, nourished her. Every word... meant something.

She looked inside of her to explain herself, but realized she didn't need to, she was standing just to the left of the tabloids.

"So?" the woman asked, her moccasin-ed foot beginning to tap to an impatient beat.

Wendy sort of tilted her head to the right toward the magazine rack.

"What is 'that'?" the woman asked, mimicking Wendy's head tilt. "What does 'this' (tilting her head) mean?"

"Um," Wendy stumbled. This woman didn't want to play charades at ten a.m. in the general store with a stranger. Understood. "Yes. You could say I'm currently in a disaster. Trying to... crawl my way out."

Finally the woman's eyes grazed over the gossips, and stopped.

"You sure look a lot like the girl in the nightgown with the wine-stained teeth being left for that 90-pound bag of legs and hair."

"That's me," Wendy said. "Not the legs and hair. I'm... Wine Teeth. And, that's a dress."

"Don't look like one," the woman said. She looked Wendy once over again with a low whistle.

"You doing any healing?"

Again Wendy asked, "What do you mean?"

"Right. Thought as much. Here's my card." Card sounded like *cahd*.

"I live on Lotus Street, near the church. Come by tomorrow, around three."

Wendy stared at her, immobile for a moment.

"Unless you got something better to do," the woman said, raising an eyebrow. For a moment, the card seemed to be frozen in the air. There was a time when Wendy had welcomed a challenge. She took the card. It had just three words on it.

"LEANNE GRACE. Healer."

Wendy looked back up at Leanne, who was looking over Wendy's wicker basket of wine, frozen pizza and Bronner's lavender soap.

"You might want to add a brush to your loot," she said.

Wendy put a hand to her mussed hair, self-consciously.

"And some fruit. Get ya-self some fruit." Then she turned her back to Wendy and walked up to the register.

"Hiya Sandra," Leanne said to the counter girl. "How's the back?"

*****

At home, Wendy sliced open the pizza box and then leaned her belly against the porcelain sink, staring out at the ocean while the cheese and bread bubbled in the oven. The sea seemed to change color every few minutes, like it held the joy and pain of the world.

By the time the sun sank into it, Wendy felt like she had watched an entire soap opera. Suddenly a familiar voice broke her trance. Her whole body seized, her cells cried out in recognition. She caught her breath and was jolted away from the Story of the Ocean.

It was Peter's new single on the radio. There would have been a time she had heard it in its every stage, from the skeleton to the full flesh. There would have been a time she had helped with lyrics and stood on the sides of the video set.

But she hadn't heard a single chord of this, and she couldn't. His songs were like landmines she hoped to avoid for the rest of her life's terrain. She rushed across the kitchen to shut it off. And then her hands shook as she fumbled in the utensils drawer for the wine opener.

She wasn't hungry anymore. She turned off the oven but just let the pizza stay in there.

She closed the curtains and returned to bed with her wine.

She turned on the television, desperate for its company, desperate for another voice to drown out the sound of Peter's that was still echoing in the cabin, as if he had been there for a moment, then gone, forever, which was what exactly what had happened.

By some grace, *Baby Boom* was on the local channel again. Wendy said *Thank You* to no one in particular.

Diane's character, J.C., was having her final breakdown in front of the frozen well — she was absolutely at the end of her rope. A scene that was once funny was now too familiar. J.C.'s foray to Vermont had failed — she had romanticized it, and now she just wanted to go home again. But home no longer existed, that bridge had crumbled behind her. J.C. had given up her apartment, lost her job, and been left by her lover. And now she had a baby and a house with a mortgage. Life had bolted her to her big yellow house in the country so she couldn't run. She had to stay. In all the unknown, in all her discomfort, she had to stay.

But the good news for Diane Keaton was she was about to end up on Sam Shepard's veterinarian table. Wendy wondered if that had anything to do with real life, that as soon as you finally hit your final wall, and totally gave up, and totally stopped trying, and stopped doing everything you used to do, that not only wasn't working, was making everything so much worse, and you just — surrendered — that that was when things finally began to change.

Wendy wondered, "What came after the death of a dream?"

6.

Wendy woke with the sun, but she kept her eyes closed, longing to sleep for as long as she could, even though her body itself wanted to wake.

Her spirit was like a buoy rising to the surface, but she kept fluttering her eyelashes closed, like blinds, against the glow of the light, she kept pushing herself back down into the dark below.

This was her habit, to only move when her flesh and bones ached from lying in the sheets too long. But she had no reason to wake. Her appointment with Leanne wasn't until three.

She had nothing to do and nowhere to be until then, all she had to do was work through the chalky, sawing headache and the stomach that churned like the high seas. That was her only purpose these days. To recover from what she had done the night before.

Like with most commitments, Wendy was now wondering how she could back out of going to Leanne's.

She thought about whether she could just not show up, and then spend the rest of the winter avoiding the general store where the woman seemed to frequent. She thought about calling the number on the card and telling her she was sick.

But being sick is why you went to healers. She thought about leaving the island, and going... where?

So at three p.m., having found no other choice, she plunked herself down on Leanne's cottage steps. She squished herself between dozens of terra cotta potted plants and beach stones and sea shells, onto a door mat that said, "You Have Arrived."

Chimes sang from the trees and a rabbit watched her nervously from the corner of its wet brown eyes, nibbling on grass beneath a rose bush. Wendy saw that life was carrying on, joyfully. She just had no idea how to get into it. There was that illusive invisible door into life again, the one she could never find but it seemed everyone else could.

Just then, Leanne's door creaked open behind her. Wendy squinted up in the sun to see the woman looking down at her, her long white hair spilling over her bosom, her white cotton dress billowing in the breath of the afternoon breeze.

"It's so nice out here," Wendy said, stabbing at conversation. "So peaceful."

"Peace is a choice," Leanne said.

Wendy's face went blank.

"Stumped ya, huh?"

"You're saying I could choose peace, instead of," she looked around at the invisible black cloud that seemed to move with her like Linus' cloud of dirt, then her hand rose over the wasteland of her heart, and she heard its pained and hungry howl. "This?"

"You fuckin' betcha," said Leanne, eyeing Wendy's hair. "Didn't get the brush, did ya?"

"I forgot," said Wendy.

"You're not helping yaself, kid." Leanne just stood there in the threshold of the cottage looking down at Wendy, who hovered outside like a vampire waiting for an invite.

"You have any idea, how to care for yourself? You ever done it?"

Wendy's eyes watered, she trembled, like someone shivering against the cold, despite the Indian Summer day. She hadn't had anything to eat that day, just buckets of coffee and four Advils. She shook her head, "I don't think so."

"I shouldn't have asked. We humans are always asking questions when we already fucking know the answer. Gotta deprogram that shit." Wendy had no idea what language this woman was speaking.

"Listen," Leanne said, "Walking in this door is making a choice. I know those ain't ya strong point. But you're making a promise to care about yourself. To have some self-worth. A little dignity. You're making a promise to try to love this beautiful life you've been given that you keep shitting all over. Can you do that?"

Again Wendy hesitated. That sounded like a tall order, one she would have already carried out if she had any idea how.

"I don't know," she said.

Leanne sighed, "Well, what do you know? Why are you here?"

Now Wendy was angry. She didn't need this. She didn't need anyone. She would go home and open a bottle of wine and turn on the television. Maybe there was a *Law&Order* marathon on. Fuck this woman. Her nostrils flared like a bull in a pen, but she was silent.

"Where ya gonna go?" the woman asked, as if she had read Wendy's mind, and wasn't impressed.

"Home," Wendy said.

"Some fancy rental? How long is that money going to last?"

"A few more months," Wendy shrugged, not that it was any of this woman's business.

"And then what?" Leanne asked.

"I. don't. know," Wendy said shortly.

"That's what I thought," she sighed. "You just gonna run from yourself for the rest of your life." Then the woman had the audacity to laugh. A deep belly roar. She tossed her head back. Wendy saw all the way down to the dark tunnel of her throat.

"You let me know how that turns out," she said, wiping a tear from the wrinkled corner of her eye.

"Well, look," Wendy said, fumbling for her keys in the bottom of the Kate Spade purse Peter had given her the previous Christmas. "I'm…"

"Okay, listen. I don't know what it is about you, kid. I'm super fucking busy. I don't like to get in the ring anymore. It's way fucking easier to just lie back and watch people get pummeled. They rarely listen anyway. But I'm gonna take a chance and get in the ring with you.

But my time is precious. Me, I actually love this life and am a choosy cunt with how I spend it. And I got a million people in here all fucking day for healing. Everyone's fucking dying. It's Grand Fucking Central. I really can't be taking in any more strays."

Just then, a cat appeared from beneath Leanne's dress and mewed, loudly and proudly, like he was playing a miniature trumpet, announcing his own presence.

"See?" Leanne said, looking down at the black silken sphinx-y creature sitting on her tan bare feet. Wendy noticed a toe ring and an ankle bracelet. She'd never actually seen anyone wear a toe ring, let alone a sixty-something-year-old woman. How… Goddessy.

"One second, Norman," Leanne said to the cat.

Wendy took a step backwards. "I understand. Maybe… maybe some other time."

"Oh yeah? You got a better time to save your fucking life? Look, I don't know who the fuck you are, or were, and I don't care who he — Mr. Big Shot Leather Pants Rock Star — is either. Don't make no fucking difference to me. You may have noticed no one around here gives a fuck either. We're used to people falling like stars from the sky onto this island to die or change. Which one is it gonna be for you?"

If Wendy opened her mouth, she would cry. So she didn't. This woman was terrifying her.

"Live or die, honey. You gotta choose. Say 'Yes,' or Say 'No.' 'Yes' is life. 'No' is death. Which is it? If you walk into this house, you're gonna have to fucking try to save your own life. I can't do it for you. I can guide you to where you gotta go, but you gotta go into those caves alone. Don't waste my time."

Norman mewed for food.

"Or Norman's. He's very busy being fabulous."

Norman looked up at Wendy, peeved.

"You look like you're on Death's Door. I mean that's not breaking news is it? You look like shit." Wendy took a shallow breath.

"Here's your chance," Leanne said. "I'm not offering it again. Take it."

Wendy stood there, the chimes singing, the seagulls calling overhead, the ocean air playing with the what was left of her hair. Norman and Leanne were looking at her impatiently. Everything froze, like God had put the tape of the movie of her life on *Pause* so she would pay attention.

Here, look, this is important. She saw her mother's hand go slack in hers as she took her last breath. She saw Peter packing his final bag indifferently, while she slumped bawling in the corner in her nightgown, feeling buried alive.

She saw herself clutching the pills on the floor the night he left. She saw herself swallow the rest of the bottle and not care whether she woke. She knew what waited for her in her rental home on the cliffs, but not what waited behind the door. So she chose the unknown. She said *Yes*.

And she thought it was as close to saying *Yes* to life as she ever had. She looked back up at the woman in white, standing in the doorway. And she walked through the door.

7.

Once inside the small craftsman cottage, Leanne ushered Wendy into a little light lavender room to the right of the front door.

A massage table wrapped in soft pink flannel sheets lay beneath a window where the white afternoon light fell. Music, a marriage of crashing ocean waves and longing cello, played from the far left corner.

There were enough green plants to make up a small garden on the chipped white windowsill, and books piled on an old driftwood bookshelf, where light pink, glistening black and glowing purple crystals lined the shelves. Leanne puttered around the room while Wendy combed over the book titles.

Goddesses in Everywoman, proclaimed one, *Be Here Now*, instructed another, and *Dancing In The Flames*, said another. At home, Wendy's floor was littered with issues of *Us Weekly* and *People*, details of celebrities' shopping lists or the demise of their private lives; Wendy binged on them like Twinkies, but they only left her hungrier and more tired.

She couldn't remember the last book she read, she didn't have the commitment a book took.

Leanne pulled back the pink sheets, and said to Wendy, "Take your shoes off, kid."

She pulled her boots off and left them by the door. She had holes in the red and white socks she had slept in for days. She had the socks and the soul of an orphan. Leanne looked at her with pity and frustration. She patted the bed. Wendy sat lightly on its side, her legs hanging off, her toes grazing the floor.

"All the way," Leanne said. "Do it all the way." Wendy complied.

"Lay back," Leanne ordered. "And go ahead and fall apart now. It's safe. All the way. When you do shit, do shit all the way. Don't hold on to anything. That's devotion. Devote yourself to your life, it needs you. Devote yourself to whatever you are doing in the moment. Right now you're healing. Devote yourself to that."

Slowly Wendy leaned back into the fuzzy flannel sheets, that felt like the skin of a teddy bear. Inch by inch, she felt herself sink into the mattress. "Let go," Leanne whispered. Wendy stared at her, wide-eyed, like, what will happen if I do?

"Close your eyes," Leanne said. "Breathe. Let yourself be held."

Wendy sank deeper. Muscle after muscle released. Tightness she'd been holding on to for what felt like since childhood. Eons of holding on, of self protection. Every cell clenching so tightly. To what could have been. To who she should have been.

And just like that, she started to cry. Not like the reserved crying she had done since Peter left, but the howling of an orphan. The crying of a child ripped from her mother, forever. The cry of death and abandonment and fear and the end of things.

The cry of her core wound, the one Peter had ripped back open.

The human wound. The I am unlovable, alone and always will be, and I will die alone wound. The one she'd been trying to cover with wine and pills and running. She wailed like an abandoned child on a battlefield. She wailed like the ocean in a storm.

She wailed like she did when the doctor said, "It's time to say goodbye to your mother." She wailed like she did when Peter said, "I'm never coming home and I never really loved you."

Over her, Leanne was just breathing, deeply, with hands that hummed with warm light over her heart. "Breathe into my hands," Leanne said. "And cry till you can't cry no more." She hadn't been touched by another woman for fifteen years. She shuddered with relief and grief.

She felt as if she was on an operating table, her heart being ripped out of her chest. She felt gutted apart like a fish on the docks of this island she had fled to. Lying splayed in her own blood.

"It hurts so much," Wendy said, gasping.

"As it should," said Leanne, as calm as the day she first met her, as cool as she had been standing in front of that dairy freezer.

"I feel like I'm dying," Wendy said, gargling for air.

"You are," said Leanne. "You have been for a while. We're just speeding up the process so you can get on with the rebirth." Wendy couldn't imagine life after this, but she kept dying, because Leanne told her to, and it felt good to feel someone in control.

It was part of the reason — no, much of the reason — why she was so attached to Peter; he had always been in control. She could be on auto-pilot. She could sleep while he drove.

She let out another gargling sound, and wailed for another twenty minutes, thrashing beneath Leanne's warm hands, which moved down her body until she got to Wendy's feet, where Wendy could feel the sensation of energy leaving her soles.

Then Leanne held her holey socks, in a way that comforted her like no macaroni and cheese *Law and Order* marathon ever had. Her touch felt so safe and loving that Wendy breathed down deep into Leanne's hands, then eventually passed out, like an exhausted child at the end of a long fit.

When she woke, she was alone in the lavender room, curled in a fetal position. Her eyes fluttered open to Leanne's altar, heavy with crystals and angels and what looked like a wooden pentagram. Over the altar, a mirror. Wendy had the daring to look in.

Her eyes were red and swollen from crying, her greasy hair knotted, her face bloated from alcohol and crying. She shook her head.

But still, she felt lighter, as if something had shifted.

She pulled herself up off the bed and padded outside to look for Leanne, who was sitting on her porch with her back to the door, looking out over the rose bush, a chenille blue blanket wrapped around her shoulders.

"Hi," Wendy said softly behind her.

"Everyone dies, you know," said Leanne, not turning around. "And everything too.'

"What?"

"I know it hurt, like a bitch, I know, trust me, you're not the first to lose someone you loved. And I can feel, you hold all that in your body and your soul and your heart. But the harder you hold on, the harder it hurts. And you're holding on like a muthafucka.

And you're drinking to fill a wound only love can fill. But everyone dies. I know it sucks, your motha, she died young and beautiful and full of dreams. But that was her fucking time. It's not your time." The words caught in Leanne's throat.

"Your motha, she told me that in there. That it's not your time, kid. She told me to tell you that."

Wendy stared at the back of the woman's head, the white curls tucked beneath the blanket. She marveled at her complexity; so tough yet tender. This woman was deeply feeling for her, and they were practically strangers.

Leanne continued. "We don't know when, and we don't know how. And you just happened to be front row as a kid. I get that. But everyone dies, at some point, sooner rather than later, and there are no fucking guarantees. I could drop dead in the middle of this sentence.

The next time you choose to take a showa — soona rather than lata, I hope — you could slip in it. And that would be fucking it. No," she shook her head. "This ain't your time. But you think your time ain't comin'? It's comin' as sure as that sun is setting."

Wendy looked up at the pink light that streaked the sky, at the orange globe that was slipping into the pine trees. "So is my time, and everyone else you love's time. We all go, sweetheart. Maybe you were given a gift to see that. And use that, to actually live.

That's what death does, if you look at it right, it teaches you how to live. You just gotta love people while you got them. "

Wendy sighed and looked down at her holed feet.

"I think," Wendy's chin began to wobble, "I didn't do that so well, love Mom, or Peter either. I think it's why I clung to Peter for dear life. I was so scared of him dying too. "

Leanne nodded. "You ran from your sick mother. Made a real escapist out of you, and tacked on some killer self loathing. And then with Peter, you did the opposite. You clung so fucking hard you killed it." Then she let out one of those hoarse throaty laughs of hers, that felt anything but joyous. "Oh, the fucking irony. You were so afraid to kill it, you killed it. You paying attention? You've got to fucking pay attention."

She shook her head, still not looking at Wendy. Then she was quiet. Wendy could hear the crickets starting to serenade the garden with the violins of their bodies. Leanne was still.

She was so calm that the grey rabbit from before had taken residence a few inches away from her foot, chewing the grass beside her.

"No," said Leanne. "That's not the answer. If you love people, you let them live, you let them go," she said. "Love lets go. Fear," which sounded like fee-yah, "that shit holds on."

Wendy breathed, deep in through her nose, out through her mouth in a long sigh. "Good job," Leanne nodded. "Way more of that. And you know, newsflash, kid. Nothing lasts forever. That love, with Mr. Rock Star, it taught you a bunch. When shit hurts this bad, pay attention.

The more it's burning, the more you're learning. Class is in fucking session. And if you're smart, you'll learn from it and gather the wisdom. But only if you stay awake in the discomfort. It wasn't supposed to last forever. It was your first love. They rarely last. They teach, but they don't last.

So the question now, kid, is what did you learn? You don't graduate until you've learned the fucking lesson. Otherwise you're in eternal detention. Muthafucking Groundhog's Day. So pay attention. And learn."

Wendy was silent. Finally Leanne turned and looked up at her, right in the eyes.

"You're no dummy," she said. "You've acted like a dummy, but you're no dummy. You're smart. You've just played dumb because it was easier. But it's time to get wise. You gotta grow up, girl.

And what a grown-up does is they figure out what they've learned, they forgive themselves, they forgive the other person, then they get back up and they move the fuck on. Here's some more breaking news. There's a whole big world out there outside of you."

Wendy looked back up at the sky, now completely fluorescent pink, the birds were calling Good Night to each other, a dog barked in the distance, and Leanne — Leanne had one tear leaving the far corner of her crinkled right eye.

"I think," Wendy whispered, "I think I learned a lot."

"No shit. Think about shipwrecks," Leanne said. "The old ones, from the days of pirates and shit. Think about all that gold at the bottom of the ocean. But only the brave ones, who dive way down deep into the wreck, only those muthafuckas get that gold.

Well, your ship has wrecked, and you're at the bottom of the ocean, kid, might as well look around and see what you find. Sometimes you gotta just thank the wreck for the gold."

8.

When she reached the rental home, Wendy felt different.

There was a new awareness to what was around her. She got out of the car, and when she closed the door she touched the Jeep's door softly, like healing love was pumping through her veins, and she could pass that love on, even to an object. She found herself thanking the jeep for driving her around.

She could swear she almost felt it respond in a humming energy.

She walked up to the front door and stopped beneath the chimes to hear them sing, as if, maybe, they were singing just for her. And she thought, "Who's to say they aren't?"

She closed her eyes and felt the sweet tinkling all over her body, like the music was healing her cells, and a small smile of gratitude crept along her face. She thought of Leanne saying to her, "Instead of complaining all the damn time, I just say, 'thank you, thank you, thank you.' And it works. Try it, kid."

So she said thank you, thank you, thank you to the chimes for their song, and she felt the gratitude peel open the doors to her heart.

Despite the cool Fall wind, she left the door open when she entered, so as to keep hearing them sing, in case they wanted to be heard. When she crossed the threshold of the doorway, she entered the space with what could only be described as a new level of consciousness. She saw the house as if for the first time. Despite the circumstances that had brought her to this house on the cliff, how lucky she was to have someplace like this to land. She straightened the blanket and pillows on the couch.

She scooped up the magazines that vultured others' lives, and put them in the recycling. She did the dishes which had piled high in the sink, and outside the window, the moon, almost full, caught her eye, glowing in the sky, the stars twinkling around it like its shiny attendants, like ladies in waiting to their Queen.

And for the first time since she'd moved in, she opened the window to the ocean breeze, and she felt it whoosh over her skin, as if it had been trapped there, just longing to touch her. She shuddered beneath its salty fingers.

One breath of ocean air felt more filling and healing than twenty gulps of inside air. She again thought of Leanne. "There's this whole big world outside of you."

Suddenly Wendy wanted nothing more than to feel outside of herself. To climb outside of the prison of herself and be a part of the world.

But like a programmed robot, she reached for the bottle of Cabernet on the counter. She pulled it closer to where she stood at the sink in front of the ocean breeze that had now begun to fill the house.

She could see Leanne shake her head. She could hear her say, "You do the same shit, you get the same shit." But Wendy didn't know how to hit five o'clock without wine. That seemed insurmountable. "I mean, baby steps," Wendy thought.

For the first time since long before Peter had left, because there is the actual moment they leave, but the leaving begins long before that, she had felt hope. And she didn't want that hope to leave her, she wanted that hope to stay.

And she knew how she felt the mornings with the wine in her body, she knew too well the Death Monster that lived within her tummy and her throat, and she knew he fed on wine, how strong he grew from the alcohol — and the stronger he grew, the more he filled her head with thoughts of death.

But she had drunk or been sedated since she was 16 years old, and not a day had gone by when she hadn't taken something to stop the pain. There had not been a morning she hadn't woken hung over in fifteen blurry years.

But this was the first time there had been a gap between just reaching for it and slugging down at least three glasses. There was something within her resisting, pausing. She didn't know what to do. So she did something she hadn't done since Sacre Couer.

With the moonlight falling in through the window sill, she fell to her knees on the white kitchen rug, she clenched and interlaced her fingers, pressed her forehead to the ground, and she asked for help.

This time, though, nothing came.

She only heard her words:

"If anyone is there, I could use some help. I want to change. I want to be better. I want to make something of this life I've been given. I'm scared I've ruined it.

I'm scared it's too late. But I don't want to be me anymore, I want to be, someone I can love, who can be loved. Please help me change."

Wendy waited on the floor with just her own words hanging in the air. She waited some more. She heard the ocean breathing in and out behind the house. She heard the chimes in front of the house. But nothing else. So she placed her hands in front of her and she rose to her feet.

And just as she did so, the wine, teetering on the edge of the sink, fell into the porcelain basin and shattered, red liquid leaking like blood down the drain. Wendy stood there for a second, and then looked around. Leanne had told her there was no such thing as a coincidence.

So she said, "Well, okay then. Maybe you are listening," to whom, she wasn't sure.

But her heart still beat like a trapped hummingbird, and her breath was still short and shallow, and her hands still shook. She scoured the fridge, there was just old pizza and rotting lettuce. She opened the cupboards. Pots and pans and coffee and... tea.

She took down the tea box. Green Tea, Black Tea and Chamomile. Chamomile would have to do. She poured water into the kettle and clicked on the burner, and while she waited she moved into the living room. Instead of turning on the television, she wandered up to the book shelf.

There were books on the island's history, photography books of local fishermen, boats and beaches, classics like *Wuthering Heights* and *Jane Eyre*, those books she always pretended she'd read but never actually had. Wendy wrinkled her nose.

She was about to give up and turn on *Lifetime*, to surely watch a hysterical, bereaved woman shoot her ex-husband through tears in a "You did this to me" rant, because isn't your life over when your man leaves? But then a title caught her eye.

The Presence Process, it said. She did that face people do, that shrug of the lips, that meh, and she pulled it off the shelf. The tea kettle sang from the kitchen. She stuck the book under her arm, pulled the folded blanket off the couch, and poured herself a cup of chamomile.

Armed with a book about *Presence* instead of the drowning glow of the television, and drinking a mug of something which was not alcohol, she headed to bed.

When the sun came in the next morning, she didn't close the blinds. She opened her eyes. She waited for the terror, but it didn't come. "I didn't drink last night," she marveled. She felt flooded with relief. She let the sun wake her, and rose with it, stumbling into jeans and a white turtleneck sweater.

She made coffee and opened the door to the porch, feeling herself pulled to the ocean. The wind whipped her hair, slapped her face with a gratifying stinging sensation. She chugged the rest of the coffee and ran barefoot down the steps to the beach, her feet sinking into the wet sand.

She began to run, hard, along the shoreline, sandpipers scattering in front of her, the water licking her feet, the icy cold zapping her even further alive. She had visions of the lacrosse field in high school, barreling toward the goal like a machine, her legs like wheels.

She could remember the track at night, where she would run when the pain in the house grew too much. She used to run away her pain, not drink it. And it used to work.

She could hear her high school lacrosse coach crying from the side of the field, "Go Wendy, Go!" and she ran faster until she realized there was actually someone screaming at her in real time, and they were yelling "Wait!! Stop!!" Wendy halted in her tracks.

Her lungs heaving, her heart banging, she looked back toward the voice. A woman with long brown hair was waving frantically, running to meet her. She stopped, twenty feet away.

"If you keep running," said the woman in between breaths, pointing at Wendy's feet, "so does she." Wendy looked down to see a small brown dog staring up at her, its tail wagging excitedly.

"Oh!" Wendy laughed. "I didn't see her!"

"She's been running with you for ten minutes," the woman smiled, hinged over, hands on her thighs, taking in air in gulps. "She can't resist a runner. Nice pace," she nodded. Wendy kneeled down and pet the cinnamon-colored dog.

"Hi," she said to the pup. "What's your name?"

"Greta," the woman said. "She's Greta. I'm Danny." She moved toward Wendy and stuck out a strong calloused hand with clean short nails.

Wendy rose and took it. "Wendy."

The woman stood up tall, a good half foot over Wendy. She was about Wendy's age, but her skin glowed like the moon and her eyes were alive with life. She was absolute vitality itself.

Her hair fell down her shoulders in shiny waves like a woman out of a romance novel, but she wore tattered denim overalls and a heavy black and red flannel jacket.

"You just get here? Never seen you before," she said.

Wendy smiled shyly. "I guess I'm what you call a washashore," she said. "I don't really love that name... it feels so transient... like I could float away at any moment like a piece of driftwood."

Danny shrugged. "You don't have to subscribe to any label," she said. "Everyone has to get here somehow. Besides, things that wash ashore can either wash back into the water or they can stay. Up to you."

"I don't know what I'm doing," Wendy said.

Danny looked at her now, with a brown-eyed gaze so powerful that Wendy shrank. "You came here to figure it out, right?" she asked. "We get a lot of those. Sometimes I wish I could run somewhere and figure my shit out. But I've got a husband and a baby and business. I'm anchored as can be."

'That sounds really nice. To be held somewhere. I don't…"

"Know where you belong? Ha," smiled Danny. "I don't have time for all those questions. And if I did, I think they would drive me insane." But now she was sort of staring at Wendy — her head tilted, her eyes narrowed.

"Wait a minute," she said. "Aren't you Peter Jackson's wife?" Wendy was so used to people not giving a shit about her that she'd forgotten how just one month ago her demise had been on the cover of *People*. She breathed in sharp, his name made her throat seize. "Ex," she said.

"Yeah, that's right. I'm sorry. I saw something about that. My husband, Ray, he's a big fan of his."

Wendy looked out at the choppy white water. "He's… he's talented."

Danny looked at her, her face softened. "If you're into that. I like my bad-ass chick singers."

Wendy smiled. "I could stand to listen to some bad-ass chick singers. I used to." When Wendy was captain of the lacrosse team in high school, she used to pump the girls up with Alanis Morrisette and Mary J. Blige before games.

One day of sobriety, and she was remembering the rebel leader she'd been at 15 years old. She was looking up to the girl she used to be, before she felt she had to be someone else. Before she became overwhelmed with the need to please and look cool.

"Well, for now, how about hanging out with some bad-ass chicks?"

Besides seeing Leanne, getting gas, or going to Al's, Wendy hadn't left the house since she landed on the island. "That sounds great," she said.

"Tomorrow's the full moon. We do a women's potluck circle at my house. Bring something."

"A moon circle? What is that? What do I need to do?"

"Just show up. And breathe," Danny said.

"I think I can do that," said Wendy.

"I know you can," said Danny.

There was silence, just the waves, and Wendy wasn't comfortable in silence.

"Well, thank you," said Wendy, her tone wrapping things up. "It was really nice to meet you."

But Danny wasn't done with her yet, she was still taking her in.

"You know what my momma says? She says, to get what you want in this life, you gotta know what you want in this life. She says, most people's problem is, they don't know what they want.

If you think about a ship crossing the ocean, and it doesn't know where it's going, it's going to get lost, bang into a ton of ships, cause a ton of chaos and get wrecked. A ship that knows where it's going, that's different. It's got a North Star to look to. It's got direction. It's got a goal. So despite the inevitable storms, it will get there."

Wendy was quiet.

Danny shrugged. "She's a ship captain, so everything with her is sailing metaphors. But they work — for the most part. But maybe you're just rebuilding your ship, and redirecting yourself, you know?"

Wendy nodded. "But I don't... I don't know what I want anymore," she shook her head. "I wanted him."

"Ouch," Danny said, her hand rushing over her flannel heart.

"I feel that for you. I had one of those. He hung the fucking moon. Then they leave, and your whole world goes dark. I vowed to never build my life around a man again. And then I met Ray. He's my equal. They have to be."

"I feel about as big as a grain of this sand," said Wendy, her toe grazing over the tiny wet rocks.

"You are," said Danny. "But you're also as big as the sky," she smiled. "You're in that cool place of the unknown where anything is possible now."

Wendy was silent. If she spoke, she'd cry.

"Hey," Danny reached out, took Wendy's hand, it was warm and tough. She only held it for a second — a momentary jolt of intimacy.

"You're gonna be okay," Danny said. "You've come to the right place." She let Wendy's hand go with a rough, pull it together shake.

"It gets better. It's not going to be like this forever. That's the one thing you can count on in life, is that it changes. Everything changes. But I guess you learned that pretty good, huh? You probably don't need some stranger on the beach telling you that."

"No," said Wendy. "I do need a stranger on the beach telling me that," she looked up at her.

"Thanks," she said. If Wendy was still in magazines, she would have put Danny on the cover. But there was such little vanity about her, which made her more beautiful, makeup-less in paint-splattered overalls, than any model Wendy had ever seen.

"You're... you're beautiful," Wendy blurted out.

"Bah..." Danny said, shooing the words away. "That ain't gonna last." She pointed to her heart. "But this is. So that's what I focus on."

Wendy kicked some sand in the silence, she wasn't used to women her age talking like that.

"Hey, listen," Danny said. "Come over early tomorrow night? I could use the help setting up."

Wendy nodded. "That sounds nice."

"619 Beechwood Road. Five o'clock." Then she scooped up Greta. "Come on, you," she said to the little dog, who looked up at her adoringly. They turned in the sand. "See you tomorrow night, Wendy."

Wendy just stood there watching them trot away, when Danny turned and called to her in the wind.

"Hey, Wendy."

"Yeah?"

"Don't worry. We're gonna get you sailing again."

9.

The next day, Wendy woke on the full moon — she could see it behind the soft morning clouds, pale white and translucent, patiently waiting for the curtains of night to reveal her in her glory.

She knew just a little about the moon, that it moved the tides. And she knew that humans were mostly made up of water. And she wondered, could we be moved by the moon, as powerfully as the ocean was.

And she wondered, how something could be so powerful just by sitting there being, and filling with light.

She hadn't looked up at the moon since she was a little girl. She had been looking in for so long that she had forgotten to look out.

She remembered being small and talking to the moon, feeling it fill her skin until it sparkled, and then letting that light fill the chalice of her heart until it swelled and glowed like the moon itself.

Despite the fearful swirling soup of her mind, she pretended she believed in magic again and she made a wish — to be free from herself and to be loved.

Then she rolled over and reached for *The Presence Process*, she'd found it helped to read someone else's clear calm thoughts when her own mind threatened to drown her.

Michael Brown was talking about how we are always either trying to sedate or control our experience, how our pursuit of happiness is really just our running from our childhood wounding. How we need to take responsibility for our experience, how we need to grow up. How being present in your body, how being present is our only place of power, not in the past, not in the future, but right here right now, and she practiced that, with attention on her breath, moving her awareness into her body, breathing into the moment and calming the storm of her mind.

She moved into the kitchen in her sweatpants to stand over the coffee pot as it gargled and then began wafting its waking aroma into the room. She chugged a mug, then ran down the back porch stairs to the water.

And then she ran for her life. She ran like her past was behind her, chasing her, and she ran so hard her lungs went ragged and her legs ached and throbbed.

Once back in the house, she grabbed the keys and left for Al's like that, dripping sweat, and red as a sunset.

She was pulling into the parking lot for eggs and juice when she felt a tug from a new inner voice, a one she had just begun to hear, one she wasn't sure was real or if she was making up. "Slow down," it seemed to say. "Pay attention."

She noted it, then stepped out of the car and crossed the dusty lot and onto the creaky wooden porch. Even before she swung the door open, she could hear Springsteen singing from the speakers, "Wendy, let me in, I wanna be your friend, I wanna guard your dreams and visions," he cooed.

On her beeline to the cooler, she passed the wine. It whispered to her, seductively in the way that ex-boyfriend who only ever brings you misery and derailment does, despite the promises of, "This time I mean it, things will be different... I love you...you know you want me."

"Shut up, wine," she thought.

She passed the newspapers. Violence erupting all over the polluted world. A world on fire. Syrian and Sudanese refugees running for their lives, and from their homes, with nothing. Just to survive. She felt sick. She felt sick of her sadness and her solitude and sick of herself. She wanted to do more, she just didn't know what yet.

She stared down at a small Syrian child in a stoic woman's arms, the child's big pools of brown eyes seemed to be looking straight at her. Her chin trembled and a wall of tears blanketed her eyes. She put the paper down gingerly and crossed to the cooler.

In the checkout line, she held the cardboard carton of organic eggs from a local farm and a jug of fresh squeezed orange juice. Springsteen was now erupting in passion, "I'll love you with all the madness in my soul," he cried.

The E-Street Band was exploding in a cacophony of sax and guitar and cymbals. Behind her, a deep voice was humming. She felt his energy on her neck and her skin bristled. She felt a sensation in her hips she hadn't felt in over a year, a loosening.

She hadn't realized her hips had been so tight, until they flooded with warm liquid energy. Her face somehow became redder. She trembled, she felt transparent. Could he see the blood pumping through her body, into her pelvis, into her face, her lips, her flesh rising to receive him?

She could smell him, too, he smelled warm and musty and safe and dangerous. Like moist earth and caked sweat. She licked her lips.

"Hi there…" the cash register girl was saying. "I can take you now."

Wendy was caught on those words, "I can take you now," and she could only think of sheets and bed and being… taken. She found herself attempting to shake herself awake, she needed a good crisp Cher *snapoutofit* slap, and with that she managed to drop the orange juice.

She knelt, and her head banged into his. She looked up. Deep green eyes that led all the way to God.

"Oh, gosh, I'm so sorry," she said. He smiled. Perfect big white teeth. Dark shiny thick hair, black as night, and huge muscled hands that lifted the jug's handle with a broad finger, a crescent moon of dirt under his finger nail.

"No problem," he said. He smiled at her, so confident and at ease with his surroundings, like a movie set he was the star of.

Sweatpants had been a bad choice.

She didn't really have many other clothes, she'd packed one bag. Her therapist had said, "Take as little baggage as possible," to start over.

Wendy had stared at her blankly.

"That's a double entendre," her therapist had said.

"I got it," Wendy had snapped.

He passed her the dented jug of orange juice.

"Good thing none of it spilled," he said in a voice so low it hit her deep in her belly. She stood there as if her tongue had been cut out, her pulse was racing, and her heart beating louder than Max Weinberg's drums. She snatched it from his hand. He was a Greek god in overalls.

What was it with all these beautiful people in overalls? What was in the water that they all glowed like characters from a *CW* show? All of them ready for their closeup, yet no desire for the limelight?

She thought of that movie *The Secret Life of Walter Mitty* she had seen on the plane to Maine, of the line, "Beautiful things don't ask for attention." And she realized her whole life she had been begging, busking, for attention, but the more she got the more she wanted, it was an insatiable hunger that only grew the more she fed it.

"You're up," he said, nodding to the front of the line.

She was flustered, and stumbled up to the checkout. The young girl behind the antique register smiled at her — a short voluptuous girl of twenty or so with dyed black hair and a gleaming silver pentagram around her neck.

Wendy stared at the necklace, then down at the girl's hands, as she rang the items up with her short chipped black nails.

"You okay?" she asked Wendy, warmly, in such an adult manner that Wendy felt reduced to a five-year-old.

"Yes, yes, thank you."

"No wine today," the girl smiled.

"Nope," Wendy said a bit shortly, pursing her lips. "Not today." She thought of Leanne. "Ya can't push a button that's not there." Well, this girl had pushed a button. The wine button.

Wendy fumbled in her sweatpants pocket for a twenty-dollar bill, and felt him breathing behind her like a panther in the jungle; she could feel his eyes glowing on her neck. She could feel the heat of his body all along the back of hers. How close was he? Inches? Nothing between their flesh but fabric?

My God, she thought, *get me out of here.*

The girl reached for a paper bag from behind the counter, just as the song on the radio switched. The familiarity split Wendy open with a knife, she had heard it maybe ten million times. It was an old song of Peter's, written just as they were falling in love. She felt her stomach lurch up through her throat.

She started to sweat at her temples. "She's the brightest light I've ever seen," Peter screamed, "and she just might guide me home."

"I don't need a bag," Wendy said, hurriedly. She took the handle of the juice, right where the beautiful man had held it, and she scooped up the eggs. She couldn't look at him. It's as if she was paralyzed, her neck in one of those whiplash braces. She felt him smiling at her with a confident coolness.

She heard that voice from within, "Turn around and smile," but she couldn't; she was frozen in fear. And then she walked — no, she ran — right by him, out of the door, when she heard the checkout girl say, "Hi Jack, how's the farm?"

She sat in her car and collapsed. She looked around at no one in particular.

"What the hell was that?" she asked. Like, who is running this show and what are they smoking? She finally meets a new beautiful man, he talks to her, she ignores him, she's in her sweatpants, and Peter comes on the radio? Jack. Jack. She always loved that name. What a strong, sturdy, sexy name.

Jack. Jack and Wendy. The coupling sang. Of course, she would have to speak to him for him to fall in love with her. She had forgotten how to be human, though. She had forgotten how to think or talk or care about anything but herself.

For a moment, she felt this nagging sense of betraying Peter to fantasize about Jack. But wait, it was Peter who had betrayed her... hadn't he?

No, Peter, she thought firmly, envisioning herself dancing in a white pantsuit along with Diane, Goldie, and Bette to "You Don't Own Me," at the end of *First Wives Club*. Peter didn't get Cassandra *and* Wendy's life-long celibacy.

If this was anyone else's life, if this was happening in a Sandra Bullock movie, she would be saying, *Move On. He has, time for you to.*

Why wasn't she? Peter was gone. He hadn't returned a single text. And that had killed her. That response, the lack of response, was the response. Nothing. As in, you no longer mean anything. You mean nothing.

How did she go, she thought, from being someone he planned his life with, someone he shared his body and heart and dreams and family with, to being someone whose text he wouldn't even return?

Sometimes the pain was enough for her to want to just Virginia Woolf it right into the ocean with stones in her pockets.

But, "After death,..." Leanne had said, "...life." And this Jack man had made her feel a tiny spark of life — no, maybe even the rumblings of volcanic lava — within the corpse of her body. She couldn't wait to get to her two o'clock appointment at Leanne's.

She decided she would drive past Leanne's house in case she was outside.

Wendy rolled down Church Street slowly, like a stalker on a stakeout, and saw what she had hoped for — Leanne bent over her rosemary bush in a white linen dress and straw hat.

She parked quietly and stalked barefoot up Leanne's grey slate path.

"Hi," she said softly.

Leanne jumped at the sight of her.

"I'm sorry," Wendy said, "Did I scare you?"

"No, not you — your hair did. Good God, girl, your life is hard enough, why do you have to run around town looking like that?"

Wendy's face fell. "I was just going to get eggs at Al's."

"Well, here Al's is like Grand Central Station. You can't go nowhere here without being seen. So... run a brush through it." She looked over Wendy's sweats ensemble. "And... tuck something in." She looked closer. "Is that zit cream?"

Wendy's hand fluttered up to the corner of her lip and she etched away at the chalky white substance with a thumbnail.

"I was running, on the beach."

"That's good. That's good news. But…" she shook her head. "I'm just trying to help you out, kid. I know I'm a little rough around the edges."

"No… no, you're right. I should… I should try. I should try a little harder."

"That's the spirit. You never know who you might run into. There might just be life after *WhatsHisName*. Leanne refused to name Peter, like Voldemort.

"Well, actually, I saw someone today. His name, I think, is Jack."

"Woo hoo," Leanne let out a low whistle. "What do you know about that! Isn't that a fine specimen!"

"So you know him."

"Every woman on the island 'knows' him, my dear. Why, if I were thirty years younger…" She turned back to snip at the rosemary. "Don't want to make the bunnies blush."

Wendy bit her lip. "So he's like, a heartthrob or something?"

"He's the main eye candy of the female community."

"Oh."

Leanne turned around. "And you saw him like 'that', huh?"

"Yeah." Wendy sighed. "Shoot." She looked down in resignation. "I don't know what I was thinking, getting... " she shrugged. "Excited. I mean, you said it yourself... I'm a mess. I probably horrified him, if he noticed me at all."

Leanne clucked.

"Look, kid, you can't give up so easy. That's the sure sign of a loser. Every winner needs something to aspire to. And desire... well, desire created just about everything in this world. Yep, everything started with a dream. You wait to be perfect, you'll wait forever.

Looks like you've got yourself a reason to put two feet on the floor and brush your hair. And that, my friend, is just what the doctor ordered. Make no mistake. That's a cause for celebration." She put down the hedge trimmers and peeled off her Crocs by the front stoop.

"Come inside, I'll make you some tea." Wendy smiled, and happily followed Leanne into the house.

10.

Wendy sat down at Leanne's kitchen table while Leanne puttered around making their tea. She stopped in front of the window over the sink and peered up at the passing clouds.

"Well, would you look at that," she said. "Storm rolling in." She turned and looked at Wendy, who was playing with scattered pieces of a puzzle that would eventually form Van Gogh's Starry Night.

The sky rumbled. "And look who just got here." She smiled, shaking her head. "Figures."

Norman slinked against Wendy's legs and pushed his wet nose into her bare foot, mewing seductively.

Leanne's hand shooed him away. "Ya just ate, Mister. None of that preying on a helpless girl." Norman looked up at Leanne with utter disgust and retired, tail up, to the living room. Wendy watched him walk away with impeccable dignity in his white-slippered feet.

"Jack Fletcher, huh," Leanne said, screwing the mason jar of tea bags closed and returning it to the wooden shelf.

"Ain't he a picture. Could stare at that one all day."

"Well, I didn't know he was prime real estate around here."

"So?" Leanne asked.

"Well, I wouldn't have shot so high."

Leanne wheeled around, and put two hands behind her on the steel handle of the oven.

"Why the hell not?"

Wendy looked down at her slovenly sweatsuit, then up into Leanne's steely gray eyes. She said nothing. She thought the way she looked said everything.

"Reaching for something high up is the only way we grow. What are you gonna do, reach down below ya? No, we reach up. And you're not hopeless, you're just a project. You're just primed for a makeover, inside and out. You're a transformation waiting to happen.

You're one of those makeover movie dreams — I love those movies. Ask the ladies at the library, I'm always renting them. 'Cuz there's nothing I love more than transformation. *My Fair Lady. Pretty Woman*. In a Beggar, out a Queen. The Pygmalion effect. I can't take my eyes off of those stories, dammit."

"You think so? There's hope?"

"Well, abandon hope, kid. Forget the future, forget the past, embrace the now. You're your hope." The tea kettle hissed and Leanne switched off the flame. Thunder cracked over the house and outside the window, the air turned black.

"Well, hot damn," said Leanne.

"You're so close to starting over, can't you taste it? Cant you feel it? A new life moving in like a storm? I mean the fact that you even noticed someone besides yourself is a great sign. That's moving on for sure."

"Well, when do I get to start changing?"

"You're like my... daughter," Leanne said, pulling down two mugs from the shelf.

"You have a daughter?"

"Had. I had one."

"Where is she?"

"Now is not the time for that conversation."

Wendy bit her lip. "Okay, I'm sorry."

"Apologize when there's something to be sorry for. Anyway. One day she's two, the next day she's twenty. And she kept saying she couldn't wait to grow up. And the whole time, she was.

We've all got one of those *Days of Our Lives* hourglasses somewhere, and it's just runnin' on out, but we act like it ain't. Change is happening all the time, it's all there is. Trust me, you're changing. You're already older and wiser than when you walked in this door five minutes ago."

"I think my whole life I just wanted things to stay the same."

"Wishing for that will kill you. Change is life. No change- that's death. No, you gotta know, you're on the ride. Put your hands in the air and say 'Wheeeeeee'."

Wendy threw her hands up lightly, like she was in a roller coaster, just for fun, but the truth was that was exactly the way her life felt. A free fall. She had no control. She laughed despite herself.

"There ya go. So why didn't you talk to The Prince of the Island?" Leanne passed her a dark blue mug of tea. "My old boyfriend Bob made that mug," she chortled. "Big Ol' Wizard. That mug has magical powers. Make a wish when you drink from it. And, as always, be careful what you wish for."

All this magic talk... Wendy liked it. It was better than believing in nothing. She cupped the blue pottery chalice, closed her eyes and wished for the second time on the full moon for love. She sipped in the wish tea deeply.

"I didn't talk to him because I was afraid, I think," Wendy said.

"Of what?"

"I thought I was the journalist," Wendy said. "I'm used to asking the questions."

Leanne rolled her eyes. "Were. You were a journalist. Eight million years ago. Now you're sitting in my kitchen drinking tea. The past bores me. It puts me right to sleep. Snooze. No more past talk around me, got it? I've got no use for it. What I wanna know is what's happening now."

"Got it," Wendy said. Although she wasn't sure what she would talk about, she didn't feel she had much of a present.

As if she could read her mind, Leanne said, "You're enough. Just as you are. Right now. We all are. Ain't gotta be nothing other than who you are right now. Now, why didn't you talk to Jack Fletcher?"

"I guess… I don't *feel* like enough. I used to be. I'm not… anymore. I was scared of him… rejecting me. I looked terrible. And that he'd think I was weird, and that I would say something really stupid."

"Oh, you kids. You think you have your whole lives to live. That's a lie. What does the Buddha say? He says, 'Your problem is, you think you have time.' When you're young you think you'll live forever. You get a little older, time becomes more precious, you have more to lose. Life can really start then, if you're paying attention and letting it break your heart.

Here's what you need to be terrified of. Not living. Not falling in love. Not speaking up. Not taking chances. Not going for something that makes your heart feel like a Christmas bonfire. You need to spend your whole life, the time you got left, following that fire.

None of the other crap, none of the fear, none of the past, none of those distractions. Just the fire. Just the desire. What you truly desire, that's your destiny. That's your destiny, and that's your true destination."

Wendy ran her finger around the rim of the mug and thought about this concept of Transformation.

"Well," she prodded again. "When do I get to start, this new life?"

"That's easy. When you finish with your last one. You done with that disasta yet? You ready to say goodbye? Now's the time to throw it all in the fiyah — all of it, no exceptions — and walk out new. I'm telling you, kid, to really change, you can't do anything you used to do."

She pondered this. She had been holding so much space in her heart for Peter to come back that there was no room for anyone, or anything, else. She had frozen time while life passed her by.

"What are you still holding on to from it?" Leanne asked. "What's left? Is there anything alive left from your old life? No. It's all ashes and death. I can tell you this, kid, it's done with you. Now you gotta choose to be done with it. Lemme tell you something else, and it's a good thing you're sitting down.

It's that actually, you were as done with him as he was with you. You just didn't know it. So stop playing the victim. Stop telling that story. Life spared you. He did the honors, but you were dead inside, and that ain't no life. That's not love, either. That's what I'm saying.

Everything has a season, and your love had entered its winter. It was begging to die. He knew it. He did you a favor. It might have felt brutal, but it was a brutal gift. So receive it, and then release it. Sayonara.

It's the perfect time to let it go. Full moon." She looked up through the ceiling as if she could see it.

Wendy winced from all the truth Leanne had just served her.

"Here's the thing about life," Leanne said. "So often, the worst things that happen to us turn out to be the best."

Wendy wasn't so sure. She changed the subject.

"Speaking of the moon," she said, "I'm going to a circle tonight."

"Oh yeah? Where?"

"Her name is Danny, I met her on the beach."

"Well, would ya look at you! Social card filling up right there."

"Yeah, she invited me to her house."

"Ah, with all the baby witches."

Wendy balked. "Witches?"

"You say that like it's a bad thing."

"Well, isn't it?"

"You ever think about thinking for yourself? Try not to believe everything you hear, my dear. And you want a transformation? Nobody does a makeover like the Goddess."

"The Goddess?" Wendy asked.

Leanne sighed.

"Well, here's one way to look at it." She gestured with her right hand, "There's a Sun," and then with her left, "and there's a Moon, right? There's a day, and there's a night. There's masculine, and there's feminine, right?" She looked at Wendy to make sure she was following. Wendy nodded.

"So there's a male God... well, I'll be, is it so insane to think there's a female God?"

"I guess not," Wendy said.

"And all that feminine nature, that's the Goddess. That's the creative, healing, transformative energy. That's what's going to change you. She... she is change. The stuff of storms, seasons, cycles... of life, of death, of rebirth."

Something moved inside of Leanne's eyes, like a plan hatching. She took Wendy's hand and led her to the side screen door of the kitchen. She opened it and a powerful gust of wind came rushing into the room.

"Just look at her, I mean, feel her in action. Feel it in your body." Wendy usually hid from storms, but she watched the wind move the trees and she saw lightning fork over the hill. "Close your eyes, and feel it," Leanne said. Wendy closed her eyes. She breathed in the whooshing air.

Then she felt Leanne's hand on her back and a swift push, and she stumbled into the yard.

"Hey!" Wendy said, almost tripping over herself in the grass. She reached for the door, but Leanne pulled it shut, locking Wendy outside with the world. The thunder roared over her head, and lightning cracked a tree less than a mile away.

"Okay, I get it, Leanne. Let me in."

"Don't be afraid," Leanne said, from safely inside the screen door. "That's life out there, and you've been hiding from it in the porch of your mind, waiting for the rain to stop. But it never, ever stops. You've got to learn to move out into it, you've got to learn, even when it's scary, to dance in it."

"What?!" Wendy cried through a crack of thunder. Her hair whipped with the howling winds and the cloud above her cracked open, in two seconds flat she was soaking wet. She threw her arms around herself despite the warm winds, she huddled against the storm.

"Nothing can protect you from life!" Leanne had to shout over the roaring.

"You feel that energy? That's Mother Nature! That's what lives inside of you! It's the feminine forces of life! The power of rebirth! And you've got it, kid! We just need to wake it back up inside of you! That's the force of creation and we're ready to recreate you! You see? And see that moon in the sky?" Wendy looked up.

It was so dark in the middle of the day; the moon had made her debut early, right over Leanne's house. "You're just like her too! Sometimes you're light, sometimes you go dark, but just to glow again! She's always dying to be reborn!

You're mighty powerful! You've got the forces of creation inside of you! But you know what's most powerful about her? It's that she's soft and open enough to receive. She receives the sun's light, and that's how she glows.

She's vulnerable and worthy enough to receive light, life, and love — that's what fills her up and then she has something to offer! Then she's powerful enough to light up the dark and move the whole world. That's the Feminine, my friend."

"Okay, I get it," Wendy panted. "Can I come in now? My sweats weigh a million pounds." Her thick Hanes sweatshirt and pants hung off her like heavy wet sandbags, it felt like trying to move through wet cement.

"Well then, take 'em off."

"What?!" Wendy cried. Now she was getting angry. She hadn't been naked outside since she was two years old.

"You might as well take them off. Because you're not coming in here until lose some of that armor and you dance."

"No. I'm leaving."

"Fine, but you can never come here again," Leanne crossed her arms.

Wendy stared at this woman through the screen. She wasn't budging, she just stared back at Wendy, as serious as an ox.

For a moment, she thought about retreating. Of never seeing Leanne again. And once again, leaving the island, and going... where. She looked up at Leanne's face. Dammit, she loved that face.

"Life is asking you to dance," Leanne said. "You gonna say Yes?"

Wendy looked around. There was no one for miles. Just pouring rain over rolling acres of green land. She flared her nostrils, then she shook her head and she started to laugh. Oh, why the hell not, she thought.

"I hate you!" she cried through her laughter.

"Oooh!" Leanne whooped. "Something other than sorrow and self-pity! I like it! Today we've felt desire and anger! We're talkin' passion, people! There might just be life in you yet!" This time, for the first time since Wendy had met her, Leanne's laughter felt truly joyous.

This woman had already given her so much. Wendy wanted to give her something back. And once, once she really knew how to bask in the light.

Leanne wanted a show? She'd give it to her. She reached for the bottom of her thick wet sweatshirt. She peeled it off her body like an old dead layer of skin. She ripped off her sports bra. The water ran over her flesh and made her nipples stand at attention.

"Oooh, kid," Leanne said, "That running's been working. You're beautiful, kid, beautiful!"

Wendy blushed but kept giving Leanne a striptease, with the gusto not unlike an empowered exotic dancer who had once danced on a table she and Peter ate at in Spain. Wendy had watched her unbridled femininity in awe, feeling helplessly trapped in her own body.

She stepped out of her sweatpants like another layer of skin, and then, for her last act, she peeled her underwear down off her legs and flung it into the rose bush.

"Ow ow owwwww!" she cried like a wild thing on the moors. She opened her arms to the moon and tossed her head back, catching the rain in her throat.

"Now here's the trick, darling. Even when you're fully clothed, stay this naked. Stay this free." Wendy shivered alive.

Inside, Leanne had moved her old beatbox radio to the table by the screen door.

"Lose the armor. Let life take you. Let it make love to you with its mystery."

The local radio was playing the beginning strains of Ben Howard's "Only Love."

"You know this man?" Leanne shouted. "He's one sexy mutha." Wendy stood naked in the warm rain and watched Leanne start to sway her hips across the kitchen floor in the glow of the lamp, her eyes closed, like she was dancing with God.

"Why, if I was 30 years younga…" Leanne mused with a satisfied smile on her face, like she was moving in warm liquid honey.

Wendy's heart filled with love for this woman. She felt it burst like a cloud and crack open with the thunder, she felt it rain love.

"You'd make the bunnies blush!" Wendy cried through the storm, howling with laughter.

"That's right, kid. You betcha. Now it's your turn. You're up to bat in life. Make the bunnies blush. Show me what it looks like to do something with your whole heart."

Leanne cranked the radio up so loud it battled the roar of Mother Nature. The music filled the backyard, filled her body. And with that, Wendy began to move, the rain washing her clean of the past, her heart as cracked open as the sky, the moon filling it with desire.

And then she moved her hips, as if she was dancing for the first and last time in her life, and once she started, she couldn't stop.

"Keep moving those hips, baby. That's where all the rebirth energy is. Keep 'em fluid and juicy!"

Wendy swiveled them with all the sensual fluidity of that Spanish tabletop dancer.

"That's it! Out of the mind, into the body! That's where the life is!" They danced together through the screen door. Leanne in the warm light, Wendy dancing in the wet dark.

"Only Love! Only Love! Only Love!" she and Leanne cried in unison.

"So," Leanne cried. "You ready to let the past go?"

"Yes," Wendy whispered into the wind.

"She can't hear you!" Leanne cried, pointing at the moon.

"YES!" Wendy screamed.

"And you're ready to say Yes to life?"

"YES!!" Wendy screamed even louder, her arms raised to the moon, shedding her skin like a snake and shaking her hips like the wind, in her birthday suit, soaked down to the very bone, to her very essence.

"Wendy," Leanne hollered through the screen, "You're going to make one damn fine woman. Just you wait and see. Look out, Jack Fletcher."

The thunder cracked and Leanne let out another whoop from within the kitchen.

Outside, awash in Nature's dark and beautiful baptism, Wendy was still crying "Yes, Yes, Yes," as naked as the day she was born.

11.

Leanne had sent her off wrapped in warm white towels fresh from the dryer, smelling of lavender.

She had one on her head, one around her body, and she drove home that way, blasting the heat and Bonnie Raitt on the local radio. She almost wanted to get pulled over, just for the story of it. Stories like that are what people who really live tell, she thought.

"I got pulled over on a full moon in a storm, wearing nothing but a witch's terrycloth towel, and had to explain, that I had been dancing naked in the rain."

But she made it home safely, and poured herself some Kava tea, and then she ran a hot bath. She still had two hours before she had to be at Danny's for the moon circle.

"Go home, and mix some olive oil with rock salt," Leanne had said as she shooed her out of the door.

"Smoothe it all over your skin, then slough it off in the bath. And bathe yourself with the gentleness you would a newborn. When you rise, let the old self you're done with run down the drain, and let her go with love and gratitude and forgiveness."

She made the special salve and rubbed it all over herself gently. She put on Nina Simone in the living room stereo and she turned her up so loud that Nina haunted the whole house.

She turned off the lights and lit the candles in the bathroom, and when she stepped into the tub, Nina was singing *Plain Gold Ring*. She felt like she was part of an ancient ritual of rebirth, full of intention for her new life.

Immersed deep in the oily, milky water, submerged but for her nose and mouth, she could only hear her heartbeat and breath.

She was remembering a watsu treatment she had done in Hawaii when Peter had played a festival there, she was being held by a large Hawaiian man in a big dark tank, just limp and trusting in his arms like a baby in the womb, and he had said, "This is how God holds you, you can let go now." And she was letting go like that, when she heard her phone receiving a text in the bedroom.

Every bone in her body knew who it was from. She rose from the bath and made a swampy path to where her phone lay on the bed.

"Hey," Peter wrote.

"Hi," she texted back.

Maybe this shivering solitude of a nightmare is over, she thought. Maybe he's coming back.

"You should know before you hear it," he said.

"Hear what?"

"Cassandra is pregnant."

The phone fell from her hands and the glass face shattered when it hit the wood floor. She fell, soaking wet and naked, into the bed. When she caught her breath, she reached for more, more pain from him, despite the little girl within her calling out, "No, please no."

She was hanging halfway off the bed as she slid the phone toward her with her index finger and slowly, with sickness in her throat, asked, "Are you marrying her?" Her fingers trembled as she typed.

With baited breath and the story of them reeling in the movie of her mind, every memory and every dream they had, and all the hopes she'd stored, that she would get her shit together and then he'd come back, she waited.

It felt like seven days passed.

And then:

"Probably," he wrote, with all the tenderness of a serial killer.

Nina's crucified heart was moaning through *You Can Have Him*, when Wendy pulled the covers over her head and sobbed like the rain that poured outside.

As if through a black mourning veil, she saw The Story of Them and she watched herself bury it, she watched herself throw dirt on its casket, and then watched the casket as it was lowered into the dark flesh of the ground.

And when she came up for air from the visions, gulping through the rivers of tears she whispered, "Take care of him, Cassandra. Please take good care of him."

Two hours later, with Danny's moon circle swiftly approaching, she wished time would just freeze so she wouldn't have to make a decision about going. The clock above her bed ticked away, loudly, impatiently, like that hourglass of our lives Leanne had talked about.

It waited rudely, tapping its thin second-hand while she struggled to make a decision.

But she never did make one. And then time made one for her. And she thought, that indecision was a decision in itself, that way. It was almost as if indecision was like deciding not to live, or not to move forward, at least. But moving forward was living. Change is life, Leanne had said. No change, death.

And then she realized, when you don't make a decision, time makes one for you, and you don't get that choice back.

Defeated, she dug for the remote under the covers and clicked on the TV. Then she rolled over and stared at the wall. She felt pain for the loss of the not-yet-quite-born friendship with Danny, but she couldn't move. Grief sat on her like a twelve-million-pound elephant.

Night fell as Olivia Benson interrogated another sex offender in the cold grey room of the *SVU* precinct. She'd seen the sexy brazen detective hand it to about five bad guys since she had gotten into bed.

She fell asleep as Benson banged the table with her fist and said, "She was someone's daughter," to the greasy angry perp in the tan Member's Only jacket who hissed under his breath, "Yeah, well seems like everyone in this world belongs to someone or someone belongs to them. Everyone but me. For once I wanted something that was mine."

I get it, she thought, repulsing herself for relating to the perp in the pervy jacket.

Ten hours later, she woke to a knocking at the door. The TV blinked across the room, there was an infomercial on, a woman with dead eyes was selling more plastic products for the landfills. She jumped up in her black lace underwear and scrambled for a sweater on the chair.

It was Danny, with a large wicker basket draped over her arm. The basket was full of eggs, green peppers, a loaf of bread, and two Tupperware containers. With her long brown braids and over-sized red fleece, she looked like Little Red Riding Hood.

Wendy had never seen anyone in real life carry a basket laden with goods. She opened the door apologizing.

"I'm so sorry," she said, wrapping the frayed black cashmere sweater tighter against the morning chill. "I…"

Danny just moved on past her, towards the kitchen. She walked gracefully, like someone stepping lightly over clouds.

"The girls laid some good ones this morning," she said, gingerly removing five large brown eggs from a red and green plaid hand towel. "And Jay-Z and Beyonce gave us fresh chèvre," she said, peeling open the Tupperware and revealing a large scoop of soft white cheese. "Those are our goats."

"And this bread just came out of the oven. Feel it, it's still warm." She put it against Wendy's face, looking into her eyes for the first time since she'd arrived so unexpectedly. Wendy closed her eyes and smelled something like the most warm loving home she'd only ever visited.

She watched as Danny whipped the eggs and poured them, sizzling into a pan, chopped the green peppers and then dropped them and the cheese into the bubbling yellow liquid. She opened the window over the sink and looked out to the water.

She stopped for a moment, closing her eyes and breathing it in. Then she sliced the loaf and toasted the bread. She moved around the kitchen like she was born in it.

"So, I would have called you, I just don't have your number…" Wendy said, still trying to apologize as Danny split the omelet in two and buttered the toast.

"Did you make that too?" she asked of the butter.

Danny laughed. "No, I bought this. I assumed you wouldn't have any." She handed Wendy a plate.

Wendy nodded. "Astute."

"You look hungry," Danny said, taking her in, stopping at her hips. "Nice undies. I should spice it up in the bedroom. I'm pretty sure I'm wearing underwear I've had since eleventh grade." And then, softly but firmly, she said, "Eat."

"Thank you," Wendy said.

"You like to cook?" She asked Wendy.

"I can slice open a frozen pizza box pretty well."

Danny shook her head. "That's not going to nourish you. You're starved."

Wendy looked down at the smaller, but still there layer of down that still covered her body then looked at Danny like she was crazy. "Um, I don't think so."

"For nourishment. For life. For your own love. For real deep comfort. You have to learn to receive it. You have to know you're worthy, of receiving your own love. If you can't receive your own love, you'll never be able to receive anyone else's."

Wendy forked the fresh eggs into her mouth.

"Oh my God. These are the best eggs I've ever had."

Danny nodded. "Eat things straight from the earth. From the Mother. She'll nourish you."

They sat on the bar stools at the silver kitchen island. Wendy crossed her legs and her right foot tapped nervously against the wood of the island.

"Should I put on some music?" Wendy asked.

"I'm okay with silence," Danny said. "I like it."

"Oh," she said, putting her fork down and turning to her basket. "I brought you one more thing," she dug into its endless depths.

"A lamp?" Wendy joked.

Danny looked up at her.

"You know, Mary Poppins."

"It's a journal," she said, handing her a small leather bound book. "I know you used to write, well I read that... in *People*. Isn't that how you and Peter Jackson met? You interviewed him? You were a writer?"

"Yes," she whispered. Her heart remembered with a raw howl, I *was* something.

"Maybe you could, I don't know, start by writing down your dreams."

Wendy took the gift. "Thank you," she said. "You mean, from sleep? I don't really have those. Well I do, but I'd rather not remember them."

"Well, what about the ones you have for your new life?"

Wendy shrugged. "Gosh, I don't really have those either. I feel sort of... dreamless."

"Oh. Like that place between sleeping and waking. Maybe that's kinda where you are. You know, in your life."

"That feels right," Wendy said. "You're very wise. This island seems to be overflowing with wise women."

"We breed here. By the dozens. It's thick with witches."

"There's that word again," Wendy said.

"We're just aligned with the earth and the moon. We listen to our internal wisdom. We're one with nature. Nothing scary about it." She finished her toast and licked the butter from her strong fingers. "Sick of people thinking that there is. Some people pray to God, some to Goddess, some to both. Me," she shrugged, "both."

"I do have one dream," Wendy said.

"Oh yeah?"

"Well, not a dream. Just an interest. I saw a really, really handsome man the other day."

"You left your house?" Danny smiled.

"I deserved that. I'm so sorry about last night... I can explain."

"Nah," said Danny. "I know you're in your... situation."

"I saw him at Al's. His name..." something told her not to say it, but she did so anyway. "His name is Jack."

A darkness passed over Danny's eyes.

"Shoulda known."

"You know him?"

Danny shot her a look, like "Come on."

"Dumb question, huh?"

"You were here what, two weeks, and we met? There's just two thousand of us in the winter. Only a few of us under fifty. Funny thing about people thinking they're coming to hide here. If you wanna hide, stay in one of your anonymous big-ass cities. Everyone knows everyone here and everyone sees all. I think, really, people come to truly see themselves and be seen, despite what they tell themselves."

"Did you grow up with him?" She couldn't contain her curiosity about Jack.

"You could say that. I'm not gonna tell you to not to go for Jack Fletcher. I'm just gonna tell you, be careful. And, you know, *you* should be your dream. Not some guy."

"You're absolutely right. I'm great at distractions."

"If you don't mind me asking, what did happen with Peter?"

"It's okay. Well, he said... he said 'I never came true.'" Wendy no longer had an appetite. She pushed her plate away, pulled her hair back from her face and longed for a big dewy glass of white wine.

"Well, what the hell does that mean?" Danny asked.

"Like," Wendy breathed in deep and wrapped her arms around herself. "I didn't end up feeling real to him."

"What, like not human?"

"I guess not." She looked up at Danny. "You're... you're a good human," she told her. "Coming over here, with breakfast, checking in on me. That's, that's maybe one of the nicest things someone's done for me in a really long time. I don't know how to do things like that. I've always thought people like you were..."

"People like me?" Danny asked.

"You're real. People like you, who do things for others, not just to get something in return, who know how to really live, who are deep in their self-created busy lives, constantly showing up, you're more real than me."

Danny reached over and pinched Wendy lightly on her arm.

"You're real, Wendy."

Wendy smiled.

"I don't feel very real."

Danny looked around at the expensive rented kitchen. "Maybe when this money runs out, and you have to figure out what you're good at and how to offer that to the world, you'll feel a bit more real. But I just live how my mother taught me. She's pretty humble and hard working. Being human is a practice. Love is a practice.

I think being human is practicing love."

"Maybe I don't know what love is."

"Everyone knows what love is. It's what you are." Danny got up and took their plates to the sink, and began to wash them in slow meditative movements. She did everything slowly, sensually, like she relished being in her body.

"So… why *didn't* you show last night?" she asked, keeping her back to Wendy.

"I… I heard from Peter."

"Oh really?" Danny placed the dishes in the drying rack and moved on to the pan.

"He and his new girlfriend are pregnant. They're… probably getting married."

"Ouch," Danny said. She dropped the sponge into the sink and swirled back around. She looked Wendy right in the eyes.

"Look, I know this happened just a few months ago. But I just, I just hope you don't make this 'your story'. Do you know what I mean? If it becomes your story, you get stuck in it. It defines you. Then no other wonderful stories take place.

You'll plug every new guy into the place of Peter and you'll be stuck in an endless spin cycle of being left by Peter, even though it will be a different face. Same story. Same, 'I got left and everyone is always going to leave me' bullshit fucking story.

I know, because my sister Emily did that. And it's been so painful to watch. Her husband left her, and now she's been telling herself and everyone else the same story for five years. It was awful, yes, but she got like, addicted to the sadness of it… like she's under a spell.

He, he moved on. She didn't. He's alive, he's living. She… not so much. She's trapped under glass, like Sleeping Beauty."

Wendy felt punched in the stomach with resonance. And then she said quietly, "I don't want to do this for five more years."

"Well," Danny said, "that's up to you. So learn what you gotta learn, so you don't keep doing what you did, but don't forget to keep living, don't stop taking chances. Don't keep telling yourself this story of victimhood and rejection." She tapped the journal she'd brought Wendy. "Write a new story."

Wendy gulped. "It's funny, well not funny, I just can't think of a better word. But for a moment last night, there was a second I thought he wanted me back and I wouldn't have to do all this... work on myself. And all the work of being alone."

Danny sighed, and rested her elbows on the island and her head in her hands. "We're all alone, really. If you don't mind me saying..."

"Oh no," Wendy said.

"What?"

"Just that that's how a lot of things you don't want to hear begin."

"Ah," said Danny, but she carried on anyway. "It sounds like things went south in your marriage when you stopped... doing the work. Caring for yourself. And being true to yourself and following your own dreams. Not just his. You know you have to do that with or without a relationship, right?"

"It's just that he was..."

Danny interrupted her. "As long as you're talking in the past, you're living in the past. And the present is the only place anything is really happening. There's no Someday, Wendy. There's really only Today. Tomorrow is going to be just like today if you don't change things now."

Wendy shut up, and then found herself staring Danny's sea-green eyes and pillows of lips. "You really are amazing to look at," she told her. "Like crazy pretty. You've seriously never modeled?"

Danny smiled and began to pack up her Red Riding Hood basket. "Nice transition. I have to go help Ray with the animals. Anyway, stop doing that. Stop complimenting me to get me to like you or something. I already do. But I won't if you keep doing it."

Amy was stunned. It's how girls won each other over in New York, they were always lavishing each other with praise, even if they didn't mean it, even if in the next moment they'd turn around and stab each other in the back.

"Right," Wendy said, standing up from the bar stool. "I should go running. Thank you. ... I'd say thank you again but it would sound insincere."

"De nada," said Danny, crossing through the living room as Wendy followed her. She turned to Wendy in the door way. She leaned in for a hug and Wendy received it. Danny was so warm.

"The truth is," Danny said, pulling away and reaching for the door, "I did model. But with all that attention on me, I became a real asshole. You think you want it, but really, it's not all it's cracked up to be. Everyone treated me like I was so special, and then I began to feel... different.

And it got really lonely, actually. I got really isolated on my stupid fucking pedestal. For a moment I forgot, well, you know, how to be human. And I forgot that I was just like everyone else. And that being like everyone else wasn't the bad news, it was the good news."

"I knew it," Wendy said, "that you modeled, I mean."

"And so are you, Wendy. You're just like everyone else, too. And that's the good news."

"You know," she said, "you can't turn your back on yourself just because someone turned their back on you. You've still gotta hold your own hand. Always."

"Thank you," Wendy said. Danny walked out of the door, and the wind was blowing cool and soft through the trees, whose leaves had turned gold and red, never so beautiful as right before they died. Somehow that felt cruel, that they couldn't stay like that forever.

And then Danny stopped and turned around.

"Oh... one trick to being human," she said. "Leave the house and let people see you and let them love you just as you are. Even when you're not feeling perfect and your life isn't perfect. Because if you wait for that, you'll never leave the house and you'll never let yourself be loved.

And then your life will be over and you won't have lived. All because some dude left you."

She fished her keys out of the pocket of her red fleece. "Okay, enough lecturing. You can tell me to shut up. I get on my horse sometimes."

"No," Wendy asked, "What else?"

"Huh?"

"How else do I be a better human?"

Danny opened the door to her enormous grey truck and put the basket on the passenger seat.

She turned the key in the ignition and the radio started singing. She turned back to Wendy, standing waiting in the door way.

She seemed to disappear for a moment, tuning into the music that sailed out of the car. she tuned back in.

"Be of service. Be a sensible person. Use your words, and don't be nervous. Find your medicine and use it."

"Hey!" Wendy laughed. "You're just quoting Medicine for the People."

"Ha, you got me," Danny laughed. She leaned in and turned up *Manifesto*, pumping out of the truck's speakers.

"Dance," she said, moving her hips to Nahko. "And don't be so serious!" she raised her voice with her arms over her head. "If you're not having fun, you're missing the point. Find your joy and let it be your North Star. When you get lost, look for it again."

They shook it together a little like that, Wendy only a bit more clothed than she was the day before, dancing in the open air. They laughed together in the wind. Then Wendy breathed in deep and felt serene, she felt like her self, whoever that was.

"I love the things you say to me as you're leaving, Danny."

"That's when the best stuff seems to happen, you know? Right at the last minute. It's why you can't ever give up."

Danny jumped in her truck and pulled away, beeping at the end of the driveway. Wendy walked back into the empty house. It was too quiet. She wanted Danny back. She noted in herself the shift from wanting to be alone to wanting company. That felt... human. And she had danced, sober, two days in a row. She felt like she was starting to have a life of her own.

She switched on the radio to fill the void Danny had left.

Tracy Chapman was singing.

"I had a feeling that I belonged.

I had a feeling, that I could be someone."

12.

Wendy was up early the next morning, and before she could think, so she didn't have to, she sprinted down to the beach barefoot in her sweats, running for half an hour to the soundtrack of the breath of the water and the breath of her lungs.

But when thoughts of Peter and his new family caught up with her and began to flood the bowl of her mind, she stopped, losing her life-force. Her knees went jelly-like and she fell into the sand.

Dammit, she thought. She sat there caked in sweat and sucking in breath, fighting salty tears as the great tears of the earth rose and fell before her. Sometimes, just like hers, they felt like waves of sorrow, sometimes joy. Fuck. It.

She rose and stripped to nothing and hurled herself into the icy late October water.

"Ay yi yi yi!!" she shrieked, as the thoughts of Peter were ripped from her mind and sank to the ocean floor. She bolted upward from the shock, laughing as she nearly ran across the water to get back to the shore.

She hadn't laughed alone, she thought, since she was a child.

She ran up the wooden steps naked, shivering, clutching her sweats, and stood, head tossed back to the sky under the hot outdoor shower.

The inside of the house felt lonely, she wanted to be outside, where the world was alive, she wanted to be in the bustle of others. So she dressed herself with actual care, black leggings and a white tank top and a long tan cardigan, and went to Al's, the heartbeat of the island.

Pumpkins lined the porch, and a little girl, whose face was painted with whiskers and a black triangle of a nose, sat with her legs swinging from the hammock. She stared at Wendy as she sucked on a juice box.

"Good morning," she said to the girl.

"Meow," the girl replied.

She got a coffee for herself and then thought to get an Earl Grey for Leanne, just in case she was home.

Deep into Fall, the crowd was thinning out to locals, carpenters and fishermen in plaid and Dickies. They had extra scruff on their faces to protect from the chill of their outdoor labor, they drank coffee in to-go mugs and thumbed through the papers.

And they all knew each other, it seemed, since birth. They spoke a low, familiar, abbreviated language to one another.

"Chuck."

"Dan."

"Martha?"

"Yep."

"Linda?"

"Same."

"Ya motha?"

"Betta." And then Chuck grunted, and Dan tapped Chuck on the back with a newspaper and that was how they said Goodbye.

She was beginning to recognize faces, and they began to recognize her too.

"Hi," a ginger-bearded, kind-eyed man her age had said as he held the door open for her. "Thank you," she'd said, and one nod from a venerable white-haired farmer to whom everyone seemed to pay special homage made her chest soar a bit.

The girl at the register told her her name was Sandra. "I like your necklace, Sandra," she'd said, entranced once again by the gleaming pentagram.

"Oh, thanks. Are you one of us?" she asked, pushing her horn-rimmed black glasses up her button nose with a chipped purple nail.

Something stirred in Wendy. "I'm not.. not one."

Sandra winked. "Well, welcome to the Lovin' Coven," she said. "Coffee's on me."

Wendy beamed like she'd won the lottery.

By the time she got to Leanne's, she nearly skipped down the path.

She knocked gently on the door. Leanne opened it in a long white nightgown and a grey shawl over her shoulders, her white hair fell nearly to her waist.

"You're up with the larks," she said. She looked Wendy up and down, taking her in.

Wendy had brushed her hair and pulled it back into a low bun. She'd even applied concealer and mascara and a trace of red lip liner. The red of her lips pronounced the blue of her slightly dancing eyes, and they hadn't shone in as long as she could remember.

"Well, I'll be damned, if it ain't the Queen of England," Leanne said. "To what do I owe this pleasure?" she asked, scooting Wendy in through the door past Norman, who slept in front of the fire in the living room. She ushered Wendy to the little table in the kitchen, where she'd replaced Van Gogh with a Scrabble game.

The man on the radio was reading the results of the Bluefish Derby and forecasting a record chilly Halloween.

"I brought you Earl Grey," Wendy said.

"Thanks, honey. But I don't drink that. I'm old. I know what I like and what I don't. Had a few years to figure it out." Then she gave Wendy a swift pat on the back. Leanne always touched her like she didn't want to get attached. A noncommittal touch that pulled away as soon as it made contact.

Wendy jumped a bit beneath her fingers. "Now doesn't that feel betta, to treat yourself betta," she asked.

"Yes," Wendy agreed, sitting down at the table and crossing her legs, folding her hands, feeling... dignified.

"I play myself, but you're welcome to replace me," Leanne said nodding at the game board.

Wendy assessed the letters.

"Oof," she said.

"Well, you're the writer, right? Make some magic."

She planted a room temperature glass of water in front of Wendy.

"Elixir of the Gods. Drink up."

"Thank you." Wendy moved the tiles around and scrunched her face.

"How was the moon circle?" Leanne asked.

"I didn't go."

"Ah, honey, that's too bad."

"I couldn't."

"Why? What you gonna do, avoid life your whole life and call it a life?"

"No."

Leanne chugged her water and banged the empty glass down on the table, the Scrabble tiles rattled. "You asked about my daughter, right?"

"Yes," Wendy said, sipping her coffee. "I did."

"Well, I'll tell you. But know I'm not in the business of flinging around what's sacred. I don't know why people don't keep the sacred sacred."

Wendy thought of her late mother, she saw her delicate, small round face. She had a perfect angelic face and tiny beautiful hands. She looked down at her own hands, so similar, they could be her mother's. She began to massage the right palm with the left thumb, and then she switched.

"Shelly. Her name was Shelly. She's no longer among us. In the flesh anyway."

"I'm so sorry."

"That won't bring her back. The only thing that would bring her back is if she hadn't drunk five glasses of wine and gotten in her car on North Road five years ago. Hit that big oak tree, the one that forks like a choice. Like, you can go this way, or you can go that way.

Every thought and every single choice we make matters, you know. It creates the whole path. Everything. Every single little thing, matters."

Wendy lifted her chin. She stared right back at Leanne and directed her heart right to hers. "I'm still sorry, I still mean that."

Leanne cocked her head, and thought for a moment. She was quiet.

"Alright. Well, in that case, I'll take it. I just don't take empty sorries."

"I get that."

"And I don't like to dwell in the past."

"I know," said Wendy.

"But you wanna do something for me better than a sorry?"

"Yes," Wendy said.

"Live ya fucking life, kid. Take some fuckin' changes. Like Audrey says in *My Fair Lady*, 'move your bloomin' ass.'"

Wendy straightened her spine and held her head up taller. She breathed in deep through her nose.

"I am trying, Leanne."

"Eh," Leanne said. "It's not really about trying. It's a choice like that tree. You think too much. You tell too many stories. Right now, all you have is stories. You know who sits around thinking and talking about the past? Old people and dead people. And they're allowed. That's all they have. You?

You don't get to do that. Look at you." Leanne pointed to the mirror above the oven. Wendy looked up in it. She could see her face for the first time since she could remember. And she had forgotten all about, and given up hope, of seeing it again. *There you are*, she thought. *I had really missed you.*

"Life isn't something you talk about, honey, it's something you live. You gotta use that body. You gotta use that heart. You gotta use those hands."

"Don't let mourning your past or worrying about your future steal one more moment from living your present."

Florence was singing *Shake it Out* on the local radio. Wendy wasn't resisting what Leanne was saying anymore. She was only resisting dancing. Her body was loving all this recent dancing. How had she gone so long without it?

"I won't," Wendy promised.

"Great. You've decided to really be here. That's great. You've accepted the invitation. So if you wanna be a real human, you have to have relationships with other humans."

"Okay," Wendy placed the letter L on the board.

"Okay then. So today's the day you join the land of the living. And you stop making excuses. Perfect timing. Because Jack Fletcher is at the Farmer's Market."

"Oh God." Wendy's face went pale and her foot stopped tapping to Florence.

"Yep. Every Saturday morning. Right around the corner. Selling his wares. Although most gals just buy a cucumber just to look at him. I suggest you and your fancy shoes," Leanne nodded down at Wendy's leopard flats, "huff it on over there and make some mother-loving contact. Otherwise it's just gonna be a fantasy. And those are dangerous. They'll rob you of your whole life. Nothing beats experience."

"I'm not ready," she said.

"Well, when will you be ready?"

"I don't..."

"That's a trick question. If you're alive right now, you're ready. Let's start this story."

"Damn you," Wendy said. "You're going to be the death of me." She placed the letter E.

"If it's the death of that small scared dried up self, well, then it would be my honor."

"Ugh," Wendy groaned and rolled her eyes.

"Norman, help me," she cried to the cat in the other room.

"That selfish asshole only helps himself." Then she called, "God bless you, Norman."

"Listen, I'm telling you. This is what humans do. They practice being human with other humans."

"Danny said being a human is practicing love," Wendy said.

"Yeah, that's right. Smart girl. For yourself and others. And if you love your self, you'll forgive her for the past, let her have a real life, a real adventure, and another chance at love."

Wendy placed the letter A.

"Love is not easy, kid. That's why most people give up on it after they lose it. But it makes you real. The hard stuff, the heart stuff, that makes you real. This is your moment. This is the place some people close off forever, after the hurt. This is the place where you get to choose to get back up again. Now or never.

It's always now or never. And it's always your choice. To stay open and feel the pain and feel the fear and let it all happen anyway."

"I've decided that's what I want."

"What?"

"To move forward. To be real. I want to be a real person with real relationships and a real life. And be a human."

"It's the hardest thing you'll ever do, being a goddamned human. I remember when they went to the moon the first time. I watched it on my little TV. I was sitting there thinking that going up to that ghostland in the sky was far easier than being down here with all these crazy people.

The moon, with not a soul around? That's the easy shit. Down here on earth? Well, god damn. This takes courage."

"Ha," Wendy laughed. "Maybe that's why I've put it off for so long. But it's true. And you told me I had to figure out what I wanted."

"You sure do, if you want to get anywhere in life."

"I want that. And I want..." Wendy licked her lips and then bit down until she felt sensation. "Intimacy."

"Ah, yes," Leanne said. "To touch and be touched. In every single way. That's what we're here for. You know what I wish for you? That moment where you go,

'I don't care anymore what anyone else does or thinks, I'm just gonna be myself'. That's the moment it all comes together. After it all falls apart. It's the sunrise. The clarity. It's the 'Holy shit, this is my one life and I've gotta fucking live it' moment. It's the Billy Joel *My Life* moment. It's the Sinatra *My Way* moment. Then you shake it all off and get clear again.

And from there on out, the only advice you take is from God, or, Love. No one else's worried, fearful, jealous, or angry projections or opinions move you. Just your own heart. Just you and Spirit, running the show. Your show. It's Your. Fucking. Show. Those are the moments we start to live again. Where we make some real decisions and act on them and un-stick ourselves and move the river and see that there was nothing ever to fear except not living our true purpose. You get rid of all the bullshit holding you back and suddenly you're you again. When how you feel about yourself and your choices takes precedence over what people say or think.

And suddenly, what does Cohen say? Suddenly, every breath you take is Hallelujah."

"Well, that sounds amazing, but I think I have to know who I am, to feel like me again."

Leanne rose from the table and Wendy rose too, placing the last letter, P, on the board. Leanne looked down.

"Exactly," she said.

"Ah, you just have to remember. And I don't think you have anything better to do than remember who you really are. And you find out through experience. That's how you know who you are. That's how the world knows who you really are. Action. It's not in the talk, it's in the walk."

"Gotcha," Wendy said, petting Norman by the fire as they walked out.

"Now, no offense, but get the hell out of here. I want to take my bath."

Wendy's leopard feet stalked slowly down the stone path, taking a left toward the Farmer's Market. Her whole body was quivering. She stopped in the street and looked back at Leanne, who shot an arm up in a wave.

"It's time to go live a new story, honey!" she called.

"I think I'm going to barf," Wendy said.

"That's good! That's the feeling you get when you leave your comfort zone! Follow the barf feeling!"

"Thank you. I owe you."

"No, kid. The only thing you owe anyone is your happiness. Your misery, that serves nobody. Your joy? That serves the world. May your cup run over, child."

13

Her first tactic at the Farmer's Market was to hide behind the lady selling fresh egg rolls. Until the woman said if she wasn't buying she had to move, and she had way too nervous a stomach to eat Chinese food at 10 in the morning. So then she slunk over to the girls selling yarn hats they'd spun from llama wool. She watched Jack Fletcher at his stand from there, as she gently grazed her fingers over a soft pink hat that she might actually buy if she weren't allergic to wool, for winter was coming and she had nothing warm to wear.

She stalked him like that for a while through the thin crowd of locals walking in the dusty parking lot of the market. Their dogs sniffed each other in greeting as they made their way across the sand lined with white tents sheltering local food and wares. But everyone was a blur compared to him, he glowed like a god, and all the voices chatting and dogs barking muffled in her mind as she tried to make out the words on his lips as he conversed with customers.

There was a frosty morning breeze blowing but he wore just a thin grey t-shirt with holes in it; it looked so soft and worn she imagined he'd had it since he was a teenager. Then she imagined back to the boy in him and her heart softened. The wind blew his thick black hair in waves across his face and his strong masculine hands caressed so carefully the vegetables he'd raised from the earth himself.

She watched him gently pass a bunch of carrots to a middle-aged woman in a white cotton sweater. He placed them atop the pile in her arms of his beets, broccoli and collards. The woman blushed as he laid them breast level in her arms, then placed a hand on her shoulder in thanks. *Keep that up and she'll buy the whole stand*, Wendy thought. As if he could hear her thoughts, he looked up across the market, directly into her eyes. Wendy dropped the pink hat and looked away, toward nothing, toward anything else. But when she looked back up he was still staring at her. He waved a thick muscled arm. She tentatively raised a hand. He waved her over to him. Wendy shuffled across the lot, pulled to him like a magnet.

"Come back when you've got more arms," he smiled to the woman in white.

Then he held out fresh squeezed orange juice in a shot-sized Dixie cup to Wendy.

"It's the Orange Juice Girl," he said.

"Well, it's Wendy," she said.

"I know," he said.

"I'm Jack," he said.

"I know," she said.

He smiled softly at her. "Welcome to the island, Wendy. Here's the best stuff in the world."

She took it, and as she did so her fingers grazed his and an electrical current passed between them. Her vagina leapt like a mummy from a crypt in a horror house. Back from the dead.

"Second chakra juice," he said. She sipped from the cup gingerly, like a Princess at High Tea.

"What?" she asked.

He rubbed his lower belly with his large dirt-caked paw and his thin grey t-shirt rode up to reveal the marble carvings of his hip bones. She breathed in through her nose and her eyes got stuck right above his soft leather belt for a moment. But he seemed to like watching her watch him. She looked back up into his eyes. He had long dark lashes that lent a vulnerability to his intense masculinity.

"You know, the seat of your sexuality," he said slowly, his eyes searching hers, like some sort of dare game. She held his gaze. She dared.

"Your second chakra. Energy center. It's orange," he explained.

"I didn't know that," she said. "That's... that's sort of German to me." She couldn't take it anymore. She had to look away. She had a feeling that he always won.

"You don't do yoga?" he asked. Then he ran his eyes along her. "You have the body for it."

That threw her right off her center. Did he just make it clear he liked her? Were they being adults acknowledging interest? She was still approaching adulthood, at 33 years old. She was a terrible flirt. She was a child more comfortable in fantasy. He had the confidence of an adult entirely comfortable with reality, and letting people know exactly how he felt.

"No, I never have. I've been… running. I mean, I'm a runner. Well, I just started. I mean, I was on the couch for a long time, running from life." Shut. Up. Wendy.

He just stared at her, like now it was she who was speaking German. She felt like Baby carrying a watermelon. Why was it, she wondered, that we were so cool, too cool, around people who already loved us, but with the people we wanted to love us, we were absolute schmucks?

"Well, anyway," he said. "Want to come to a class with me? I'll pick you up tomorrow. Ten o'clock. There's a good one down island."

"Okay," she stammered.

"You're renting the Pearse's place. On the cliff."

"Yes," she said.

"Jack," a woman's voice purred from behind her. "Any leeks?" Farmer groupies, she thought. A whole new ball game. She'd dealt with Peter's groupies, who showed absolute loathing and contempt for her, and whom she loathed in return when he was on the road without her. She had never wanted to deal with groupies again.

"Well, I'll see you tomorrow," she said, shuffling away in a daze, as if she was waking from a lifelong nap.

She approached the road back to Leanne's and folded the Dixie cup with her right hand, pushing it down into her sweater pocket. She walked dream-like into the street until a car horn blared and she looked up, like Bambi in the lights.

"Yo, Yo, Wendy!" It was Danny, waving coolly to her from the wheel of her monstrous grey truck. She pulled the beast up to the side of the road, in front of the post office.

"Get in. We're going oystering."

We was her and Greta, who sat in the wicker basket on the passenger seat with her long sleek nose out of the window, sucking in the fresh air.

"Scooch, Greta," Danny instructed. Greta leapt into the backseat and Danny moved the basket to the floor for Wendy, who climbed in with a groan. Danny wore an over-sized black sweatshirt over overalls and a big pair of yellow rubber boots.

"Nice boots," Wendy said.

"I've got an extra pair for you, city girl."

"Thanks, I left mine at home."

"I figured. But you do... you do look nice," Danny said, looking Wendy over as she pulled back onto South Road. "Did you do something different?"

"I brushed my hair."

"Isn't that amazing, what it can do?"

"Apparently," Wendy laughed.

"But it's something else though…" Danny kept looking at her from the corner of her eye. "What else is it? I don't think it's physical. Did something happen? There's something new inside of you."

"Oh well," Wendy touched the folded paper cup in her pocket. "I might be hanging out with Jack tomorrow. Maybe it's that."

Danny's foot came off the accelerator, and the truck slowed down around the curve; it was almost like she forgot she was driving for a second.

Then she came to.

"Well, that was quick. You manifest pretty well."

"What do you mean?" Wendy asked.

"You made that happen."

"Well, he did, I think. One minute I was drinking his orange juice, and the next minute I was going to a yoga class with him."

Danny nodded. "Sounds like him. He moves pretty fast. You ever done yoga?"

"No."

"He probably just wants to see what you look like in those pants." Wendy thought she saw her roll her eyes.

"Well, I don't have those. Tomorrow's outfit will be styled by Target's loungewear department."

Danny pulled onto a small dirt trail, and she drove them — bumping and twisting — all the way to the banks of a small sheltered pond that looked like a tiny patch of paradise, with tall green grass, tree branches falling into the water and herons proudly stalking the edges on stilts.

"Here we are."

Danny and Greta jumped out into the sand. She slammed the door shut, but as it was her tendency, left the radio on. Wendy slid out after them and flicked her flats off into the sand. She scampered onto the hood of the truck and watched Danny wade into the water.

The radio started playing *Hungry Eyes*. Danny didn't turn around, but said, "Turn that shit up."

Wendy rolled onto her stomach and reached through the window to press the volume button on the steering wheel. Danny swayed to Eric Carmen in the water.

"Best. Movie." Danny said.

"Best." Wendy said.

"Nobody puts Baby in a corner."

"No. Body." Wendy said.

"You were in the corner for a while," Danny said.

"I think so."

Danny held a dripping scallop and moaned to it. "I look at you and I fannnntasize, you're mine tonight…"

Wendy laughed and it carried over the water. She sank back onto the window and crossed her ankles, the truck hood felt like it was made for reclining and watching people oyster. She wanted to close her eyes and replay the scene of Jack asking her to yoga, when Danny said, "Hey. Get in here. Grab Ray's boots from the back."

"But I'm comfortable. I don't actually have to do this, do I?" Wendy whined a bit.

"No. But do you always say No to things you don't know how to do? How are you going to learn anything new?"

"Does everything you say have to be right?"

She slid off the truck and landed with a thud in the sand. She grabbed Ray's gargantuan boots and pushed her feet in them. She waddled over to Danny.

"Quack, quack," Danny said. She stood next to Danny as the water lapped gently at their rubber legs.

"Well, I said *yes* to yoga, didn't I?"

"But that involved a black-haired Ryan Gosling. If he had offered you heroin, you probably would have done it. Wait, have you done heroin?"

"I'm proud to say I have not."

"Mother Teresa."

"I feel like a nun these days. I'm on a tea and Eckhart Tolle diet. I've been so good I think I'm gonna rob a bank or something if I don't cut loose pretty soon."

"Uh oh," Danny said.

She pulled another dripping oyster up from the water and retrieved a knife from her pocket. She wedged the shellfish open. She looked up at Wendy. "So this is what Ray and I were doing when he asked me to marry him."

Wendy looked around. "Right here?" A heron left the water in a graceful ascent. She could barely hear the flutter of its enormous white wings. It hardly made a sound, she had forgotten it was there. *Beautiful things don't ask for attention.*

She thought of her own proposal. She had been late to meet Peter at dinner because she'd been out drinking with a friend. She'd shown up tipsy and blown the whole surprise, and he'd asked her when he was angry. She'd said yes, apologizing, and crying, through what she wasn't sure were happy or sad tears, she was so disappointed in herself for ruining another beautiful moment. That was maybe the moment she helplessly felt her life slipping through her hands.

"Pretty beautiful," Wendy said.

"Look, I want to show you something," Danny said. Wendy studied the open oyster in Danny's hand.

"He said I was like this. That he had to peel open my hard shell, and it took him a long time, but he was patient. And that nothing has ever been more worth it."

"That's romantic."

"And then look what he found." Danny produced a tiny pearl.

"Me," she said. "Deep past my shell and through all the gore. He said I was a beautiful mystery, that every day he felt himself walking deeper into — getting closer to — my heart."

"Holy shit," Wendy said. "Ray's a poet."

"He can be. I guess I just wanted to say, don't, don't give him the pearl of you right away. Is all."

"Who? Jack? We're just going to yoga."

"Anyone, Wendy."

"Well, maybe I don't have a pearl."

"Everyone has a pearl, Wendy. It's your heart. Protect it. Not just anyone deserves it."

She held Wendy's palm open and placed the pearl in there, then she closed her hand around Wendy's fist.

"We want to earn things. It's how we're made. It's human nature. And we only care for the things we work for. If it comes too easy... we don't care for it."

"I didn't think you had a tough shell," Wendy said. "Like I didn't have to pry you open."

Danny kept watching the water, but said, "No. I opened right up to you. Some people we're just drawn to and it's a mystery, at first, why. But I think we're drawn to everyone for a reason.
Think of all the billions of people in the world, that you just walk by everyday, the ones you'll never meet. But then think of the ones you do actually cross paths with. They always have something to teach you, and maybe, you them."

The wind picked up and she watched Danny raise another dripping scallop from the water. This relationship to a woman felt different from ones she had before. She wasn't jealous or intimidated by Danny, and she certainly didn't feel Danny wanted her to be small and un-threatening. In fact, she felt Danny wanted her to be bigger.

"Thank you," she said to Danny.

"I'm just saying it's okay to be a mystery. To let others be one. To let life be one. You don't have to give it all away right away."

A darkness covered the pond.

Wendy was shivering. "So, is it a mystery how long we are going to be out here? I kind of feel that oystering is like math class. Like I'm never going to use it, so I can't pay attention."

Danny rolled her eyes but you could tell she was endeared by Wendy, who felt her real personality emerging, like it was safe to come out and play.

"Your life starts to happen when you choose it. You just have to choose this life, Wendy."

"Have you chosen yours?"

"A long fucking time ago. And I never looked back. Looking back makes you crazy."

"I've noticed," Wendy said. "If looking back makes you crazy, then I should probably be locked up."

"You kind of are. I mean you've locked yourself up."

"Geez, you're so fucking deep, even standing in shallow water."

"And if you choose this life, this isn't so bad, is it?" Danny asked her.

Wendy looked around at the quiet pond and down at the pearl in her hand.

"No, no it isn't."

Wendy thought a minute. "It's a beautiful story, about you and Ray, but I don't get it. Are you asking me to be like you?"

"No, not at all, Wendy. I'm saying, be you. Totally you and true to you."

"Ugh," Wendy let out a cry over the water. "I'm so frustrated! Everyone keeps telling me that, to be me. Peter and Leanne and now you. It's easy to tell someone that when you know you are. I don't."

"Wendy." Danny put a calm hand on the back of Wendy's neck. It was cold from the water. At first she bristled, then she softened into Danny's touch.

"Everyone deeply knows who they are. It's about undressing from who you aren't. You, most people, had to be someone else for a very long time. Why don't you spend the winter letting that all go to become who you really are? It will be the most worthy time you ever spend. Most people never stop to do it, they don't have the chance."

Then she took her hand from Wendy's neck and pushed her finger deep into the sludge of the oyster. "It's about removing all this shit. To get to your truth."

She touched the hand Wendy held the pearl in.

"To get to the pearl of you."

She took off her sweatshirt and wrapped it around Wendy's shivering shoulders.

"Okay," Wendy said. "Can I go wait in the car now?"

14.

Wendy stood in the kitchen having coffee in one of Peter's old cotton t-shirts, so big that it fell to her knees, and the sleeves came to her elbows. There was such a comfort to clothes that ballooned her; she felt so tiny and safe in them. It was the t-shirt of one of Peter's opening bands that was way too metal for her taste. Wendy remembered trying to watch them from side stage next to Peter, and even with earplugs she felt her brain about to hemorrhage through her ears.

"Why does it have to be so loud?" she'd mouthed, cupping her ears in pain.

"If it wasn't so loud, it wouldn't be metal," he'd screamed.

She'd left to check out the wine bar across the street from the venue. He'd kissed her on her forehead as she left. She realized she'd taken all those tender forehead kisses for granted. She hadn't known there was a timer on them. She was finally realizing there was a timer on everything. Wendy and Peter had acquired hundreds of t-shirts of his tour mates over the years, they were their easy autopilot wardrobe — tour shirts over jeans, accessorized with sunglasses and an eternal hangover.

She knew she should throw all these shirts out. She highly doubted he had anything left of hers. It felt as if he had bleached and Brillo-ed her out of her life, like someone covering a murder scene. Erased all evidence of her. I watch too many crime shows, she thought. But she just couldn't bring herself to toss everything. If Wendy closed her eyes, which she did, and sniffed hard enough into the fabric, which she did, she could smell their old life. She could be in their old life.

She opened her eyes. A kitchen on an island off Maine. Alone. With a beautiful farmer coming in half an hour to take her to a yoga class. Back to the not so bad present. *This is happening*, she thought, which was something she was beginning to whisper to herself to acclimate to her ever-changing reality. *This, right now, is happening.*

She had that feeling when you don't just think something big is going to happen, you know it, but you don't know how or exactly what. She stood in this quiet place before change, she felt like she was in the blank space in between chapters in a book, like the pages of her life were turning. So this is what moving on feels like, she thought.

To move on, you have to make a move. And going to the Farmer's Market and saying *yes* to Jack was the move. And she knew moving on was what she was supposed to do, and she knew there was no logical reason to wait. But it was bittersweet. It felt like taking something beloved off of life-support, even something that had no chance of living again. Something nothing could save but a miracle. Peter had left the hospital long ago, but she had sat by their comatose love and held vigil.

She missed many things about Peter. She missed his playful King of the Jungle bravado. His silliness. Everything had been a game, life was full of joy and surprise. He was a deep thinker and deep player who loved art and wordplay and creation in a myriad of forms. She missed her playmate. She missed her best friend. Did we always have to lose things, to realize how much we loved them? Was that just the way life worked?

She felt the instinct she had been honing, alive and talking within her. There was a close-off when it said *No*, and an opening when it urged *Yes*. There was dread with something dark on the horizon, and there were butterflies with something new and life changing was near. But this morning she couldn't discern if she felt butterflies or dread. She felt she had a cloudy connection to herself. Like she couldn't quite makcalle out the picture on the internal TV screen, or hear the words coming through the inner phone. But something was certainly going to happen today.

She could only stomach half of her coffee. It might be that she might kiss someone who wasn't Peter. Either way, she was thinking about dating again. She was going to have to try out... new people. With new personalities and new senses of humor and new ways at looking at the world and new ways of kissing and new families and new friends. New worlds. It had taken her so long to find Peter. And she had finally found the one that fit. Did she really have to get back in the game? She thought of *When Harry Met Sally*, of Bruno Kirby and Carrie Fisher sitting up in bed.

"Tell me I'll never have to be out there again," Carrie says.

"You'll never have to be out there again," Bruno replies.

She had asked Peter to say the lines with her once. She had said Carrie's line casually as they walked, but he, he had done it with the usual way he did everything, full on, full in, staring into her eyes, clasping her hands over his heart, kneeling on a busy Manhattan street until she laughed and cried "Get up!"

He had an *O Captain My Captain* Robin Williams on the desktop way of delivering himself to the world. It was all his stage. Every corner of it.

"Wendy," he had shouted, "You will never have to be out there again."

She put her coffee down on the counter. *Liar,* she whispered, and walked into the bedroom.

She finished her outfit with sweats, she had never been to yoga and didn't have any of those fancy pants or halter tops women wore.

Then she stood in the bathroom mirror squishing the flesh of her face up with the heels of her hands, wishing things would fight gravity a little harder.

Grav-ity, she thought, the pull to the grave.

She applied concealer, mascara, blush and some light lipliner. Then she scoured the bottom of the makeup bag, but she had run through all its tricks. She looked in the mirror at the tired, older version of her in the reflection. She still only partially recognized herself. But it would have to do. She would have to do. She sat out on the back porch watching the cold grey ocean sprawled out to forever until she heard wheels on the gravel driveway.

Jack was here.

She could hear Leanne. "Follow that barf feeling," she had said. "It means you're leaving your comfort zone and that's the only place life happens."

This is happening, she thought. Whatever this is. She didn't feel ready. She didn't feel beautiful. But Danny was right, if you waited until you felt perfect you'd never leave the house.

So she rose from the recliner and walked out to meet him. He stood on the porch in well-tailored light brown sweatpants and a grey tank top that revealed arms that were comic book hero carved. He held a white coffee cup and wore an easy confident smile. She, on the other hand, felt like she was being punked. Like Ashton Kutcher would show up with a camera in the bushes, or a bucket of pig's blood was about to fall on her head.

"Hi," she said.

"Morning," he said. He passed her the coffee. "Ran by Al's for you."

"That's so nice," she said, almost astonished, "that was so nice of you to do."

"Well, that's what people do, right? We do nice things for each other."

"Yes," she said. That made sense. She had been used to love as drama, not friendly gestures. This felt mature. "I suppose you're right."

She feigned a sip despite a resistant stomach. Straight black. No cream. She preferred buckets of cream.

"Thanks," she smiled up at him.

He held the door of his old black truck for her, the bed was piled with bags of mulch and a bale of hay.

"Excuse the... farm," he said.

As they pulled onto the main road he thumbed through his iPod and selected a twangy song full of banjo and melancholy.

"Know these guys?" He asked.

"No," she said. "I'm out of the game. Who are they?" Her mind danced back to when it was a job to know bands. What a funny living it had been. She had done it because she didn't feel there was anything else she could do in life, but listen to music and write about it.

"Friends of mine," he said. He fell quiet, just tapping his leg to the music and watching the road. Wendy wanted to fill in all the empty space with bumbling, tap-dancing-monkey words, but thought of Danny.

"It's okay to be a mystery." She decided she wouldn't entertain. She chose discomfort over comfort. She breathed into the quiet and pretended to sip the black coffee.

She thought again about being a music journalist. Do we choose our livings or do our livings choose us? And what happens when you don't feel called to a calling anymore? And why is it called a living when most people feel so dead in their jobs, and their jobs leave so little time for true living? Shouldn't making a good living mean making a good life? It had been a good life, until she got to the top, but then she got too powerful. One paragraph from her and someone's record could be doomed or shoot to the top of the charts. All that power made her very uneasy. It was just her personal, usually tired and hungover opinion, and it could decide the fate of someone's life's dream.

"What are you thinking about?" he asked.

"What we're always thinking about, I guess," she shrugged. "Life."

"I'm not always thinking about life," he said.

"Oh, I thought everyone was."

"I could tell that about you," he said. "You're a thinker. You seem- lost- in thought."

"I guess so," she said.

"That's okay," he said. She hadn't thought it wasn't. She felt sort of awkward and suddenly alone, next to him. But just then he reached over to where her hands were in her lap, and he closed his right hand over her left wrist, his finger tips resting on her thigh. She got distracted by the warmth of his broad calloused hand easily encircling her entire wrist. The feeling of being held. She sighed loudly, despite herself. You don't realize how tightly you are holding yourself until someone holds you.

"I'm more of a do-er," he said.

Clearly, she thought. She hoped he couldn't feel her shake. Her body always gave her away. It talked so loud. They ambled into the harbor and Jack pulled up to a tiny shingled shack with a hand-painted driftwood sign that read: *Release Yoga.*

"I've never done this," she said.

"You'll feel like you've done it forever," he said, climbing out of the truck.

"It's like sex," he said through the open window. "The body just knows."

She blushed.

"It's true," he said, as if he'd never been wrong, about anything.

She reached down for her purse, and before she knew it, he had opened her door for her. She stepped out into the sand parking lot and looked up at a group of four sleekly pulled together women who all looked slightly younger than her. They wore skin-tight patterned yoga pants and brightly colored bras, and they stared at her, slack-jawed.

"Heyyy Jack," cooed the tall one with Kennedy teeth and a lustrous wave of brown hair. You could hang coats off her collar bones. Wendy sucked in her stomach. The other girls were looking her up and down like a zoo animal. When Wendy caught their eyes, their heads snapped back down to their iPhones.

"Hey Amanda," he nodded at their ring leader. "Ladies," he gave the group a brief wave.

"I wish I could just walk around in sweat pants and not care," Amanda said to her friends, who snickered as they stole glances at Jack. Wendy's stomach fell. She was back in freshman year, being stonewalled by the senior girls on the hockey team. She was back at *Rolling Stone*, being boxed out by the other assistants. Back being death-glared and ignored by the women back stage. *Leaving the house sucks,* she thought.

"Didn't see you at Luke's last night," said Amanda. "We missed you."

Wendy was doing her best to make eye smiling contact with Amanda, but Amanda only stared right at Jack like Wendy was wearing an invisible cloak.

Wendy wished.

Any minute now Jack will introduce me.

Any minute now Amanda will introduce herself to me.

Any minute now…

But Jack just said, "Couldn't make it," and made his way to the studio door. Wendy assumed she as just supposed to follow.

"Oh. Well, Josh is having a barbecue tonight…" Amanda called behind him. "I can pick you up."

"Dinner plans," he said.

"Come on," he whispered in Wendy's ear. "Let's get a space."

They crossed into the small sunny studio and she looked at him, big-eyed. "Um," she said, jutting her neck out a bit, incredulous.

"What?" he asked.

"Did I just meet... well 'meet' is a stretch because I think technically someone has to speak to you for you to meet them... is that the island's Regina George?"

"What?" he asked.

"Never mind," she said.

"I have a little sister, I get the reference. They just have to get used to you," he said.

"To be human?" she asked.

"People here, they kinda wanna make sure you earn your place here."

She tensed up. Her inner child threw a tantrum. She crossed her arms over her body. Well, I don't even know how long I'm going to be here so, she thought. The last time she'd felt this way Leanne had said. "Oh, so nice of your four-year-old self to come out and play."

"What, like I have to pledge? Get hazed? Are they the Freemasons?" she asked Jack.

He didn't laugh. His eyes were blank. She was noticing he didn't seem to get her... jokes.

"We're all pretty close," he shrugged.

"Like how close?"

He was quiet.

"Like dated? Did you date her?"

"Let's get you on a mat," he said.

15.

Wendy found yoga horrifying.

She had laid her mat down in a back corner because that felt like where the secret door to *Anywherebutthere* could be, but sadly she wasn't taken into an alternate world; she was still visible, in her sweats, in the tiny yoga studio with the cast of Mean Girls and Jack, who did her no favors by laying his mat right alongside of hers. She didn't have the courage to ask him to practice where he couldn't see her, like China.

She flailed around on the mat like a slick rubbery whale while the girls from the parking lot moved like synchronized swimmers in the front row. It was if they had each been born in crow pose and spandex. And instead of Wendy's withering grunts, they breathed gently and smoothly, chatting to each other easily as they moved.

The teacher, a strong thin tan girl in her early twenties with blond bouncy hair, wearing head-to-toe Lululemon, was named Leslie. She knew each girl by name and delighted in sharing inside jokes with them. At one point, she even said to Amanda, "You're holding that pose a lot better than you held your liquor last Friday," and the room tittered with laughter.

When Wendy's arms quivered in downward dog, Leslie stared at her and said, "This is your 'home pose.' You should be able to relax here, this should feel good."

If good meant you had been set on fire as your limbs were quartered in town square while the villagers watched, then Wendy felt fantastic. Leslie seemed to point out everything Wendy did wrong, constantly prodding her to use her core, which could have been in Wendy's foot for all she knew. She wanted to beg Leslie to pay attention to anyone else but her, but Leslie seemed addicted to her like watching a moth burn in a flame. At one point, she loomed right over Wendy and said, "For the beginners, feel free to go into child's pose when things get too difficult."

When Leslie turned her back, Wendy glared at her with the fury of ten thousand fires. And as she looked at Leslie, she could feel Jack's eyes on her, and she burned in mortification. Her internal tears manifested themselves in a sheet of sweat coating her entire body, pooling on the mat beneath her. She had never used any of these muscles before in her life, and she had never had any desire to be aware of them either.

She wanted to be anywhere but there in that stuffy room down in the harbor. She would kill to be taking the SATs. In line at the DMV. Being reamed by a dodgeball in eighth grade. Being stood up for the homecoming dance by that sullen, passionless boy, even though she had pity asked him. Getting a root canal. What. Ever.

Finally, she chose her dignity over dying on that sweaty rented piece of rubber.

She stood up and left the mat and walked out to the water, where she sat, wondering, if Jack abandoned her, how she would get home. But a few minutes later, she felt him approaching. She swiveled her head and looked up at him, her eyes appealing for mercy.

"I'm not ready for that," she said.

He sat down next to her in the sand, rested his arms on his knees. He didn't say anything, he just let the warmth grow between them. He was really good at saying nothing while saying everything. She could feel his heart beating, she could feel the blood coursing through the veins of his body. His bare sweaty arm pressed alongside hers, their sweat sticking their flesh together. Their breath synched up as one. She was about to burst when he finally looked her in the eyes.

Then he leaned in and pressed his warm soft lips against hers. There was that smell again from the first time she saw him at Al's, of moist earth and caked sweat, of something both safe and dangerous.

When he pulled away, she sucked in the sea air.

"It means union," he said.

"What?" Wendy asked, watching the vein pulse in his neck.

"Yoga, it actually means Union. Of things," his gaze went deeper into her eyes, "merging as one," he said. "But sometimes, sometimes people forget that."

He stood up in the sand and offered his massive paw of a hand for Wendy to grab. She slipped hers in his and he pulled her up.

"Come on," he said, leading her back to the car. But when he saw the girls letting out of yoga, he released her hand. They were milling about in the parking lot, texting their boyfriends about where to meet for brunch. They looked up at Wendy and Jack, and they did that pinched faced smile that was really no smile at all. Wendy wondered why they even bothered, she preferred no smile to a fake smile.

He held the door open for her, and she found she was getting used to that. She was getting used to Jack, despite their moments of disconnection. She slid into the truck and her body trembled with a feeling she hadn't felt in far too long, of delicious anticipation, for what was almost certain to come. He had his usual air of calm satisfaction, like everything was always going perfectly to his plan. He flicked on the radio.

Mumford and Sons was singing, "there will come a time, you'll see/ with no more tears/ and love will not break your heart, but dismiss your fears..."

And Wendy thought maybe that was a sign, that really, everything would be okay now, that Jack would be her lover and she wouldn't feel so alone. That the hard part was truly over.

They didn't talk the whole drive, her lips were burning with the sensation of the kiss and their energy filled the car. Ten minutes later, he pulled up to a grey shingled house on the outskirts of a sprawling farm. She stepped out of the truck and smelled sea air; she couldn't see water but she could feel it. All over the property were grazing animals. She saw horses, pigs, rabbits, sheep, chickens. Wendy started to walk to a large black horse who hung its head heavily over the fence, fluttering its luxurious Kardashian eyelashes at her.

But Jack took her hand.

"Later," he said.

"Who's that?" she asked.

"Princess," he told her, leading her toward the house. She looked back at Princess who kept her large, deep brown planets of eyes on Wendy, almost as if she had something to tell her. Wendy stole one last look at her, and then let herself be led into the house by Jack. For a moment, she didn't mind being led or directed. She didn't mind not thinking. She'd been working so hard on herself, in all this transformation, that she just wanted to let go, and not think for a moment. She'd missed the masculine presence of just... presence. And maybe, she thought, just letting go was the transformation.

He walked her through the door and up the steps to what looked like a messy bedroom of a boy, and then he kissed her again; this time his mouth opened, this time he pulled her against him, and she had to stand on her toes to meet his kiss. Their bodies began to speak to each other, their mouths passing secrets. He pressed his hands deep into her back, underneath her shoulder bones. It opened Wendy's heart to lean into those large hands and fall back weightless; it cracked her open, and she opened and opened and opened.

And it felt like exactly what she needed and had been waiting to do. And then she started to talk. "I didn't think I would ever feel this way again," she said as he pulled her shirt up over her head.

"I thought I was broken forever."

And the less he said, the more she said. It was as if when he opened her body, he opened the dam in her heart and she had no control over the words that flooded from her mouth. And the more Wendy spoke, the less he did; she felt her power dwindling, and his strengthening. Somehow, she always lost her power with men, she always got so tiny. And here she was doing it again, dooming herself, repeating herself with a pattern. She felt a sinking, like in quicksand, but she couldn't stop the sabotage. She couldn't stop telling her same, sad, small story.

"When my mother died, I felt... abandoned, and then ... then when my husband left me, it just doubled that... I just felt so incredibly unlovable... discardable, you know?"

He fumbled off her sports bra, but still said nothing.

"I thought I was just going to drink myself to death in the corner of the world," she said, as he kissed her breasts.

"I didn't want to be close to anyone again, because of the pain of being loved and left. But then I realized, you know, we all lose each other at the end, so while we are here we should attach, we should lean in, we should let ourselves be seen and see others... do you know what I mean?

I think that's what the brave do. I mean, people who are really alive." She paused, as if he might respond, but he just gnawed on her shoulder.

"I never thought I would heal. But I feel like things might be okay... like I might be okay... I mean, I hope, we all hope, right? That we're not alone and we matter and we're okay?"

He finally put a finger to her lips as he laid her down on the bed.

"Shhh..." he said.

"Oh, Okay," she said. "I'm sorry."

And she was suddenly so embarrassed. Even as he undressed the rest of her body, it seemed he didn't really want to know her soul, and for a moment she felt she should stop him, before she gave absolutely everything to him. Even though her body wanted it, something was saying No. And even as his tongue painted her neck and she began to slip away, she wrestled with all the thoughts that boys never had to have. She wrestled with all the sex shame that had been passed to her, from a society where men could freely have sex but women couldn't.

She wrestled with the, *I should waits,* and the *he won't respect mes,* the *he'll think I'm cheap and easys,* and the *girlfriends don't give it all away right aways,* and, *what if he tells everyones,* but she didn't really know whose rules they were. They had been handed to her but they had never been hers.

So she lost her mind and she followed her body's lead, because it begged to be touched, held and opened, so she just closed her eyes and they made love.

At one point he said, "We move really well together," but that was as close as he got to saying anything tender, so she turned it into something, she made it a metaphor in her head. That they made sense together, that they, as people, worked well together. But it was all he said, and when it was over, she didn't know what to say. So she said, "Thank you." But as soon as that came out, it felt wrong. Suddenly, everything was feeling wrong, and she was powerless to reverse it.

"You're welcome," he said, casually.

She wanted to take the *Thank You* back, because it made her feel like a charity case he had made love to, like he had done her a favor, but it was already out there. She rested her head on his chest and listened to his beating heart. She loved nothing more than a heart pillow, and couldn't help but remember lying on Peter's heart. She even almost said something about Peter at that moment, but he stopped her.

"Want to see those horses now?" he asked, moving out from under her, scooting to the edge of the bed and slipping into jeans.

She felt she had no choice. "Sure," she said, pulling the sheets up over her body, like she could take back what she'd already done. He stood up and pulled an old cotton fishermen's sweater over his head and she felt like she was watching a walking J. Crew men's ad. Then he reached into a bureau drawer and pulled out a pair of women's jeans.

Alarm bells sounded within her.

"Whose are those?" she croaked, sitting up.

"A friend's," he said.

"A girlfriend's?" she asked.

He paused. He shook the jeans out but didn't look at her. "Do you think I would take you in my bed if I had a girlfriend here?"

"Here?" she asked. *Like, is she elsewhere?*

"Come on," he said. "Give me a break." He handed them over to her.

The traffic light inside of her went from green to red. But the abandoned part of her, that just felt so grateful to be loved and didn't want to rock the boat with questions, that accepted crumbs and called it love, that was so scared of losing she clung, took the jeans.

Wendy stepped into them warily. She had to suck in and lay back on the bed to zip them up. From that horizontal view, she started to look around the room. Now, she saw. There weren't only men's things, the way it had looked at first. There was a silk gold scarf on the desk chair, there was a small silver ring on the nightstand. She felt a little dizzy, her throat went dry.

She didn't feel like she was allowed to ask more questions. She felt like an outsider who was only allowed to be so... loud. She didn't really belong here, her privileges could be revoked at any moment, so she'd have to behave. She'd have to walk on eggshells. At a certain point way back in her story, Wendy had gone small to be loved. She felt muted. She felt the dread that she had felt standing that morning in the kitchen.

Something is going to happen, but I don't know if it will be good or bad, she had thought.

That feeling she had felt, but ignored. And she was beginning to see. The internal picture was coming into focus. And it wasn't good. He ambled down the stairs and called at the foot.

"You coming?"

She walked down in a daze, clinging to the railing, step by barefoot step. She didn't feel safe or loved or seen. She felt numb. And a little scared. When she and Peter made love, they came together, they became one. But now Wendy felt more alone than ever.

He walked in front of her through the kitchen, then out of the back door, where the two horses roamed in the back pasture — a smaller sturdy white horse and that proud ebony one who had stared at her on the way in.

"Princess," he called.

He clucked gently until the midnight mare sauntered over to them. He slipped a bridle on her, and the bit into her mouth with a clink, as the metal hit the teeth. He interlaced his fingers and bent over, making a step for Wendy's foot.

"No saddle?" she asked. "I haven't done this since I was twelve."

"Just take a stroll around the pasture," he said. "She's the gentlest horse you'll ever meet."

"Okay," Wendy said, completely out of touch with who she was and what she wanted.

"Anyway," he winked, "I know you can ride."

She gave him a limp smile.

Gross, she thought.

She stepped her bare foot into his hands, threw her leg over, and sank onto Princess' wide black back. She looked down at him as he adjusted the mare's bridle. He now he looked and felt like a stranger. She felt a coldness from him, a distancing. He was treating her like an acquaintance, and she had that feeling when something is over before it had even begun. A small death. They were together but worlds apart, and Wendy longed for the love where you could be worlds apart but still together.

Her mouth tasted like metal and her body was weak. Another rejection. She wanted to be alone in bed, crying and processing what had just happened, not in another girl's jeans in Jack's backyard, on his horse, listening to his orders. He was always in control. Now more so than ever.

"Give her a little kick," he said. "Just walk around."

But she did as he said. Wendy kicked the horse gently, "Come on, Princess," she whispered.

Princess lazily ambled them away from Jack.

"Only one thing," he said to her back. "Don't let her feel your fear."

Wendy turned to look at him, wild-eyed.

"Why?" she asked.

"Just trust me," he said.

That's a tall order, she thought.

"She feels everything you feel."

She and Princess moseyed along the fence of the pasture.

"Sit up tall," he said. She raised herself.

"Open your heart." She tried, but the gates were back.

"Keep your spine straight, but let your hips move with her." She felt anything but regal, but let her hips go soft. She ignored him and focused on the beautiful animal beneath her. As a little girl, she had ridden three times a week after school, but had stopped after a scary fall.

But she didn't feel afraid on Princess, who felt as sturdy as a Buick.

"Good girl," she whispered into her massive velvet ears. She reached down and gave her a soft pat on the neck. They sauntered along the fence until Wendy's mind began reeling.

Did he have a girlfriend? Who was she? Did the mean girls know he had a girlfriend? Is that why they were so cold to her? Was she the stupidest girl in the whole world? Or was she just paranoid?

Suddenly Princess lurched down to graze on the grass and almost took Wendy sliding down her thick neck.

"Show her you're in control," he called.

Wendy yanked at her bridle and tried in vain to pull her up from the grass.

"Hey!" she cried to Princess, "Hey!" she kicked her lightly but frenzied. "Listen to me!"

Princess continued to graze, ignoring Wendy.

Jack walked over and touched Wendy's thigh. She tensed up.

"If you don't trust yourself, she won't trust you," he told her.

"Take a breath. Calm down. Get back in your center." And then he had the nerve to say, "Use your core."

Wendy and Princess both flared their nostrils.

"She felt your distraction," he told her, pulling the mare's head up himself. "You have to stay present."

She couldn't take his orders anymore. She just wanted to scream.

"This is all body language," he said, immune to the storm brewing inside of her. "All you have to do is focus on the direction you want to go. And just look in that direction. She'll feel it."

Look in the direction you want to go, she thought. There's that question again.

She closed her eyes. *Where did she want to go?*

"Come on, Wendy," he said. It almost felt as if he was mocking her. "Show me what you got."

She could hear Peter, "You were something. Now you're nothing. What happened to you?"

"Okay," she said.

"Okay, what?" Jack said.

She couldn't tell if she was talking to Jack or Peter anymore, but it didn't matter. She was done with this story, of falling apart, of abandoning herself for love, of being so small. She was ready to be free of it. She was ready to feel wild and big and possible in control again.

Whatever lay ahead was far better than living like this one more day.

I'll show you, she thought.

Wendy looked ahead and sat up tall. She gave Princess a swift kick. "Let's go, darling."

Just like that, Princess took off in a gallop, like she'd been waiting for this. She went buckling across the field in a streak of midnight. Wendy held on through her thighs, which, with the yoga and sex and now riding, had done more work than they ever had in her life. She felt like she was flying, like the whole world was below her and she was up above it, where she was free of everything. She and Princess moved as one, in true union.

"Whoah!!" Jack called.

She smiled, until she realized Princess was headed straight toward the fence and she wasn't slowing down. Wendy clung hard and closed her eyes, and she felt the mare soar clear over it, and they sailed in the air for a frozen moment in time, as if she had wings. Then they ripped into the forest behind the pasture, and all she could hear was Jack calling like a maniac from far, far, far behind her.

"Wait! Wait!" he cried.

But Wendy was done waiting.

16.

Wendy woke up with a throbbing pain in her head that was far worse than any hangover she had ever experienced. Her body lay flat, and she tried to open her eyes, but they struggled against it; they were too heavy, it felt like trying to lift iron gates with tiny thin strings.

She was greeted by an unfamiliar feminine voice, "Good morning," the woman said.

She squinted harder into the light that seeped in through the slats of her eyes, and tried to sit up to see, but she could barely move her head, and her whole body felt immobilized, like when children bury each other in sand and just leave the head peeking out. Barely, through the blinds of her eyelids she made out the form of a woman in white, whose silhouette looked just like an angel. And the last thing she could remember was... the horse. Galloping on the back of Jack's horse Princess, as they tore through the forest and met the ocean.

Then she remembered... a fall, a flinging of her body at the edge of the cold sea. And she hadn't remembered anything after that.

For a moment, she wondered if she was dead. Had she missed her own death?

Had that been her whole life? Divorced and dead at 33? But, she lamented, she hadn't ever figured out what she wanted, and gone for it completely with her whole heart. She hadn't written that book. She hadn't made a difference in the world. She hadn't found good, healing love that stayed. She hadn't gotten happy. She hadn't had a baby.

Wendy began to mourn the life she hadn't lived when the woman in white touched her hand, with what felt like warm breathing flesh, and she finally fluttered her eyes open to see. Standing by her side was a blinking machine with tubes that pumped into her arm, and she was in a soft blue hospital gown and both of her legs, both of them, were wrapped in white plaster casts.

"Oh my God," gasped Wendy.

"Let me get the doctor, dear," the nurse said, "just wait right here."

Wendy winced at that with a panicked smile. She was practically strung up like Sigourney Weaver after her skiing accident in *Working Girl*. Moving wasn't on the menu. The nurse shuffled back into the room in front of a man of about forty, or maybe even a little older, she couldn't really tell. He looked so tired, and perhaps that added age to his appearance. Boyish, but tired. Like someone you wanted to both be comforted by and comfort at once. He had thick sandy brown hair and lightly tanned skin. His kind blue eyes twinkled like the surface of a lake beneath handsome tortoiseshell glasses. A navy cashmere sweater peeked out from under his white coat, and he was scribbling on a clipboard he carried.

"Hello Wendy," he said. He had a nice voice too, warm and calm and low. "I'm Doctor Weaver."

She felt heavy and underwater like her system was pumping with sedatives. She'd lost time, and she wasn't sure how much.

"Hi," Wendy croaked slowly; she tried to reach out her hand but her arm weighed a thousand tons.

"Sorry," she said.

"No, no," he said, shooing her hand down, "Try to rest up. You had a really hard fall. And you're on a lot of medication too, so you probably feel pretty woozy."

"That explains it," Wendy said. "Um, do you know what happened to me?"

"You broke both of your legs in your accident. You're going to be in those casts for a good two months."

"Oh my God," she said.

"It was pretty bad," he nodded. "You had us pretty worried."

"I'm sorry," she said again.

He shook his head. "You haven't done anything wrong," he said.

That softened her. She felt so soft she felt drunk.

"Like, ever?" she asked hopefully.

He let out a surprised laugh.

"I can't speak to that, but I'm going to say that's true, that you've just been doing your best, just like the rest of us."

Her chin wobbled. She looked down at her broken body in horror.

"Everything is going to be fine," he said. A tear fell down her right cheek.

"I think I've been waiting to hear that for a while now," she said.

"The good news is, this is something we can fix. Your only job is to heal. And I don't get to tell everyone that."

"How did I get here?"

"Jack Fletcher brought you in. He caught up with you right after you landed in the water, which is a good thing. It's good he found you so fast."

"Oh," said Wendy, her heart racing at his name. She tried to sit up, shaking as she pushed her hands into the soft white bed. "Is he... is he still here?"

"It seemed he had to go," Dr. Weaver said, and Wendy flopped back down onto the pillow like a fish. She barely concealed her disappointment, which the doctor seemed to register.

"But he said that was some pretty reckless riding you were doing." The doctor's eyes grazed over the bedside machine's numbers and he took down more notes, "What," he smiled softly, "were you trying to kill yourself?"

Wendy was quiet, like she had to think about her answer. He stopped writing and put down his pen.

"I was kidding," he said. "But, now I'm worried."

"Well, I don't think I was." She looked up at him. He held her gaze, empathetically curious.

"But I... I just couldn't be me one more day," she told him, her voice starting to shake.

He placed his hand on her forearm and her skin grew warm under his touch, like all the blood rushed to the spot where his fingertips rested. She had been touched by men her whole life, but in ways that were sexual, or joking, or with force; it was never this, this sort of masculine healing. Another wet warm tear rolled down her face. She breathed in for the first time since she woke. She was exhausted.

"I hadn't done anything brave, in so long," she said. "Too long. I was tired of being told what to do and how to live, I knew if I could just get free and quiet enough, I could hear myself, what I really wanted. And I am dying to know what I really want and I am dying to do it."

She realized he wasn't a psychiatrist, but she couldn't stop herself. He nodded along with her words. She was feeling so deeply heard. He was such a patient listener. So she kept going.

"You know when you get so sick of yourself, and you're just dying to change? I guess I was just... dying to live, do you know what I mean?" she asked him.

"That's a lot of dying," he said.

"That's what it's been feeling like. For a long time now. And I'm just, ready to live."

When he didn't say anything right away, she she felt that familiar pit in her stomach. She'd said too much. Once again, she had given too much of herself away, to someone who didn't want it. To someone who didn't ask for it. She even over-gave laid up, broken and immobile in a hospital bed. She opened her mouth to apologize.

But then he said, "I know exactly what you mean."

"Are you just saying that because you're my doctor and you have to?"

He laughed again. His kind eyes smiled down at her. "No, I understand you. I get you," he said.

"I love being gotten," Wendy exhaled.

"It's rare," he acknowledged.

Then he scanned her eyes, like he was recognizing something of him in her. She kept his gaze. She was high as a kite, so she didn't know how long they looked at each other — it could have been only two seconds, or it could have been two minutes. Wendy wasn't sure what the standard amount of time to look in someone's eyes was, before you were supposed to look away. Most people could barely last a second, because any time after that, it meant something, and something happened. At a certain point, it became intimate — they saw you and you saw them. And maybe that's why most people avoided it.

The nurse cleared her throat.

"Wendy, is there anyone we should call?" she asked.

Wendy heard her but she was still taking the kind doctor in from behind her velvet veil of meds. He seemed like the sort of man she would set up with a friend, just to keep him in her world, but still just out of reach. And then she'd be secretly jealous she herself couldn't go for someone so nice and stable and loving.

If she didn't like nice guys, did that mean she liked them mean? And what did that say about her? What did that say about how she felt she deserved to be treated or how she treated herself? He seemed like the sort of man who would love you just as you were. And she couldn't let herself be loved just as she was, because she didn't love herself just as she was. Even before Peter, she was always hiding parts of herself from her lovers, but what would it be like, she wondered, to be seen completely, and loved for every part, even the dark and weird ones? Even the ones that made her feel like a hopeless, crazy, unlovable, messy, lazy loser?

Wouldn't that feel like being held in some golden net of love, wouldn't that feel so safe, like the world itself had taken you in its arms and there was no fear of falling ever again? That you'd been found, you were safe, and you no longer had to wander like a vagabond through your own life?

She always felt like she had to be better, get somewhere else, achieve more, look better, before she let herself be loved. She was always holding herself to this impossible elusive standard, and then, when we she reached it, which was never, only then would she let herself be seen and loved. She could love, with her overbearing needy panic, but she couldn't be loved, she couldn't... receive. And she had no idea what she was waiting for. Meanwhile her life raced by like that horse tearing through the woods, and she had no idea when it would just stop, abruptly, and she would be thrown into death's sea.

Somewhere along the line, she began to believe that being loved was something she had to earn, and she walked just outside the edges of it, endlessly trying to prove herself worthy of entrance to its secret garden.

To his credit, Peter had tried his best to love her, and convince her of that love, but one day, he gave up. He just had to. She wasn't something he could fix. She was something she was going to have to fix herself. And he couldn't wait around forever. Wendy felt she was always begging at the gates of love, and never sitting in its golden throne.

"Wendy," said the doctor, who had taken his hand off her arm and returned to jotting on his clipboard.

She returned from her trance and looked up at him.

"Word is, you're a writer," he said.

"Looks like you're going to have plenty of time to do that now."

"Oh," she said, gingerly raising her arm to massage her temples, "I was."

Her head felt swollen to the size of a Zeppelin.

"Is my head like, as big as this room?" she asked, squinting up at him.

"It feels like that, I'm sure. But it isn't. I promise. You look..." he looked at her again, this time like someone standing in front of a painting in a museum, he turned his head to get another angle. She waited. She held her breath. He dropped his eyes to the floor.

"Fine," he said, "just fine."

She exhaled and dropped her hands into her light blue lap.

"I did write. I mean, I guess you could have called me a writer once."

"I don't think that's something you ever stop being," he said. "You either are or you aren't, is my opinion."

"Well, I wrote about other people, I wrote about their passions. I think that's all I can write about. I don't think I have anything to say."

His body language told her he was beginning to leave the room, he put the pen in his pocket and nodded at the nurse.

"Well, Wendy, I don't think that's true," he said.

"You don't?" she asked.

"No," he said.

Emboldened by the drugs, she pressed him.

"What do you think is true?"

"That everyone has a story to tell, and something to say, and we find pieces of our selves in everyone's story. We've all learned and survived a lot more than we even realize. And when we tell our story, somehow we free ourselves, and somehow, it frees others too. So it's almost, or it is, our birthright to tell it."

"Holy shit," Wendy whispered under her breath.

When he moved through the door, she wanted to cry, "Don't go!"

But he had lives to save.

And Wendy had a book to write.

17.

Leanne picked her up from the hospital in the morning; the air had gone cold for the winter, and when they wheeled her out in her chair, she could see her breath. An attendant loaded her into the back of Leanne's old silver Subaru. With Wendy's plastered legs laid out gingerly in the back seat, Leanne laid an old red and yellow crochet blanket over her.

The car pushed out into the November frost, and Wendy watched her slowly take the turn onto Main Street. On the dash, Leanne had collected a small altar of seashells and crystals. Leanne pressed in an old cassette tape. A buttery rich voice of a deep and fiery angel floated into the car. Leanne took in a huge gulp of air then sighed with an *ahhhhh.*

"You know this shit?" she looked up at Wendy in the rearview.

"Um, just that it's opera," Wendy said.

"*Carmen,*" Leanne said. Then she shook her silver head.

"Ooooh, dog," she said.

"What?" asked Wendy.

"The Goddess sure knows how to ground a girl to her room so she can get some things done."

"I guess," Wendy said meekly.

"Well, I know." she said. "When you're on the wrong path, She'll stop you in your tracks. It's time you stayed in one place and didn't even think about running. Because you literally can't!"

Leanne indulged in that guttural laugh. Wendy was in no mood for the guttural laugh.

"You writing that book," Leanne continued, "that's some real self-actualization right there."

"What's that?" Wendy asked, watching the harbor glide by out the window.

"Becoming the person you were meant to be," Leanne said. "Cracking your own code." The opera singer's voice soared through the tinny old speakers like a woman on fire, singing for her life.

"Living your truth. Putting your inside dream on the outside. Becoming whole."

"Mmm," Wendy said, closing her eyes and resting deeper into the seat. She thought about the doctor's warm touch on her arm, and the way he'd held her gaze.

"What do you know about Dr. Weaver," Wendy asked.

Leanne was quiet. Wendy opened her eyes and looked up, she saw Leanne's strong wrinkled fingers squeezing the steering wheel tight.

"Why do you ask?"

"Well, just that he's so nice," Wendy said.

Leanne sighed. "And handsome. You gotta be blind as an old bat not to see that."

"Well, yes," Wendy pulled the blanket up a little defensively.

"And the whole island knows Jack Fletcher's horse is what landed you with two broken legs," she said.

"Forget it," Wendy said.

Leanne didn't.

"Just like getting bucked off of the love rodeo," Leanne snorted. "You ignore too many red flags, and that's what happens."

Wendy thought about that. There had been, she realized, a lot of flags she had blazed right through, but they were subtle, internal, and she hadn't yet learned to trust that inner voice.

"That's the running I'm talking about. Running to men to save you. Looking for it all outside of you."

"You're just not ready. You're healing," Leanne said. "And when we ignore the signs to heal our soul, the body stops us until we do it. The inside always creeps on out to the outside."

Wendy had an itch on her right thigh, and stuck a finger under the plaster, helplessly. She gave up and tossed her head back. She rolled down the old window and sucked in the late autumn air.

"Listen kid, you gotta fall in love with yourself first, like the way you dive headfirst in with men and give them everything, it's gotta stop. If only you loved you the way you loved men, so absolutely, with abandon, so curious and forgiving. Fall in love with you like the way you fall in love with men."

"I don't want to talk about this," Wendy said.

"Well, you're in my car, so we can talk about anything I want."

Wendy sighed.

"Here's some breaking news, kid. Love doesn't have to hurt. Love can heal. I think you've been looking for the hard kind. But there's a soft kind too. And I'm saying until you love yourself, you're going to be looking for love outside of you for the rest of your life. And you're never going to find it. The kind that sticks and stays, anyway.

If a woman can't be her own best friend, it's a long and lonely road, take it from me."

"Okay," Wendy said.

"I know you don't wanna hear me right now, but I'm quite fond of ya. I was happy by my fire this morning, but here I am, picking your broken butt up. Anyway, what are you going to do, get out and run?" Leanne howled again as Wendy let herself float away to the opera music.

The passion lit something deep within her. Her heart swelled with the crescendo. Leanne was tuning in, too. She tapped the speakers where the music poured out.

"You write from this place. You strike where you've been struck. You write from the place that burns. And I think you know a thing or too about things burning."

Out the window, the cliffs crashed into the grey sea, and a flock of seagulls soared over the car.

"You know what she's saying?"

"No," Wendy said. "Just that it's beautiful."

"She's saying that love is like a wild bird. And it's true. You can't control it. So stop trying to choose it. Let it choose you. When you choose love, you're in control. And love isn't about control. No, it's the ultimate 'Let Go'. When it chooses you, you're terrified, you have no control. And that's how you know you're onto and into something real. But no, it's a wild fucking bird and you can't chase it. But just when you've given up all hope, when you've finally stopped looking for it, it will land right on your shoulder. But first, girl, find you. To find your true love, you've got to find your true you."

18.

Leanne propped Wendy up in her bed with chamomile tea and a linen bag full of dried fruit. She bustled over to the window to the right of the bed.

"You need some fresh air after a night in that contaminated hospital," she said, cracking it open a sliver so the early winter air could seep in.

"Thank you," Wendy said, softening under Leanne's care.

"And ain't no music like the singing of those trees in the breeze," Leanne said.

It was true, they had become Wendy's favorite sound, she had grown to love the soft feathery rustle of the leaves as the wind whispered through them. It was like the leaves were the hair of the trees, and as the breeze swept through them, she could feel those fingers through her own hair. It relaxed her whole body, to feel that breeze. It was as if when the earth exhaled, so could she.

"I've got two poor fellas to heal then I'll be back," Leanne said, tapping the foot of the bed with a turquoise-laden hand.

"You got everything you need?"

Wendy sank back into the soft village of pillows and looked out the window.

"Yes..." she said. "I think knowing you literally can't do anything is somehow really calming. Like there's nothing I can do but be. Gosh, Leanne, I think I could say for the first time in my life, that I do, I do feel like I have everything I need."

"Now we're talkin'," Leanne said. "This, right now, as it is, is far more than fuckin' enough," she said. "Always wanting more is your hell. And knowing that is your ticket to paradise. Some wise fucker once said all of man's problems are because he can't sit alone in a room with himself. You're 'bout to put to that test."

Wendy nodded. "Before mom got sick she used to say she felt like the whole world was swirling around her and she just wanted to stop for a moment and lie down in cool white sheets, in some quiet corner of the world. She said she'd be standing at a cocktail party or sitting in the office and just start to dream of cool white sheets.

She said she felt too guilty about resting in such a fast-paced world. Sometimes I wonder if she had let herself rest more, if she still would have gotten so sick."

"Sounds like you're onto something kid. Ignore the body's whispers and one day it will start to shout. Best listen to what your body has to say. It's as wise as the earth herself. It's trying to tell you when you're in trouble, when to slow down, it's trying to tell you what you need. Smart folks listen in, not out."

"Now sink on into those cool white sheets and remember what the doctor said. Your only job is to heal. It's like the Universe is saying your only job is to let yourself be loved. Not that most folks find that easy. Most folks find it to be the hardest job in the world. It's why everyone's so sick. It's why I never have a day off. Everyone's so starved for what's right in front of them."

"That's a really nice prescription," Wendy said. "Be. Loved. Doctor's Orders."

"Yup," Leanne said.

"The secret to life. Okay, I'm out."

Leanne strolled down the polished wood hall.

"Well, la di da," she called from the living room. "You know I don't really think I'll mind hanging around this joint till you get your sea legs back," she said. "Always did wanna know how the other half lived."

"Thanks again, Leanne," Wendy called back.

"Don't go nowhere now," Leanne laughed.

Wendy gave in. "Hahaha," she said.

"That's the spirit. Gotta laugh at this shit. Or else you'll cry. And who wants to do that on a beautiful day like today. That laughing will heal you faster than any pills."

The door slammed and Wendy was alone. The unfinished books she had begun to collect; the *Power of Now*, collections of Rumi and Hafiz, Leanne's borrowed books on the Goddesses and Feminine Awakenings, sat now like dogs at her feet waiting to be touched. She had nothing else to do now, but to receive the wisdom.

And, well, write. Write that book. God, it wouldn't go away. Once you knew you had to do something, you simply had to do it. It wouldn't leave you alone. It seemed there was nothing to do but that thing you had to do.

But how?

She looked over at the bedside table, where the journal Danny had given her lay waiting, unopened. She picked it up, held the soft brown leather book in her hands. It spilled open, revealing its empty pages, like a life waiting to be lived.

Just… start. That was the only way to do anything, right? Was to just start it.

But she had never written about herself before. Only others. She had never started any writing with "I." She could write a celebrity profile in her sleep, she'd start with a quote, or what they were wearing, or what they were having for lunch. She had never told her own story.

But she had told an older male editor once, she had told him of her dream of telling her story. He had laughed.

"What story do you have to tell?" he had asked her.

"I mean, like a memoir," she had said.

She figured the word memoir came from the word memory, and everyone had memories, right? And she figured it would be a good way to expunge some of the ghosts that rambled through the halls of her body. He chided her like a child. He had told her she'd barely lived, what was there to write about? He told her wait until she was eighty, wait until she had actually done something with her life. Wait, he said, until she had something to say. But what if there was no time to wait, or waste? But what if she didn't last that long? And what if her story might mean something to someone else? What if, what if her story was actually enough?

And maybe writing about that last chapter of her life was as good a way as any to close it, before she started a new one. Just maybe, it was the only way to start a new one. She felt a little wiser than she ever had in her life, like she might be able to offer something. It felt as if things were finally coalescing, like she had stopped and found a place of stillness. Leanne was right, she had been grounded. There could be no drinking, no chasing men, no possibility even of thinking of leaving, no last night to recover from.

All the lessons now had time to stop and settle into the bones of her body. And maybe they hadn't all been for nothing. Maybe they had been for this.

She picked up the pen.

"Strike where you've been struck," she heard Leanne say. Well, that would be her heart. She would write from there.

She placed the black pen to the white page.

"Start where you are," she thought.

"Both my legs are broken," she wrote. "They seem to just be an outer reflection of my inner brokenness."

And then she wrote: "How did I get here?"

She thought of Carmen.

"Well, if love is a wild bird, then I held it too tight. And it couldn't breathe, and it couldn't fly. If love is a wild bird, then I captured it, and I, I let it die."

She paused. Even the heartbeat of her pen seemed to race. And there and then she decided to do something radical, that she would tell the absolute truth. She would write as if she would never show anyone, like she was just sharing her secrets with God. She would empty every skeleton from her closet. She wouldn't worry about characters' names or getting anyone in trouble.

She wouldn't worry about any of that stuff that might slow her down or censor her. She wouldn't worry about what people thought, or what they would say, or if they would think her strange or sad or crazy. She would just write until she felt free, she would empty herself out until there was nothing left to say..

She wrote until she heard Leanne's wheels on the gravel outside. She heard Leanne rustling around making a fire, before she came in and helped Wendy to the bathroom, and then back to bed. She disappeared again only to come back in bearing a tray of two bowls of soup and soft white buttered bread.

"Got you some nice fresh minestrone," Leanne said.

"Did you make it?" Wendy asked.

"Hell no," Leanne said.

They sat together that night on the bed, sipping soup in silence. When Leanne's spoon clinked down for good, she looked down at the books at the end of the bed.

"How 'bout we read a little poetry?" she said, sifting through the titles, opening up Hafiz, rifling through the pages.

"'K," said Wendy.

"Mmm, this is pretty," she said.

"Ahem," Leanne cleared her throat, lifting her reading glasses from her generous breast, resting them on the tip of her nose.

"The subject tonight is Love," she read.

"And for tomorrow night as well,
As a matter of fact
I know of no better topic
For us to discuss
Until we all
Die."

"Well, how about that? I sure think he's right. What do you think?"

"You know what I think," Wendy said. "I think I don't know anything about love," Wendy said.

"Oh, hush now with that story," Leanne said, stroking her fingers through Wendy's hair.

"Stop trying to be something you already are. Which is love."

"You're right," Wendy said.

"Lemme give you a hint," Leanne said. "Everything you're looking for is always right under your nose."

"You really think that's true?" Wendy asked.

"Why would I say it if I didn't?" Leanne said. "I respect myself too much to lie."

"Ah," said Wendy. "Well, you're right here and I love you," Wendy said.

"You ain't so bad yourself, kiddo," Leanne mustered.

And then, even though it felt wrong, even though the intuition flashed red, Wendy said it anyway:

"I feel like, you're kinda like my mother," she said in a voice as small as a doll's. Leanne's hand stopped mid hair- stroke. It was like a moment which had been floating happily in the air suddenly crashed to the ground and shattered like a porcelain plate.

"Don't say that," she snapped.

Wendy was quiet.

"I'm, I'm sorry," she said.

Leanne sat up off the edge of the bed.

"I had a daughter. And you had a mother. I'm not your mother. And you ain't my daughter."

"I know, I'm sorry," Wendy said.

"You're a grown woman. At least in body. The rest of you needs to catch up and learn how to care for yourself. I'm just here because you need someone right now, and truth is," her eyes hardened. "Truth is, kid, you ain't got nobody else. Your life is damn right empty. And that's something you need to look at."

Leanne walked out the room, snapping the lights out as she passed through the door. Wendy sat there alone in the pitch black emptiness, looking at it.

19.

Right before dawn, Wendy rolled herself off the side of the bed and into the wheelchair that sat beneath the window. She ripped a blank page from the journal that rested on the bedside table, and placed it with a pen on her lap. Then she wheeled herself into the living room where Leanne slept by the fire. And she continued to sit there by the fireplace, with her legs out straight like a plaster doll's on the couch, until the sun rose light yellow into the room and Leanne woke up.

"Holy shit," Leanne said, peering at Wendy from within her nest of cashmere blankets. Then she started to laugh. "Oh, you are a pathetic little thing," she told Wendy. She said it sweetly though, as if to say the previous night had been forgotten.

Wendy smiled weakly, but she was still thinking about what Leanne had said; she'd spent a sleepless night in the dark with those words, looking at the emptiness, taking responsibility for it. And thinking about changing, about how badly she wanted to. She was still feeling bruised when she raised her head and looked straight at her, but she had resigned herself to Leanne's teachings like a thirsty woman at a well.

"How do I grow up?" Wendy asked. She raised the pen over the paper.

"Well, hot damn," Leanne said, "that's a good question. Let me get some tea, wake the brain up."

Then Leanne stood up and as her long white hair fell to her hips, her long white gown fell to the floor in one big rustle. She wedged her feet into her sheepskin slippers, and shuffled into the kitchen and switched on the kettle.

"You want some?" she asked.

"Yes, please," Wendy said, the fire crackled next to her and she closed her eyes for a minute. She focused in on the sound of the hot wood cracking and the sizzle of the flames. She was beginning to practice that meditation in bed, to just find one sound and stay with it, like the breeze, or the fire. Any sound but her thoughts. Mostly she just mediated on her breath. She just stayed with the sound of her breathing, and sometimes she pictured the ocean, rising and falling with her breath. And she found that she couldn't listen to both her thoughts and her breath at the same time, and that was the point. To choose the breath over the thoughts.

Practicing meditation was becoming her way to stay sane and calm, to not react, to not drown in fear, to let the small stuff simmer away and what was important to rise to the surface. She found that from that quiet space between her thoughts, a new self was beginning to emerge. One she actually recognized and trusted, like a long-lost friend. Leanne brought her tea in a light blue pottery mug. She sat back down on the couch and pulled a grey blanket like a shawl over her shoulders.

"Good question," Leanne muttered again to herself. "Okay, here's what I, personally, think makes an adult."

She crossed her legs and stared in the fire. She took a moment, letting the thoughts bake in her mind's oven.

"Well," she started, "an adult doesn't just think about herself, she thinks about others. But she doesn't care about others think of her. She knows she's the one who needs to approve of her own life. Like I said before, she gives precedence to what she feels over what other people say or think.

She knows how to care for herself, and that only from that place can she care for others. She knows what her body needs, how to listen to it. She's got boundaries, borders you need her trust to cross. She protects what's sacred to her and others. She knows what she needs to be safe and happy. She has no problem saying *No*, and when she says *Yes* she means it. Oh, and her happiness, it's not reliant on other people.

It's not subject to external whims; she's at peace with herself so she can be at peace with others. She knows how to make decisions in her life. She follows through with what she's promised herself and others. Oh... she's on time. She meets you when and where she said she would. You know, she shows up.

And... when she fucks up, she owns it and apologizes. And she doesn't blame other people for her problems. At the same time, she's unapologetic. She tells the truth. She's kind but clear. She isn't sniveling around looking for approval or permission. Or forgiveness for being different or living her own life. She knows this ain't no dress rehearsal.

She doesn't sit around begging you to tell her who she is or what she needs. She makes her own decisions. She cleans up after herself, literally and figuratively. She gives without agenda, she's of service to others and the world. She knows the other is herself.

She has a calm confidence about herself. She believes in herself and in her dreams. She's got her own back and she's comfortable in her own skin.

When shit gets hard, she doesn't run. She deals. She can commit.

She knows she can handle whatever comes. You know, she faces things, faces what she fears. Oh, and she can't be abandoned. Because she stands on her own two feet. You know, she's got herself. She can lose someone or something without losing herself. She can depend on herself and you can depend on her.

She's compassionate. She has a big strong, soft heart. She'll take breathtaking, heartbreaking tangible reality over imaginary untouchable fantasy any day.

She doesn't just dream, she does. She likes who she is in the lonely moments walking through her house, when no one else can see her. She likes her own company."

Leanne brought her mug to her lips and slurped.

"That's all I can think of for now," she said. Then she paused, still holding the cup in front of her lips. "She relies on herself and can be relied on. She trusts herself, and you can trust her."

Oh," she said, "She's left Neverland. You know, the fantasy that can rob you of your whole life. Responsibility ain't a bad word, you know. It's Power. With responsibility comes power, and with power comes responsibility.

She's entered the real world where she's truly living. So when her time comes to die, she can say she truly lived. She can say she was real. That she touched and was touched. That she loved and was loved. Again, she didn't just dream. She did. She's aware of her hourglass, of the sands of time, spilling so damn fast."

"Thank you," nodded Wendy, still scribbling.

"It's a waning moon, by the way. A 'let go' phase. A perfect time to practice letting go of all that small childish stuff. You want a spell?" she asked her.

"What do you mean?"

"Well, when we do ritual, we signify to our unconscious that we are ready to mark a change, or an important passage in our lives."

"Okay," Wendy said.

"Write down the small parts that you are ready to release.

"The parts that complain, that are too passive. The tiny 'shrinking in fear' parts. The messy, lazy parts. The gluttony. The scarcity, the lack, the mother wound, the destructive patterns in relationships. Get specific, what keeps happening.

What's the story, the story you need to burn. What needs to die so you can live again. Or maybe for the first time.

Write down all the small scared parts, the parts that refuse to let you bloom. 'Cuz you were meant to bloom, we all were. Just like everything in nature.

Okay, Burn that. Burn that paper. Offer it up. Release it.

Then, on a second piece of paper, write down who you're ready to become and speak it in the present tense. Whatever you want to be and do…" Leanne waved her hand in the air, like she was beckoning the words to come to her.

They came and landed on her tongue. "Speak present tense. I am powerful. Calm. Confident, successful whatever you deem success to be. I have found my joy. I am Loving, Loved. Kind. Of service. Write those down and keep them somewhere where you look at them everyday. And then, don't just dream it, align your actions with her. Align yourself with the higher dream in thought and word and deed.

Self-actualize. Remember, do the thing you're here to do. If you can, you must."

Wendy nodded.

"Alright now," said Leanne. "Wheel on back to that room. An adult commits, remember? She stays with it.

I'll bring you breakfast. Whatever you do, don't stop writing. Just keep going 'til you can't no more. I'm telling you, that book's your ticket to walking with confidence."

"I'd take just walking for now," Wendy said.

"Remember you're on bed rest for a reason. The answers don't always come when we demand them. But if we relax, they do eventually come. The more we can accept what is happening right now, the less crazy with resistance we tend to go."

Wendy complied. She picked up the journal again, and plunged back in. She wrote for half an hour, until she hit the part about her pill addiction. The moment she got her first Xanax prescription had been the downfall of... everything. Now Wendy was blocked. Where she was once swimming along, she had now slammed into a brick wall.

She took a deep breath. The pen scribbled slowly in an ink whirlpool in one place.

Fuck it, she thought, *be fearless.*

She tried again.

It started innocently, she wrote. And she wrote. About how the pills made her relationship with Peter and life itself go fuzzy, how as she lost herself, she helplessly witnessed herself losing him, and the terror of that, of not knowing how to stop it, how to stop the loss.

The quicksand of her life that followed: the blacking out, the getting fired, the lying, the fights, the depression.

She stopped again; she didn't know if she had the heart to do this, to write it all out. It hurt so bad to remember. She could barely take a breath, like her throat closed off. How brave one had to be to write about the darkest saddest parts of her life, the ones she had tried to forget, especially the ones she herself had been responsible for.

She hadn't just hurt herself, she had hurt others. And how shameful and terrifying it felt to momentarily face it again. But somehow relieving, too, to pull it out of herself and place it onto paper. The pen somehow acted as a surgeon's scalpel, touching each wound. Pulling the stories out felt like taking tumors from her body.

And she wrote and healed like this, for days.

There were times she felt as if she was sitting before a dark cave she was too scared to enter. But she couldn't turn back now, she didn't want to give up. There was nothing else to do but write this book, so she wrote through it. She kept finding, too, all that was in that cave, waiting to be faced, was herself.

She walked her pen across the paper like a sword with which she slayed her dragons.

When she carried on, despite the pain, she felt like a knight to the grail.

More days passed. Leanne had ordered her a little laptop with Wendy's credit card. The small, slick silver machine came, light and thin as a coaster. She typed out her diary pages and kept going.

A few weeks later, the first snow fell.

Wendy was writing thirty pages a week, and spending the other time reading, talking with Leanne and napping. She even took Leanne's advice and started making a vision board. Leanne had been kind enough to bring home old magazines from her volunteer shift at the library.

Wendy sliced the pictures and words that called to her with scissors, and glue-sticked them onto a large piece of cardboard, which she kept by her bed. Slowly a vision actually did begin to appear. She would add words and pictures to it day by day, and tell Leanne about it.

"Saying it aloud makes it real," Leanne had said. "Looking at your dream every day reprograms the Universe. It begins to roll out a yellow brick road for you to follow toward your visions. When you can see your dream, step by step, the path emerges. Take one step, and another one appears. So you know, keep seeing it.

Hold the vision, trust the process."

20.

Through the window she watched Doctor Weaver's truck drive right over the snow and park in front of the house.

She heard the door swing open and a whoosh of wind enter before him, then Leanne taking his coat and offering him tea in a voice even shorter and snappier than usual.

Wendy cringed a little for the Doctor, she sure knew what Leanne's cold fronts felt like, they were so frosty your teeth chattered. That was her joke with Leanne when she got tough, Wendy would say, "Hmm, seems like a cold front coming in, pass me my sweater?"

But in two months of invalidism, she had grown to feel an intense compassion for and understanding of Leanne. She knew Leanne didn't even like to be so hard around the edges, as she herself called it, but she had built up a wall of armor over years of doing battle with a lifetime of loss.

But Leanne never liked being too tough. "No one actually likes being a shitty monster," she said. "It's just my ego defending my wounds. The only thing that really feels good is when love is in charge, not fear."

Still, all her life's adversity had brought her much wisdom, which Wendy soaked up like a sponge. Leanne liked to say that the world had cracked her hard enough to let a *fuckload of light in.*

Wendy waited for the doctor in the bedroom, in her tan cashmere sweater and silk light blue nightgown which Peter had bought her for their honeymoon. She hadn't been able to take it off; it was a symbol of their innocence, of his mad romantic love for her, he had bought it in London before sweeping home to marry her.

Leanne had told her how unhealthy it was, to wear something that symbolized something dead. She called stories about Peter ghost stories.

"Why you telling me ghost stories?" she'd ask when Wendy would tell an anecdote about Peter. "Why you bringing up the dead?" Leanne was careful to toss dead flowers and quickly fix things which broke around the house, like the kitchen chair that split when she had landed in it too heavily in the middle of a particularly dramatic story.

"Don't want nothin' with dead or broken energy in this house, especially when you're trying to heal, and start a new life," Leanne had said. "What I want to know is what is happening now. That's the question a gal's always gotta be asking herself in order to get present and take care of business.

Otherwise you're floating around in the past or future, and neither of those exists. Don't muddle over the past, darling, and don't you dare believe in the future. Ask yourself: What. Is. Happening. Now. Otherwise, you'll miss your whole life."

But Wendy still wouldn't take the soft silk blue nightgown off.

Before the doctor had come, Wendy had brushed her hair, but that was all. She was in this new place of not trying to be anything more than who she was, of being enough as she was. She was starting to realize that trying had never worked. And besides, she didn't really feel there was anything she could do to feel attractive for the handsome doctor.

It was hard to feel desirable with two splayed out plaster legs, despite them being draped with a light lavender blanket. Maybe it was simply because she had to, but Wendy was finding herself letting a lot of things go.

Leanne had told her, "Fear holds on. Love lets go."

And Wendy was letting go of things she had clutched tightly her whole life. Her obsession with looks and how others saw her. She was even starting to see beneath others' shells as well; she wasn't so focused on their outsides, but their insides — if they meant and did what they said. If they cared about something besides than themselves. If they were kind.

"Remember, with this Doctor Weaver character," Leanne had said after Wendy had brought him up again, *"all that glitters ain't gold."*

She barely looked in a mirror anymore, and beauty was becoming a different definition to her, one she had never thought of in her prior world of materialism and cool. She and Leanne talked about what true beauty was. "This culture just strives for a beautiful outside," Leanne had said, shaking her head.

"What about a beautiful inside?" she said. "The body goes. You're stuck with the soul." She hadn't read a magazine in months, the TV was way out in the living room and she could only listen faintly to the dialogue of Leanne's shows.

She'd been listening to Ram Dass meditations and reading real books, books on mystic poetry and consciousness and evolution, on the Goddess and the feminine and having real, intimate conversations with Leanne. Some days she was feeling like she and Leanne had more of an intimate relationship than she ever did with Peter.

Leanne didn't storm out of the room and go drink when Wendy made her mad, and Wendy couldn't storm out of a room and go drink when Leanne made her mad. They both stayed. Neither of them stormed away from the storm; the storm eventually passed, and their anger turned to forgiveness, and even laughter.

And after each storm, somehow they knew themselves and each other better.

Everything about her was softening in this cocoon of plaster she was in, and Leanne had even explained to her that that was exactly what she was doing, was cocooning.

Leanne told Wendy that she was perfectly aligned with the seasons of the earth, to cocoon up and metaphysically die in winter, along with all of nature.

And Wendy felt quadruple-cocooned really, by the cast, the cabin she hadn't left in eight weeks, the thick blanket of snow on the ground, and the island which seemed to hold her apart from the world, deep in the sea like a womb. Beneath all these layers, her old self felt like it was dying and a new one forming, and all Wendy could do was be patient with the process.

"It's almost like you've been mummified like some Egyptian priestess for rebirth," Leanne said, giving her left cast a little knock with a fist.

The doctor declined the tea, he sounded anxious to just see Wendy.

"Our girl's in the back," Leanne told him. Wendy's heart beat a little as he entered the door. He had a light dusting of snow in his hair and he wasn't wearing his glasses. He seemed more nervous than the last time they saw each other. He checked her vitals quickly, then asked about her emotional health.

"I have the best nurse around," Wendy said, nodding to Leanne in the doorway.

He told her she had about one month left in the casts, and then he cleared his throat as he removed the lavender blanket, absentmindedly running his hands over his handiwork. "So," he said, "Wendy, I was wondering about something."

"Yes?" Wendy asked, feeling her cheeks burn hot.

"Peter Jackson's playing in Portland next week, and..."

Her heart fell. She knew this way too well. She was so used to this scenario — people using her to get to Peter.

"I, I wouldn't have any way of talking to him," she said. Peter hadn't returned a text in three months. It seemed he hoped she would just disappear. He wouldn't even know if she was dead.

The doctor's eyes went dark. "That's too bad, my girlfriend and I were hoping to go."

"I'm sorry," Wendy said, staying stoic as to not to reveal her disappointment, "I can't help you."

Leanne stepped into the room.

"Well, Doc, guess we should let the patient get some rest."

He wasn't so kind when he left, as if there wasn't much Wendy could do for him. Her eyes watered after she heard the door shut, and Leanne sat down on the side of the bed. "Honey," she said, petting her knee, "it's good when there are no men left to dream of in your heart. It's when you finally turn into the reality of you and learn to love her, warts and all. Abandon these fantasies of men. Turn all that energy back towards you and becoming a woman you love, the woman of your dreams."

Wendy let herself cry a little. "I know, Leanne," she said, "he just reopened that wound. For years people were nice to me because they could get to Peter," she said. "I feel like I was only worth something because I was Peter's wife." She wiped a tear away and inhaled deeply. "When Peter left me, everyone else did too."

"Baby, you have so much more to offer than being someone's wife. And sometimes, people have to leave us so we can find ourselves." Leanne nodded at Wendy's laptop, then pressed her hand into Wendy's heart.

"Sometimes I think he's just going to walk back in the door and say *'just kidding'*."

With that, Leanne reached over to Wendy and pulled the sweater from off of her.

"What are you doing?" Wendy asked.

Leanne didn't answer, just shook her head and murmured something about ghosts. Then she lifted Wendy's hips and jerked the blue nightgown up and off them, then hoisted it over Wendy's head. She bustled out of the bedroom, then out of the cabin front door.

Wendy saw her trod out in the snow in front of the bedroom window. Her mane of white hair whipped in the wind and she held up the blue nightgown like a flag, and seemed to be mumbling some sort of ritual.

Then Wendy watched Leanne hold a lighter underneath the gown and set it aflame. Wendy just watched the show silently from bed as the flames crept up the dress and then engulfed it completely. The hot flickering orange was brilliant against the blanket of white. Wendy sat there naked, watching this wild crone burn the last material piece of her old life, up in flames.

There was now literally nothing of it to hold on to. There was nothing Wendy was holding on to any more at all. In fact, instead of holding on, Wendy felt naked and held like a baby in the womb. By Leanne, this bed, by this island that cradled her in the sea, and this new force she could feel within her, that always seemed to be right there when she needed it.

She leaned back into the bed, into that silent presence within her, and closed her eyes, with a small, peaceful smile on her face.

21.

The gown had burned down to black ash in the white snow.

Wendy sat up still naked in bed, but didn't long for any clothes; she was getting more and more comfortable in her naked form, more in love with her body as some sort of wild creature. It felt sensual, free, natural, to be naked.

She didn't know how her body looked in the mirror, but it felt beautiful, and that felt more powerful than anything a mirror could tell her.

The clock on the wall said four pm, and as usual she was pressed with the question of to read or to write. But she felt too tired to write, although there were still so many more stories to be told, about how she ended up in that bed on the island, sober and single with plaster casts for legs.

But she was daunted by where she was in her diaries; she was finally delving into her relationship with male power figures in her childhood and career. She had twisted dark tales to tell, of how she had used and been used for her sexuality in a male-dominated world. But she hadn't the energy to look back now.

Instead she reached for Starhawk's *The Spiral Dance* — her obsession with the Goddess was becoming more insatiable than her thirst for white wine ever had been. Maybe the absence of the Goddess was the very hole she was always trying to fill with all that intoxicating liquid. Well, one of them.

Wendy had begun to feel as if she could actually hear the Goddess, as a strong loving feminine voice, inside of her. Not outside of her, like in Church, but inside, as if that divine power lived in her body. Reading about the Goddess made her feel in-powered.

It didn't feel like homework to read, instead she was hungry for this feminine wisdom, and she flew through the pages. The discoveries took her breath away, and the word *Witch* — not an ugly warted hexer, but a powerful autonomous woman aligned with the earth, moon, and Goddess — unlocked endless portals within her.

Each book felt like uncovering hidden mysteries, tombs of truth, that she somehow knew, but it was as if they had been buried within and without. She was re-membering herself. Piecing herself back together with each book.

She opened *The Spiral Dance* to an Ostara ritual just as Leanne came storming back into the house and burst into the bedroom. She picked up the lavender blanket and wrapped it around Wendy's naked frame.

"Leanne," Wendy said, "I need to rest."

Leanne ignored her and clumsily plopped Wendy into her wheelchair by the side of the bed.

"Leanne," Wendy protested, "what in the world?"

"You haven't properly done it, you haven't let him go."

"I have, I swear. He let me go, a long time ago. I get it. Please leave me alone."

"Exactly. He let you go. You didn't let him go."

"Leanne, I'm tired of talking about Peter. Honestly. I'm at peace, I've surrendered."

"You need the fresh air anyway," Leanne said. "Come on, baby. Do this for me."

She wheeled Wendy into the living room and stopped at the hall closet. She tossed a big black puffy coat over Wendy's lap and pushed her outside, crunching over the snow, stopping at the ashes of nightgown.

"Welcome to the Funeral," Leanne said.

Wendy sighed heavily and shuddered in the frozen yard.

"He's lying in front of you. Peter is dead. In your life, anyway. Now what do you say?"

Wendy couldn't say anything. She was shivering and angry, but she wouldn't say anything. She was mad, but didn't want to make Leanne mad. So she bottled it up and she felt it stewing in her body.

"If you can't do it for you," Leanne said, "do it for all the women who stay huddled in their shells waiting for and dreaming of the man who has long gone. One man rejects them and they feel rejected by the whole dang world."

Wendy felt a pit in her stomach. That wouldn't be her. She shot a look at Leanne. She was so tired of literally being pushed around. Worse, she could tell Leanne knew she was angry, but didn't care.

Her teeth chattered.

"Do it," Leanne pressed, "and we'll go back by the fire and watch something trashy."

She bit her lip. Maybe she could use a tiny break from her spiritual studies. A part of her wondered what was shaking on *Lifetime*. She wouldn't mind watching a good jilted woman seeks revenge tour de force. But she wasn't in the mood for whatever this was that Leanne had forced her into yet again.

How weary she was growing of this weakness, how restless she was growing of rest. Her dreams were forming inside of her and she was impatient to act.

"Please," she said to Leanne.

"That's your problem," Leanne hollered. "You're a pleaser. It's not your fault, all women are programmed by the patriarchy this way. God forbid you're a strong passionate unapologetic woman. That might not be sexy. Men might not want you. Other women will be threatened. People will talk. People you don't like might not invite you to their parties that you don't even want to go to.

Fuck that. Are you angry? There's a lot to be angry about. Anger is your change agent. Feel it. Let it burn. Are you sick of being sick? That's when you heal. Are you mad at me? At Peter? Show me! Trust me, baby, I can take it."

Wendy looked down at the imagined coffin.

"Peter," she whispered.

A a satiny black crow circled over head. Leanne looked up.

"That's some fine company for a ceremony," she said.

"Go on," she gestured at the ashes. "He's in the coffin in front of you. I'm here mourning with you. This is your time to say Goodbye, so you can let him go for good. I'd offer my condolences. But death brings birth."

Wendy shook her head. "I've done this," she said.

"Not with power, not with belief," Leanne said. "The only way things become real is by believing them. Believe it this time. It's all about intention. He's gone, it's over. He's dead. And the only way you're going to truly live is if he's truly dead. Otherwise you'll wait at your life's window forever, waiting for him to come back.

And that will have been your sad lonely life."

"Maybe tomorrow. I'm freezing."

"Girl, you know I don't believe in no tomorrow," Leanne snapped, growing cold herself and pulling her black sweater up under her chin. "Can't do it for you? You said you wanted to grow up. Growing up is about your story becoming the collective story. Growing up, it's no longer just about you. It's about serving the other and realizing the other is you.

This is not just about you. It's all the women hanging out in their broken heart with the shutters closed, not letting life's light in, not letting their own love in. Still hearing his voice in their head when he is long the hell gone.

And as long as they stay tiny inside of themselves mourning some man, they can't use their powers for bigger things, outside of themselves. Like healing the world. So go on. Don't do this just for you.

And if you do this, I'm talking really trashy TV. Lots of sex."

Wendy thought of the way he left her, without remorse, about the unreturned text messages, as if she had not only never even mattered to him, but never even existed. About the affair with Cassandra, and all those horrible tabloids, and then of the last two and a half months in bed. Her blood began to boil, and the air began to stir around her.

"Can this be the last naked crazy outside ritual I ever have to do?" she asked Leanne.

"Hell no. But this is the last skyclad ceremony ever about him," Leanne promised. "If you make it real. If you make it count."

Wendy closed her eyes and raised her arms into the air, the blanket falling from her body.

"Peter," she said into the wind.

"Excuse me? I don't think he could hear you in the Underworld," Leanne said.

Wendy took a big deep breath in.

"Peter!" She screamed, reaching her arms even further to the sky.

The trees around her seemed to dance in the breeze, like Goddesses huddled around her for ritual.

Wendy opened one eye and stole a look at them, it was almost as if they were leaning in, inching closer for ceremony.

"Peter!" she bellowed to the ends of the earth. The wind moaned and the crow descended from the air, landing by her chair in the snow.

Wendy could hear Leanne's ragged, heavy breath.

" I RELEASE YOU!" she cried.

"I FORGIVE YOU! I FORGIVE ME! I DID THE BEST WITH WHAT I KNEW. WE DID OUR BEST. WE WERE WOUNDED CHILDREN PLAYING AT LOVE. WE DIDN'T KNOW ANY BETTER! I'M SORRY I LOST MY LIGHT. I'M SORRY I LOST MY FIRE. I'M SORRY I DROWNED IT IN SUBSTANCE. I'M SORRY IT KILLED OUR LOVE.

I'M SORRY. I'M SORRY. I'M SORRY!!!!!" she screamed.

Suddenly the once cold dead ashes burst back into flame. The crow screeched. The tree branches rustled and crackled in the wind.

"Holy shit," she heard Leanne whisper, but Wendy kept going, taken by that fierce feminine force deep within her. Inside, the light she'd once lost rose and swelled with the flames in the snow.

"I RELEASE YOU INTO THE LIGHT. I RELEASE ME INTO THE LIGHT. WE ARE BOTH FORGIVEN. WE ARE BOTH FREE. OUR CONTRACT IS OVER. OUR CONTRACT IS SURRENDERED. IT IS DONE.

BY THE POWERS OF THE EARTH, WIND, AIR, FIRE, WATER, SPIRIT, BY THE POWERS OF THE GODDESS, BY THE POWERS OF THE ANGELS AND THE ANCESTORS, I RELEASE YOU. I RELEASE ME. WE ARE EACH FREE TO LIVE THE FULLEST LIFE AS SPIRIT INTENDED. WE ARE HEALTHY WHOLE AND FREE.

AND FOR ALL THOSE WOMEN LEFT WAITING TO LIVE, LONG AFTER LOVE LEFT THEM, FREE THEM NOW — MAKE IT SO. FROM THE DEPTHS OF MY ANCIENT SOUL, I IMPLORE YOU — HEAL THEM! MAKE THEM WHOLE!

GO IN PEACE. BLESSED BE. FOR THE HIGHEST GOOD OF ALL, IT IS DONE!

AND SO IT IS."

Wendy's hands dropped by her sides. She sucked back in her breath, her heart still beating madly like a shaman's drum. The fire died its final death. The wind stopped. The trees were still again, the crow took flight.

She looked over at Leanne, whose jaw was on the ground, in the snow.

"I choose the movie," she told Leanne.

"Fuck me," said Leanne. "You're a goddamn Priestess."

22.

Wendy was surprised to hear a knock at the door.

She was perched in front of the fire in the living room, with the printed out chapters of her stories in her lap. But she found she could barely look at them again, it had been like unanesthetized surgery to pull them out of her body the first time. Her eyes kept glazing over to *Practical Magic*, muted on the TV.

She had been waiting for Sandra Bullock to kiss Aidan Quinn. Then, she had told herself, she'd turn it off for good and get focused.

Leanne had gone out to Al's to fetch fettuccine for dinner and more tea. It was their last night before Leanne left Wendy's and moved back into her home. So, tonight they were celebrating, with carbs and kava. Or so Wendy thought.

"Hello?" she called out to the front door.

The knock persisted.

"Hellloooo," she called louder.

"It's Danny!" Danny called from the porch.

"Oh!" shouted Wendy. "Come in!"

"I brought a few peeps," Danny said as she entered, that big wicker basket of hers dangling off her elbow, "I hope that's okay."

Wendy's face fell and she felt her walls go up, she was not in the mood for meeting anyone new, which she realized wasn't a healthy habit. But she figured herself in transition mode; it was okay to be half-alive. She wanted to feel better and look better when she met new people. But Danny would tell her if she waited to be perfect... she'd wait forever. She was promising herself she wouldn't let that isolation pattern stick, she would be careful about becoming agoraphobic like Kim Basinger. Wendy peered around Danny and saw a triad of unfamiliar women standing in twilight's fuzzy purple light on the porch.

She caught herself. She had read you should break a pattern as soon as it arises, not "next time."

She unfroze her face and relaxed it into a smile. "I'm happy to meet your friends," she forced herself to say. " Thanks for bringing them over."

Danny laughed. "Good work," she said, "how boring is fear and self-loathing, anyway?" She rolled her eyes. "Leanne told my mom you've been evolving butterfly-style in this cocoon of yours."

"Hope so," Wendy said.

Danny gently patted Wendy's leg, which was now bare, cast-free. Both of them were.

"So, how did it go?" she asked.

"Easy," said Wendy, smoothing the black blanket over her legs. "I had a nice nurse, she sawed them open with this round little buzz saw. Pretty weird, they're like white light emaciated twigs. So tiny and pale. But I'm practicing walking. I hobbled like a baby fawn from the car to the house this morning when we got back. Leanne's out getting dinner. I'm... editing those stories I've been working on."

Danny glanced down at Wendy's lap. "Oh, you finished those?" she asked.

"I guess so, I mean, I can't actually physically look at them anymore, so I guess that means I've finished them."

"Damn," Danny said, running a finger through them. "That's like three hundred pages. What are you gonna do with them?" she asked.

Wendy shrugged. ""Nothing, I think. It was mostly a self-healing exercise. To be able to look at my life honestly and take responsibility for what I did, learn, and move on. Grow up."

"Well, you should do something with them," Danny said.

"I can't even think about that right now," Wendy said. "I'm pretty exhausted with..." she looked around at her gilded cage of the last three months, "... stuff," she said.

"Well, that's why I brought the girls. We brought you a door-to-door moon circle! I figured you weren't going to ever come to me, so I brought it to you."

"Ladies," Danny called to the porch, "come meet Wendy."

They bustled in laughing and shivering from the cold in a cloud of silk and velvet. Wendy took them in from her nest on the couch: she liked how they each wore kimonos, like modern day witch's capes, and didn't use brushes, it was more like their hair had been groomed with tree branches, and they were draped in crystal jewelry, big hunks of turquoise, slabs of ruby and clear quartz. They were like mini-Leannes.

Danny gestured to a long-haired brunette in a red velvet kimono.

"This is Alice," she said. Alice smiled big at Wendy. Her lipstick was blood red and she wore colossal turquoise earrings that skimmed her collarbones.

"And Sam," she pointed to a woman with wild, scraggly long blond hair, and a light freckled face in a blue silk kimono. Sam shone her green eyes down at Wendy and flashed her the peace sign.

"And Kelly." She gestured toward a woman with short brown bobbed hair in a black fringed velvet kimono. "Hey," Kelly said.

"Ladies," Danny said, "this is Wendy."

"Hi Wendy," they chorused, and then the three of them leaned over the back of the couch to one by one to peck a kiss on her cheek. When they stood back up, they folded their arms across their bodies, and looked down at her, empathetically, under her black blanket. Wendy smiled back, feeling like a newborn foal in a manger.

"I would get up," Wendy said.

"No!" they protested.

"We're here to help you," Sam said. 'This is a healing circle."

"Wow, this is so nice of you," Wendy said.

"Great movie," said Kelly, pointing at the screen with an index finger wrapped in a massive gold moon ring.

"The best," Wendy agreed shyly, jabbing the power button on the remote just as Danny switched off the lights and pulled candles out of her basket.

"Mmm, romantic," Kelly purred, as Danny lit them in the dusky grey light of the front room.

"Just how *She* likes it," Danny smiled.

Wendy kept stealing glances at the girls while she thought they weren't looking. There was a warmness to them, and old soul familiarity. They all looked her in the eye. There was no catty weirdness like the girls from yoga in the fall.

There was no competition like the women from the city- where she had been friends with a woman until a man, a job, or a place on a guest list came between them. Then one of you was road kill.

"Okay," said Danny, "you girls wanna go ahead and sit?" She nodded toward Wendy on the couch. Sam and Kelly took the floor, and Alice sat on Wendy's right, leaving her other side for Danny. Danny walked a slow path around them, drawing a circle with her index finger. Then she sunk in next to Wendy and smiled softly at her.

"See," she said, "This is perfect," she looked around the circle. "Five pointed pentagram. Earth, Air, Fire, Water, Spirit. Perfect." Three months ago, Wendy wouldn't have had any idea what Danny was talking about. Now, she felt, she could speak the language.

"Yes," she said. "Perfect."

"Okay, ladies, let's start the engine so the Goddess can drive it. Wendy," she patted Wendy's arm, "You be North."

"No!" Sam chirped. "She should be South! The fire! We need her fire back in those legs, it's time to move, girl."

Danny nodded. "Totally, what was I thinking, North? You don't need to be any more grounded than you've already been for the last three months." She winked at Wendy.

Wendy smiled. She was in her first moon circle and she loved it. Sam reached for Wendy's right hand and Danny took her left. They gave her welcoming squeezes and inviting smiles when their eyes met. Sam and Alice took Danny and Kelly's hands, and then the circle was complete.

Danny closed her eyes, and Wendy and the girls followed her lead. "Wait, Wendy," she whispered, "do you know what to do? I had almost forgotten you were new."

Wendy kept her eyes closed and whispered back, "Yes, I think I do. I almost, don't feel new."

"Okay, great," Danny whispered back.

Alice started: "To the powers of the East, of air, of breath, of wind, of truth, we ask you to be with us now. Bring us positive healing words and the power to stand in our truth. To the powers of the east, hail, and welcome."

Alice gave Wendy's hand a little your turn squeeze. Wendy cleared her throat.

"To the powers of the South," she said, even as her voice trembled a bit. "To the powers of the South: fire, desire, purification... and, Change," she pressed, "bring us your primal passion and your call to action. Powers of the south, be with us now, hail and welcome."

Danny called in the West. "To the powers of the West, of water, of intuition, of healing, of blood, we ask you to be with us now. Bring us your soft strong courage, your powers of rebirth and emotion, the wisdom in our blood. To the powers of the west, hail, and welcome."

Kelly and Sam called in North with its grounding energy and rebirth, and Spirit, the higher self and the Goddess, and when they were finished, Danny spoke again.

"Mother Goddess," she said, "thank you for being with us. We've gathered tonight on this under the healing light of the Aquarius Full Moon to ask for the healing of our sister Wendy's legs. As you know, she spent a long winter in casts and is ready to move again. We'd like her to get her strength back as soon as she can."

She gave Wendy's hand a little shake. "Right, Wendy?" Danny asked.

"Um," Wendy said, "Yes, Mother Goddess," and even though she had thought she might, she didn't feel silly, speaking this way in front of the girls. It really felt like there was an energy with them, a similar powerful feminine energy that had been inside her at her nightgown bonfire, and similar to the fire that had building in her bones all winter.

"I would love, Goddess, to be healed so I could move my body again. But thank you for the lessons of my rest, of my brokenness, I see how I broke so I could heal. Thank you for my time to stop to change direction, thank you for what feels like, an awakening."

That was the first time Wendy had said it out loud. It felt weird, but it felt true, too. She finally understood presence, and felt as if her consciousness had expanded. She was beginning to understand energy, and the cyclical nature of life, and how to center herself in love, how to find that sacred center in herself where she could feel the Goddess breathe.

Then they put one hand on their hearts and one hand on the earth, and Wendy followed suit.

"Mother Earth," said Danny, "we send you all the loving healing energy from our hearts, and ask that you fill our hands with the power to heal ourselves, each other, and you." They repeated the mantra nine times and then they moved their hands onto Wendy's legs.

They hummed and chanted healing mantras over them and Wendy felt a light sparkle move through their hands into her legs, like an electric current. She jumped a little and her eyes opened. They were all smiling so sweetly down at her, like a gaggle of angels.

They sat back in circle and re-held hands, and Alice started to sing a call and response song about feeling the Mother under her feet. Alice would sing a verse, and then the girls would sing her one back. Wendy felt like she was back at summer camp and she was thrilled. She hadn't sung in public since she was wasted at a Peter show.

This was different, this was sacred, and it didn't matter how they sounded, just that they meant it. And because they meant it, they sounded beautiful, and they kept singing.

Wendy closed her eyes as the song filled her head and she felt lost in its rhythmic chanting. Eventually, she realized the girls had raised her up off the couch and she was standing there, on her own two legs, swaying on the floor, eyes closed like in a trance.

Suddenly she heard the front door swung open.

"Well, would you look at that?" Leanne said, stopped in the threshold holding two paper grocery bags.

"It's a downright seance."

Wendy stared at Leanne blankly, like her mother had broken up a sleepover.

"Well, well, well! Standing up like a real live human!"

Wendy fell back down into the couch, suddenly exhausted again.

"Girls," asked Leanne, "how much longer you all gonna be? I like to eat before seven for my digestive tract and such."

"We got what we needed done," Danny said, looking over at Wendy.

"But we didn't do council," Alice said.

"It's okay," Danny said. "Let's let them eat."

"Thanks, kiddos," Leanne said. "Best release those powers and hop up on your brooms." Wendy shot her a look. It was her first social interaction — besides their nightly spiritual readings which hardly counted — in three months. She'd have thought, or hoped, Leanne would be supportive of healthy social time.

They took hands, creating the circle again, and closed their eyes. This time they went counterclockwise, releasing the elements one by one. As soon as they closed circle, they leapt up and left in a flurry of swinging crystal necklaces and fringe and double cheek kisses.

"Bye!" Wendy called to her coven as they fluttered down the driveway. "See you soon!"

Leanne closed the door silently behind them and moved into the kitchen to unpack the groceries. From the couch, Wendy stared at Leanne's back as Leanne sat the blue speckled pasta pot under the faucet.

She had liked the girls from circle a lot. She hadn't felt they were sizing her up, no one was holding back kindness, or being cold, just to make Wendy uncomfortable, to put her in her place, as an outsider. She didn't feel the old judgment and competition she was used to with women from back in the scene.

She didn't think they would take digs at her and then pretend they hadn't meant to, *sorry if it hurt.* They didn't seem eager to say something to box Wendy out, to remind her she was just on social probation by making some inside joke. They didn't seem to want to ignore her or hurt her. In fact, they genuinely seemed to like her, too.

"I feel those beady things on me," Leanne said, not turning around. "What?"

"Well, you could have been nicer," Wendy said.

"Oh please, I was fine," Leanne said, watching the water rise in the pot.

"Well, you weren't June Cleaver."

"I told you, I'm not your mother," Leanne shot back.

Wendy sighed. "I know," she said.

"But I'm not... I'm not blind to hostility. It's an energy, you can feel it. It almost really doesn't matter what you say, it's more how you are. What you do."

"Fuck, I created a monster," Leanne huffed.

Wendy was quiet. Leanne ripped the pasta box open.

"Leanne?" she asked.

"What? I gotta make dinner."

"Well," she asked gently, "is it possible you're getting a little territorial? I don't know, a little overly protective?"

"Hogwash," Leanne sputtered. "Can't wait to get back in my own bed. I just hate when people don't call ahead. It's rude. What was that anyway, a flash mob moon circle?"

"Haha," Wendy said flatly, onto her.

"How did that go, anyway?" Leanne asked, her curiosity winning.

"Fine," Wendy said.

"Did they act like they knew what they were doin'?"

"Yes, very much so," Wendy said. "I mean, they did. They did know what they were doing."

"Well, what else have you been doin' since I left?" she asked. "I mean, before the cast of *The Craft* came over."

"I was trying to go through and edit down those stories of mine you printed out," Wendy told her, as she started fumbling for them on the couch.

"And?" Leanne said. "How'd you do?"

Wendy came up empty-handed under the cushions and was now looking down around her feet. Nothing. She slid herself up the back of the couch, and hung over its spine to peer behind it.

"Well, it's so weird," she said, craning her neck to look at Leanne, "but they're gone."

23

Wendy hung up her phone and looked up at Leanne from the couch.

"Danny said she doesn't have the printouts. And none of the other girls do either."

"That's some hocus pocus," Leanne said.

"Too weird," Wendy said. Then she shrugged. "They'll show back up."

"Everything we lose comes back around in some form," Leanne said. "Rumi says somethin' like that."

Wendy shuffled over to the table and plopped down in her seat. "They were just printouts, I have them on my computer."

She picked at her fettucini.

"What?" Leanne said.

"Nothing," Wendy politely smiled back. She looked around the elegant little kitchen. It was nice to eat sitting up in a chair, at a table, in the glow of candlelight, but she was antsy. Out of bed had been one giant leap, into the kitchen another, but now she needed out of the house.

And she had plans, big ones, that had been stewing in the cauldron of her body all winter. She could see the yellow yolk of the full moon bleeding over the water outside. She couldn't wait to run down the beach again. If she closed her eyes, she could feel her feet sinking into the sand and the cool rush of salty air on her skin. She rubbed at her thin legs under her long white nightgown.

"It's been agony to live by the water all this time and not be able to go in it," Wendy said.

"Most people live their whole lives that way," Leanne said. "Life is right there but they never even dip a toe in. They just watch it from a window. Don't realize the door's wide open. Anyway, don't dodge. I know you too well for it to be 'nothing'," Leanne said. "I sat you down on the toilet all winter for God's sake. You could say that's knowin' someone."

Wendy breathed deep through her nose, she had grown so impatient of being babied. "And for that I am grateful," she told her, letting out a long stream of air from her mouth.

Leanne and Wendy were in that all-too-familiar push-pull. Wendy had needed Leanne all winter, and now that she didn't, Wendy was pulling away and Leanne was pushing her to stay in her old role. It felt unconscious on Leanne's part, but Wendy had noticed her relishing in the caretaker role, the... well... Mother Role, as much as she had denied it.

Wendy recognized how good it must feel to take care of something outside of yourself, to be needed. Wendy could see that. She'd never felt that way, but wanted to.

"What's going on with you?" Leanne pressed. "There's a storm in your head. It's filling the room."

Wendy dropped her elbows on the table and rested her head in her hands.

"Are you lonely, Leanne? I mean, with no man?"

"Nah. How could I be? All my clients, you, that monster in a cat suit at home. Why?"

"Well, I'm thinking about... being celibate. Just calling the whole Love Search off. I just don't want to do it anymore. The men thing. I'm scared it will derail me. I finally feel... centered. Good again, even. Like I might know a few things — myself, at least."

"Well, as soon as you think you know something, life comes along to remind you you know jack shit."

Wendy sat back heavily in her chair and crossed her arms, like she wasn't going to talk anymore if everything she said was naysayed, if everything turned into a lecture. She'd been lectured all winter and she'd had enough.

Leanne sipped her tea, unfettered.

"Well, go on," she said. "Tell me what's up."

Wendy sighed and tried again. "Well, I do feel like I'm finally understanding life a little bit, like things make a little more sense, but I know nothing about men.

I'm just giving up. On all of that. On them. I was crazy to leap back on the horse so fast with Jack. And even crazier to go back into it exactly the way I used to, which never, ever worked."

"How so?"

"Ugh, it's so… painful to think about. I don't know."

"Yes, you do. We know all the answers to our own questions."

"Okay. Fine. I was tiny. Needy. Weak. Like a fucking orphan who wanted desperately to be adopted. Ready to latch on and give up everything for them before I even knew them. To devote my whole life to them. Like a hitchhiker on Love's Highway, instead of a grounded woman welcoming a man into her own loving space. Fantastical.

Obsessed with the image of them in my head. Trying to be whatever they wanted instead of really me, because I didn't even know who that was. Starving on tiny scraps of attention they threw me, calling it love in my delusional fantasy. Drawn to the ones who abused or ignored me. Desperate to prove myself to them. Self abandoing.

It's so gross I want to throw up. I give up on all of it. Never doing it again."

"Giving up on love. That sounds like just straight up giving up on 'you'."

"I don't get it. You wouldn't say that to an alcoholic, you wouldn't say 'oh, come on, have another, keep trying to drink'. Men and alcohol do the same thing to me, they kill me. I look back at my life, and every time I met a new man, it was a fucking catastrophe. Just like drinking.

It's okay at first, and the next thing I knew I was in bed, mourning, bludgeoning myself over everything I did wrong. I don't have time for that anymore. I can't lose this good momentum. I don't have time to die over a man anymore, to fall in that ditch. The last two quite nearly killed me. One broke my spirit, the other my body."

Leanne looked around.

"What are you doing?" Wendy asked.

"Lookin' for the goddamn cameras. Are we filming a soap opera? I mean cue the fucking drama."

"Leanne, stop making fun of me, please. It doesn't feel good."

"Oh, come on. So your first love went down in flames. Story of everyone's life. Keep remembering, your story ain't that different from anyone else's. Things get bad when we think we're so different, that we somehow got it worse than everyone else, and we think we're separate. Then we isolate. Then we slowly die.

Life owes you nothin', honey. You owe life somethin'."

"Well, okay then. I'm only gonna date the ones that have no chance of breaking my heart... or legs."

"Ha. I've tried that. We've all tried that. Can't hide from heartbreak. Can't hide from life."

"Can't a girl try?"

"Nope. Anyway, liking the 'safe' ones don't work. It's just like those cloudy days at the beach; you think you don't need sunscreen, it won't hurt, but then they end up burning you the worse than the hot sunny days. No such thing as being safe. Safety's the great illusion. That, and that we're promised a next moment."

"Well, I'm serious. No more men."

"I don't feel like I can persuade you anymore. That fire in you is big. I gotta say. I'm impressed. Even a little in awe."

"I'm going to take that as a compliment," Wendy said, straightening her back.

"It is one. I'm serious. You went from Maiden to Mother, Victim to Heroine, Princess to Queen. All archetypal speaking, of course. I sure like it. I told you no one does a makeover like the Goddess."

"Thank you. What do you mean Mother?"

"A grown ass woman who can handle whatever life throws at her. I mean someone who can care for something besides herself. You'll see. You'll get there. I don't just mean a woman who has had a baby. It's not a physical journey."

"I do want a baby, someday."

"Well that's damn fine boot camp, surefire way to grow the fuck up. I mean, if you accept the invitation that's truly being offered. Nothing raised me like raising my daughter. Every day a new test, a new trial. But I wouldn't have traded it for the world. Her daddy left the day he found out she was on her way. And it was supposed to be that way, me and her, taking life on together. We didn't need no man to be a family."

Wendy nodded. "Right," she said. "Men aside, I feel good, Leanne. If I'm not focused on them, I have so much more energy for me. For my dreams. Like, I can feel spring within me. That rebirth. Like when a baby chicken hatches. Like when things hatch and can come outside of themselves. Break out of the dark enclosed tomb of themselves, out into the world.

"Yep. That's part of the process. So what do you want to do in the world?"

"Well, I have a few ideas. You know, from my vision board. A picture came together, a dream."

"Well, just look at you. Tell me," Leanne said, as she forked a gigantic spool of pasta into her mouth.

"There's this retreat center... it's in Vermont. It's a healing place for people and animals... all rescue animals. Horses, cows, dogs, chickens, rabbits. The people and the animals sort of... heal each other. There's yoga, reiki, gardening, all that stuff. And, even more wonderful, they run a charity that profits the NRDC.

The people who run the farm are all about nourishing the feminine. Women, creatures, the earth. I'll learn to tend a garden, practice reiki on the animals, and I can ride again, like I did when I was little."

"That is wonderful," Leanne said through a stuffed mouth. "Movin' from the red carpet to the green. A real trade-up if you ask me. Which you shouldn't," she said, pointing a fork at Wendy. "Don't ask no one's advice about your personal dreams. They might sway ya different. And you'll regret it and resent them. Just follow the voice in the heart. As scary as it fucking is, like the first time you rode a bike without training wheels."

Wendy nodded.

"No resistance here," Leanne encouraged. "So... no going back to New York, is what you're saying."

"I think that life is over. I mean, it must be, because I'm not living it anymore. And I don't have fire for journalism anymore. It feels dead within me. And this new life, it feels alive. Like it's waking up inside of me. '*We must be willing to let go of the life we planned so as to have the life that is waiting for us*', right?"

"Joseph Campbell. True. Well, you look just as about as happy as a hippie in a hand basket."

"I am. It feels so good to be excited, I think this is what feeling alive feels like. Having a life you want to leap out of bed for. I want to do something outside of myself. For something much bigger than me. Maybe it's all the Campbell I've been reading. And newspapers. Fuck, I had this awakening within my awakening. A humanitarian awakening. When I finally looked outside of myself, I woke up and looked at the world. I couldn't believe how much I had, yet how sorry for myself I'd been. It was like, 'I can't believe I thought I had it bad'. I felt like Goldie Hawn in *Protocol*- before her transformation. You know, I used to just read the newspaper for the horoscope. I was so insular. Everything was about me, I was the center of my own universe, and that was a really lonely, boring place to be. I forgot this world's story was my story, and that I had a say and that I could be of help."

"Guess so. I prefer not to read the news."

"Well, I think we should. I think we should be involved in our world. I think the feminine should stand up and shout. I think the world needs the feminine's voice, the voice of the Mother- more than ever. I think the rising of the feminine- that nurturing compassionate love in action force- I think it's the answer."

"That's your prerogative, to get involved. And you're gonna be around a lot longer than me. You're signin' up for a real Heroine's Journey, is what I do know. But it ain't gonna be what it looks like in your head. Nothing is, well, if it's real."

"I know."

"Ain't gonna be all patchouli and roses."

"I know."

"I'm just sayin' it ain't gonna be easy."

"Leanne, I know."

"Worth it, but not easy. Fulfilling, but not easy. Life-changing, but not easy. People really screw themselves when they forget that life is supposed to be an adventure. When they think it's supposed to be easy it's nothin' but *Why Me* suffering."

"Got it, Leanne."

"And… don't come cryin' to me when Love done hits you over the head again."

"Well, what I'm telling you is that's not happening. My heart is occupata. Closed up shop. There's a sign on its door that says 'Gone fishin'.'"

"You think you can control the most powerful, mysterious force in the universe?"

"What?"

"Love."

"I'm just saying I'm not there, anymore, in my life."

"Child, you best lose that ego."

"What ego?"

"Oh, please. The one that thinks it's in control. Then you really will miss out on life. Let go, baby. Control stifles the soul."

"Can I take your plate?" Wendy asked, anxious to be anywhere else.

Leanne put her hand over her half-finished meal. She was clearly savoring their last dinner together.

"So, this farm. You goin' in search of that real life you were talking about?"

"Yeah, I guess, I think I am."

"So you have some idea of what one is."

"Well, I know what it isn't. What I used to think it was."

"Which was what."

"It's... embarrassing," Wendy said.

"What good does embarrassment do ya?"

"What?"

"You gotta ask yourself how something you're carrying around is serving you. Is embarrassment doing anything for you?"

Wendy thought for a minute. "No," she said, "it's not."

"Then let it go. Once we realize something isn't serving us, it's our job to let it go. So, tell me, what did you think real life was?"

"I thought it was… fame. I thought that people had made it in life when they got famous. I thought that was the goal. And I thought maybe Peter would want me back if I got… sort of famous again. I mean, he left me for someone famous, and he was always pressuring me to 'become someone'. And I thought that meant 'someone famous.' I think that's kinda what our culture tells us success is."

"I can see how you would think that," Leanne said. "It's not stupid to think that. Give yourself a break."

"At the time, I thought that's what he meant by 'you didn't come true', you know, what he said when he left me. And then, after he left, I thought if I were famous like him, I wouldn't be lonely. Even if I didn't get him back, if I were famous, I wouldn't feel so alone.

He always had this entourage of people who just adored him. Laughed at every joke, clamored for his attention. And people knew him wherever we went."

"No, honey, that's what people got all wrong. Fame doesn't make you less lonely — it makes you more lonely. And it doesn't make you real, more like an illusion. It's a nightmare, really. People think they know you, but they don't. And then, worse, you think you know you, but you realize you really don't.

You forget who you really are, when you're a star."

Wendy finished her plate and pushed it away.

"And when their audience moves on, because they're fickle, and they will, you're still left up there forever in the cage of this stage you can't ever really get off. Even when no one's left watching. You're trapped up there in your lonely ivory tower of an ego. No one can get in and you can't get the fuck out. Talk about death by isolation. What does Stephen Cope say? 'We cannot become real in isolation.'"

"I know. It seems stupid now," Wendy said, shaking her head, "I thought if I had fans, I would, somehow have 'made it'."

"Remember, this island is full of people running from themselves, trying to pick up their pieces. I know more fallen stars than I can count. Ain't their fault. Society teaches you that fame and fortune mean success. Nope. Then you get there and you find it was all a sham. All you want is peace and love, like every other person on the planet. And self-love and to feel of service — that's true success. Not fame, baby. One day they love you, the next day they leave you. Love you, hate you. The spotlight is no place for someone with abandonment issues."

"I guess I know a thing or two about those."

"Everyone's wounds are the same. We're scared of being frauds, not good enough, not worthy. And we're scared of abandonment. Of never being loved. Of dying alone."

Wendy gulped. "Resonates," she said.

"Honey, you never talk about your father, what happened?"

"He and mom split, then she got sick, and everything fell apart."

"That's some timing," Leanne said. "How it works though, I guess."

"I think that's how I got programmed this way. To fall apart when love falls apart, to lose me when I lose him. For the world to end when love ends. For my self-esteem to be wrapped up in someone else's approval of me. And I felt the same way about my mother and father as I do, or did, about me and Peter.

I didn't think they should have broken up. I felt if she could have loved herself, she could have loved him. And I felt like if I had known how to love and care for myself, I could have loved and cared for Peter."

"Probably could, babe. But knowing that ain't gonna bring him back. You just have to make it right the next time it comes along. Which, I'm telling you it will."

"If you say so. I'm just saying I'm not looking for it. Ever again," Wendy told her.

"And that's when it finds you," Leanne smiled. "Okay, we're telling stories again," she said, tossing her napkin over her plate. "And now we're back in the past, like ghosts. That's what happens, every time you tell a story. You're back in the past. You ain't alive. Let's come back to the place where we're breathing."

"You're right," Wendy said. She raised her mug of kava in a toast. "Thank you, Leanne. For everything. From the bottom of my healing heart."

"You're damn right welcome." Leanne said, clanking her mug to Wendy's.

They chugged the last bits of tea.

"So," Leanne slammed her mug down. "When you going back into the world?"

"Soon as I get my sea legs back," Wendy said.

"Good," Leanne said. "Can't just let the Peters of the world have all the adventures."

"And, Leanne?" Wendy said softly.

"Yes, babe."

"One more thing about Peter. Last thing, I swear. And it's not really about him, but like, who I was with him."

"Shoot."

"I think I know now, what he meant by 'you never came true'. I think he meant, I never came true to me. I never acted on my dreams. I never did what I said I would do. All talk, no walk. You know, how Carl Jung says, 'You are what you do, not what you say you'll do.' I was in a nest on the couch like something dying. I stopped... doing. Living.

"And you started drinkin' and pillin. Hard. You were a God damned addict. Wasn't his job to stick around and fix an addict. No an addict gotta hit rock bottom all on her own."

Wendy sucked in her breath and her nostrils flared, even though she realized it was true. Had he stayed with her, she would never had changed, because she wouldn't have had to. She almost could thank him, like, *thank you for leaving me so I could find myself,* she thought.

"Not one for subtlety, are you Leanne," she smiled.

"Who's got time for that?" she asked. "Anyway, you know what helps to self actualize? Figure out what you loved about him. What did you love about him?"

Wendy knew immediately. "His courage. His confidence- his unfailing belief in himself and his dreams and his art. His ability to play. He loved to play." She bit her lip but her eyes watered. "Maybe, maybe we don't have to 'Get Over' people. Maybe our heart can hold a whole lot more than we thought. Maybe we can always love them, but still move on."

"Don't know if that's possible, to love someone and still move on," Leanne said. "But after all that ritual..." she shook her head. "Ritual only works if it's meant to be. Maybe you just ain't supposed to be over him yet. Maybe you're still learning the lessons of that lost love. Maybe you're still supposed to be burnin' and learnin.' But I do know you can emulate the things you loved in him. Thank the man for showing you what you're missing. Become those things. Confident, courageous, playful."

Wendy nodded and pressed on.

"Anyway," she said, "He left me also, in addition, well because, of the drinking and pilling, nothing I said became realized. All my promises, they were lies. So I wasn't real, I wasn't true. To me, or to him. We don't just dream, we do. That's how we become real."

"Makes sense," Leanne said. "And I know something you can do right now."

"What?" Wendy asked.

"These dishes. Time to start using those gams again."

Wendy sighed and tossed her napkin on her plate and rose. She took Leanne's plate and shuffled over to the sink. The water ran warm over her hands and Leanne said, "Hey."

"Yes?" Wendy said, looking   through the window, out over the backyard of endless ocean.

"What did your Mother do anyway?"

Wendy soaped the sponge and started on the silverware. "She was a writer," Wendy said.

"Did she ever get to write her book, you know the one all writers dream of?"

Wendy felt the catch in her throat.
"No," she said. "She didn't."

"Damn shame," Leanne said, and it just hung in the air like that, sad and alone, but true. It was a damn shame.

Wendy absent-mindedly scrubbed the dishes and when she finished, she turned around Leanne was looking at her with a tear in her eye. "We sure as hell don't have forever," Leanne said. "Don't let that death be in vain. Let it teach you something. That we think we have forever but we damned sure don't."

24.

Wendy and Danny had lunch down island, overlooking the harbor.

It was a cold March day, bright but frigid, and they sat bundled in sweaters by the window in a polished wooden booth. Wendy sipped her clam chowder and gnawed on french fries, while Danny tucked into beer and a burger.

"So you're headed into the farm life, huh?" Danny said, wiping ketchup from the corner of her supermodel bee-stung lips.

Wendy nodded, relishing the fries she stuffed in her mouth, a decadent treat after months of Leanne's health food.

"You ever had your hands in the earth?"

Wendy blushed a little defensively. "No," she said.

"Ever worked with farm animals?"

"Horses. When I was young. Anyway, they train us there."

"That's good," Danny nodded, "they pay you?"

"A tiny bit, but there's room and board. Which is great, because I'm down to my last dollar."

"You'll be okay," Danny said, "I have a feeling you're going to be just fine. Anyway, it sounds amazing. Maybe I'll come visit. I haven't left the island in way too long." She slumped back in her booth and took Wendy in. "You're glowing. You look... healthy. And I dare say, happy."

"Thank you. I had my first beach run since the accident yesterday. It was more like an impassioned power walk, but it felt amazing."

"That's awesome, Wendy."

"I think the moon circle expedited my healing. That was some powerful energy."

"The more women who focus on the same intention, the more powerful it is," Danny smiled, "that's why we circle. And," she winked, "why people are so terrified of women circling, why covens were illegal for so long- shit really happens when women gather. I'm so proud of you. You've come a million miles, like you walked them all in that bed. Ha. I love a good transformation. We really turned a city rat into a country mouse, huh?"

Wendy breathed deep. "Yes. Thank God," she said, "I think I've always wanted a more literally grounded life. This winter I was trying to decide what I was going to do, so I looked at what I get jealous of people for. Because I realized jealousy's just inspiration hiding in shadow. And I think I get jealous of people who use their hands for a living. And I get jealous of people actively making a difference in the world. And I get jealous of people living happily in community with each other. I didn't want to become one of those died-alone-eaten-by-rats in-her-New York City-apartment-people."

She dumped another packet of oyster crackers into her chowder mug. The chowder was really just a vehicle for the salty, air-puffed crackers.

"You know, the Super finds her and no one misses her. Or I'm in the *New York Post* for one day before I fade away and my story lines a litter box. 'Depressed Divorcee Dies Under a Bridge in Brooklyn'. No, thank you."

Danny stared at her, big-eyed, and picked up her beer and pretended to chug the whole thing. "That's some dark shit right there," she said.

Wendy laughed, "Exactly."

Danny plunked the pint back on the table. "Well, I get jealous of people who can sit down for a living," she said, "making a living with your body is exhausting."

"Well, maybe I'll find a balance. Maybe I'll get back to more writing. I mean," she thought of Leanne in the kitchen the night before. "I definitely will. Maybe I'll even write about my time there."

"That's a good idea." Danny sipped the foam off of her pint. The printouts of diaries flashed back into Wendy's head. They had been right there, right on her lap, right on the couch.

"I still think it's weird," she said, "about the journals. None of you girls took those pages by mistake?"

"No," Danny shook her head, looking out at the water, "I'm sorry."

"It's okay," Wendy said, "just spooky. I didn't know I was 'that' out of it."

Danny turned back around and set her big brown doe eyes on Wendy.

"Hey, so don't go away forever. We want you back."

"I can't promise anything," Wendy said, "I don't know what will happen in Vermont."

Danny smiled. "Well, I'm not worried. This island has a way of calling the people she wants back. If she loves you, you can't ever really leave her. She might kick you off for a time to get your shit together, but she'll call you back. And when she does you can't ignore it."

"We'll see about that," Wendy said.

"Go ahead and try to leave," Danny laughed, "I love to watch people try."

"I am," Wendy said, "I'm even all packed up. It feels so good to move again, I did it in one morning."

"Okay," Danny said, "but the thing about here is that once you leave you realize there's no better place to live. That this place has everything you could ever want, and there's no place else like it. You ever heard of Avalon?"

"The mystical isle of the Goddess?"

"Yeah. Well, think about it. This is about as close to Avalon as you can get in this dimension. Green cliffs that crash into blue sea. A misty island you have to ferry to, filled with witches. Certain people get spiritually herded here. Especially women coming to heal. You'll see. You'll miss the fuck out of it. She'll call you back like a lover."

Just then the door swung open, and with it rushed in a cold gush of crisp March air.

"Brr," Danny said, looking back over her shoulder. Then she said, "Ugh."

Jack Fletcher had walked in in his big red flannel jacket, and he wasn't alone. He was holding a thin shiny blond girl's hand whom Wendy recognized from that awkward morning at yoga. He nodded at Danny, but his eyes moved right over Wendy, like she wasn't even there.

Danny rolled her eyes. "Pathetic," she said, "a 33-year-old man playing the ignoring game. Anyway... do you want to go?"

"No," Wendy shook her head, "I really don't. I really don't want to run anymore."

"That's the beautiful thing about an island," said Danny, "you can't run from anything."

Wendy had thought she would hurt when she saw him again, but she didn't. She shrugged. "He really doesn't bother me," she said, "really. I've decided to be celibate, anyway. I'm done with men."

Danny smiled.

"No, you're not."

"Why is it so hard to believe? I am. I'm no longer interested in what hurts me. They've never done me any good. "

"That's 'cuz you haven't met the right one yet. They are all wrong until the right one."

"Speaking of," Wendy said, "Did you and Jack ever...?"

"Yes, of course. He was the last wrong one before the right one. I think Jack is that guy a woman has to be with before she finally realizes she deserves a nice guy. At least for me he was. I had to give up completely before Ray showed up at my door."

"I'm sorry, I didn't know, or I wouldn't have..."

"Don't be. It's a small island. Overlap is inevitable and no one owns anyone."

"Still," Wendy said.

"If it had bothered me, I would have said something. I'm a grown woman who can express herself. Don't worry, Wendy. I was just worried about you. I guess, well, I guess for good reason."

"Exactly," Wendy agreed, "consider me in Man Rehab."

"They should have those," Danny nodded.

Wendy looked over at the back of Jack's head. He had great, thick, shiny black hair. She remembered what it was like to run her fingers through it. And she remembered his hands in her hair, and her trying to relax, but holding on too tightly to the hope that he would like her, that she was pretty and skinny and cool enough for him, to let go.

She shook her head and turned back to Danny. "I'm done with my story," she said.

"Good," Danny said.

"You know, you sure sound a lot like Leanne," Wendy told her, "you share similar wisdom. Women's wisdom. I'm sorry she was so weird about the moon circle... but you really would like her."

"I've known Leanne forever, of her, anyway, and I have a lot of respect for her. But she's from that old line of traditional witches who thinks us younger ones are in it for the fad. Or, just because it's cool right now. But that's not why we do it at all, it's genuinely in honor."

"I know," said Wendy, "I can tell."

"But she doesn't like how out of the broom closet we are about it. The old witches are big on the sacredness and secrecy, but I'm not so into secrets. Sacredness, yes. Secrets, no. Something about keeping it so secret makes me feel like there's shame around it. We were shamed about it long enough. And I've got no shame for being an earth-loving goddess-worshiper."

"Me either," Wendy smiled.

"I think she thinks we don't take it seriously enough. But the Goddess is about joy and pleasure, too. Some witches forget to have fun."

"I can see that," Wendy said, "but I owe her a lot." She looked down at her legs. "Everything, really."

"Well, she really took a liking to you. I hadn't seen Leanne with anyone for years. She kept to herself. After her daughter died, she just walled up. Went hermit. I get it. I think it's easy to close up and stay closed after pain like that. I guess it seems safer to numb out and turn in like that, but I actually think it's a whole lot more dangerous."

"She's doing her best," Wendy said, protectively.

"I'm sure she is. Anyway, we both love you," Danny said. "You're lovable. Know that."

"The thing is, I actually believe that now. And thanks, you were kind to me when you didn't have to be."

"That's not totally true," Danny shrugged, "I mean, at first I thought I got to go home and brag to Ray that Peter Jackson's ex wife had washed up on our shores."

"Okay, yeah, but after that. You didn't get anything out of being kind to me, but you still were."

"That's not true either," Danny said, looking her in the eyes. "I got you."

Wendy was quiet for a moment. Then she said, "True. And I got you. Look what a little random kindness to a stranger can do."

"Exactly. So you really leaving tomorrow?"

"Tomorrow morning, 8 o'clock boat."

"Did you say goodbye to Leanne already?"

"She said she doesn't do goodbyes."

"Sounds like her."

The ferry horn bleated over the harbor, and they turned to watch the big white ship leave the dock and slice a smooth path through the cold blue water.

Then Danny reached across the table and gave Wendy's arm a squeeze.

"Hey," she smiled, "looks like we got you sailing again."

Wendy smiled back. She grabbed her hands and returned the squeeze. "We did," she said, "thank you, Danny."

25.

Her jeep was packed and she stopped at Al's for one last cup of coffee before making the boat.

She stepped out into the sunshine of the dusty parking lot and squinted in the bright March air. Then crossed the porch through the screen door, and it slammed behind her as she moved across the creaky floor boards where she first met Jack Fletcher. She could almost see the ghosts of them, banging heads over the dropped carton of juice.

She shook her head, watching the movie of them. Girl, she thought, you have no radar for trouble.

She poured a lukewarm cup of coffee and doused it with soymilk. Then she winked at the girl behind the counter with the gleaming pentagram pendant.

"Sandra, right?" she asked.

"Yep."

"Wendy," she reminded her, pointing at herself. "Any Ostara plans?" she asked Sandra. The Spring Equinox was coming up and you could feel it, like life boiling beneath the surface of the earth, and Wendy felt it in herself and others — an excitable, awakening energy.
The girl was taken aback for a moment.

"What?" Wendy smiled, "do I have to be wearing a black pointy hat?"

"Ha," Sandra blushed. "I don't get to talk about it much in the open, is all," she said. "Just a picnic at the beach. Maybe an egg hunt."

"Beautiful," Wendy said.

"You?" she asked.

"Well, I'll be in Vermont, but I'll definitely be outside," Wendy said.

"That's all you have to do," Sandra nodded, then she waved Wendy's two dollars for the coffee away. "Are you going to Vermont forever?" she asked her.

"I don't know," Wendy said. "I just know I'm going right for now."

"You're the girl Leanne looked after this winter, right?" she asked

"I sure am," said Wendy.

"You all better?"

Wendy thought about that, about the last time she had been to Al's, and when she met first Leanne, and she was circling her like a cat, waiting for someone to notice her. She hadn't been sure if she were even visible anymore. She felt like a ghost in limbo, trapped between here and the afterlife.

She had hoped to die, but hadn't the courage to do anything about it. And she'd been hungover, on a break from a *Law and Order* marathon.

She looked into Sandra's eyes.

"Yes," she said. "I am." There was power in those words, and they both felt it.

"Well, blessed be," Sandra said.

"Blessed be," Wendy blushed.

The ferry line was short; there wouldn't be long lines until the summer season roared in, when the island sagged and groaned beneath the weight of a population that swelled to nearly 150,000. She parked right on the white line at the front of Lane Six and waited to be ushered into the steerage of the boat. She switched off the jeep engine but left the radio on.

The Lumineers started singing, *"I belong with you, you belong with me/You're my sweetheart."*

"That's what you think," Wendy thought. She'd become a 400-year-old woman completely disenchanted with love. She looked in the mirror and still barely recognized herself. 10 pounds thinner, but no makeup, and the black hair dye had drained out and left her hair straw-like and mousy brown.

She reached for a hair tie that was circling the gear shift and pulled her hair from her face, wondering if she would ever feel sexy and desirable again, or if that time had passed and she shouldn't have taken it for granted.

"Took a bus to Chinatown," The Lumineers sang, *"I'd be standing on Canal and Bowery."*

She remembered standing in front of the Bowery Ballroom venue a million times, under-dressed, over-made-up and teetering in heels, getting her name checked off the list for a show before she headed in to drink 10 free vodka cranberries in the air-conditioned dark backstage, make eyes with some guy from the opening band, leave with him, tangled up in a taxi, end up in an after-party bar, making out in a booth, then back to his hotel room.

Then she'd go into work in last night's clothes the next day and puke in a bathroom stall. Then she'd repeat it all over again that night.

She did that, of course, until that final time she walked into Bowery Ballroom, the night Peter played, before she got swept off on a tour she didn't think would ever end.

She wondered if love was the worst or the best thing that had ever happened to her. She realized Leanne was right. Often the worst things turn out to be the best things, and the best things can turn out to be the worst. She closed her eyes and slid down a little in the driver's seat, when there was a rap on the window.

She rolled down the window. "I must have summoned you," Wendy said.

It was Leanne, wearing a long tattered grey sweater over her white nightgown, holding a crinkled paper bag.

"What do you call that look?" Wendy asked.

"Witch chic," Leanne snapped back.

"I love it," said Wendy.

Leanne reached through the window and cupped a turquoise laden hand tenderly beneath Wendy's chin.

She looked Wendy in the eyes. "Fuck you," she said.

Wendy didn't flinch. "Why?" she asked.

"Because all night I couldn't sleep thinking about you, and I broke my own 'No Goodbye' rule just to see this face one more time. In case I never do again."

Wendy's eyes watered a little.

"Danny said that's impossible," she told her. "She said once the island has a hold on you, it never lets you go. She said I'll be back in four full moons or less."

Leanne shrugged. "It's a nice prediction, but no one really knows. Maybe you're strong enough to break the spell. But you know," she said, "sometimes you gotta leave to come back."

Wendy kept an eye on the ferry attendant, the boat was leaving any minute. "I'm glad you came to say goodbye, Leanne," Wendy said. "It means a lot."

Leanne shoved the paper bag through the open window.

"Betcha didn't pack any healthy road snacks."

"Nope," Wendy said. "I still haven't been domesticated." She raised the paper cup of coffee. "I've got this though."

"Well, if you want more wrinkles and early menopause, drink up," Leanne said.

Wendy rolled her eyes. "No one wants either of those."

"Gotta line up what you want with what you do. People say they want one thing and do another. For instance, they say they wanna be happy, but then they keep thinking shitty thoughts and saying sad mean things."

"Noted," Wendy said.

"Here's some fresh carrots from the garden, with an apple and a little Tupperware tin of my latest batch of hummus."

'Thank you, Leanne."

"Listen, you've learned a lot this winter. But you ain't out of the woods yet, kid. It's one thing to think about these things. To talk 'em. It's a hell of another thing to walk 'em. It's real fire-walking. And it ain't for the weak.

Stuff is gonna come up; the gnarly shit, like fear and discomfort and conflict and rejection and abandonment, and you're gonna wanna go back to sleep and react and fall back into blame and numbing and running and shit like that. Don't do it. Call me."

Wendy felt defiant. "Well, I think I'm ready for the world again," she said, as she watched the cars in the lanes ahead of her begin to roll forward.

"What I'm saying, kid, is it's all a process. You learn this shit, you read all the books, you talk about it, you think you know it. But it's just in your head, it's not in your body yet. It's easy in your head. It's different when it's living breathing staring you in the face.

And you're gonna know what's the right thing to do because it's going to be the hard thing. It will probably be uncomfortable. So sometimes you're gonna fuck up. And that's okay. Get up and try again. Consciousness is a practice. Like exercise.

You don't just go to the gym once and then you're fit. No, you gotta go everyday. You gotta practice love everyday. So just don't be one of those assholes who just talks it and doesn't walk it."

Wendy sighed and started the jeep again. "Thanks for one last loving bitchslap from the Goddess, Leanne."

"You betcha."

Wendy reached for Leanne's hand and squeezed it. "I'll call you when I get there."

"Do or don't. Not gonna be waiting by the phone."

"Okay," Wendy said, attempting to pull her hand away, but Leanne kept squeezing it tight.

"So," Leanne said, clearing her throat, not looking at Wendy, instead she appeared to be watching the seagulls swarm over the boat.

"Yes?" Wendy asked.

Leanne looked down at Wendy then back over her shoulder.

'"Hey Johnny," she called, to an old man in a red pick up.

"*Leanne,*" Wendy pressed.

"Well," she said, turning back around and squinting into the sun. Then she let the words topple out of her mouth really fast, like apples toppling from a sack. "It's just that if I ever had another daughter, I'd want her to be just like you," she said, then she dropped Wendy's hand.

Wendy felt a throb right in her mother wound, then a childlike glee that gobbled up the long-sought approval, and she felt part of her wanting to jump out of the car and be held. But she didn't. Instead she rubbed her own heart where it ached, and she said to Leanne, "The old me wants to crawl into your lap and howl like a baby."

Leanne looked around, as if suddenly she didn't want to be seen.

"Please don't," Leanne said.

"I won't, is the thing," said Wendy.

"That's right, I forgot. You're a goddamn grown-up," Leanne said.

Wendy laughed. "Yes. I done grew the fuck up."

Then they both stared straight ahead, into the gaping mouth of the ship.

"You know what that always looked like to me?" Leanne asked Wendy.

Wendy sipped the coffee that had gone cold and shuddered it down with a grimace.

"What?"

"The belly of the whale."

"It does," Wendy agreed. Then Leanne leaned down and kissed Wendy's cheek.

"Bon voyage," she said. Wendy smiled softly at her, then she put the car in gear and drove straight into the dark mouth.

26.

Halfway to Vermont she took the top down off the jeep, and she soared up the eastern seaboard like that, in the open air, bundled in a sweater with the heat on, Patty Griffin was singing, "hey Peter Pan, I'm going home now, I've done all I can, besides, I'm grown now..."

And then Lucinda Williams' *Sweet Old World* came on the radio, with Lucinda listing the things we lose when we leave this life, and her heart panged for her mother. She remembered the dimly lit living room her mom had danced in in her childhood, and she couldn't have been much older than Wendy was now.

Her mother loved Lucinda and Neil Young and The Band, she specifically loved *The Last Waltz*. When she came home from work she'd take off her power suits, put on her white jeans and an over-sized soft t-shirt, and pour herself a glass of white wine. Then she'd pad into the living room with a book, which got tossed aside for dancing barefoot on the oriental rug.

"You won't understand this now," she had said to Wendy, "but Robbie Robertson is all. man." But when Wendy got older she found herself drawn to the vulnerable boyishness of Rick Danko.

How she used to cringe as a child when her mother danced. But now she'd give everything to watch her dance again, and now how she wished her mother had danced more. She remembered the last time her mother danced, not knowing she was at death's door.

After that, her mother was too tired to dance; she was mostly in bed, at home or in the hospital, until the end. Wendy's pulse raced when she realized, how could any of us ever know whether or not we're dancing our last dance? *Be more playful*, she remembered.

How could we ever know if we're at death's door, and why does anyone act like a long life is guaranteed, when time and time again it's proven not to be? Wendy thought about the last time she had danced in the rain in Leanne's backyard. It was too long ago. She made a note to do it again as soon as she could.

She suddenly had this messy mix of pain and joy for feeling scared of dying; she realized her feelings about death had changed since she last thought of it. For the last few years she had had an apathetic stance on it, almost a relief at the thought of slipping out of this world. She hadn't really cared about living, it was too hard, she was terrible at it.

Now she grasped at life like a drowning woman, she wanted to suck its marrow and stay forever. Now she wanted In, not Out.

Four hours in, she started to see hand-painted wooden signs for Harbor Bay Healing, and eventually she followed a dirt road down to its entrance, marked with a chipped red fence. The closer she got, the louder she could hear a banging in the distance. It was methodical, like the ticking of a clock.

Bang, bang, bang, bang, like time's second hand ticking away the moments of our life, or, like the footsteps of someone approaching. The kind of footsteps you could almost feel, more so than hear. Deep within her, she could feel someone or something coming.

The sandy dirt road snaked down to a smattering of dozens of wooden cabins, with one large main cabin in the center. Horses, sheep, and cows grazed on the sprawling green hills surrounding a blue placid lake that sparkled in the early afternoon sun.

That banging echoed across those hills, and even across the water, where a small sunfish and two canoes, one red and one green, idled by the dock.

She put the jeep in neutral at the gate, stopped, the way people pause at thresholds, idling between one world and the next.

Suddenly she thought about turning back. She missed Danny. She missed Leanne. What if she never saw them again? It was still early, before the season, and she could still find a rental back on the island.

Why had she left a place that had taken her in so lovingly? And why had she left the two friends she had in the world? Who was she to go work at a healing center? It was she who needed healing. She wasn't ready to offer it to others. When were you ready to heal others, she wondered. Did you have to be totally healed? Was anyone ever totally healed?

The butterflies swarmed in her belly, and she thought about a writing teacher of hers who said that if something didn't give you that butterfly feeling, it wasn't worth it, it was a waste of time. That the best things in life all caused butterflies. Butterflies were symbols of transformation. Feeling them meant our life was about to change.

She picked up her phone and called Leanne.

"Give a gal time to miss you," Leanne answered.

"What am I doing?" Wendy asked. "Why am I doing this?"

"Right now? You're second-guessing your instinct. Don't do that. Never do that. Always go with the first instinct. First instinct is love. Second instinct fear. Never act on fear."

"Okay."

"I gotta go," Leanne said. "And so do you."

"Leanne," Wendy pleaded, "tell me something else."

"That most people are so afraid to fail they never fly. And that's a damn shame. We were all born with wings. Leap. You'll fly." The phone clicked, Leanne was gone.

Well, that answered that question, Leanne decidedly did not miss her. And Danny, Danny was preparing for summer season, swamped with birthing farm animals, scheduling workers and her clients calling her with summer garden plans. They had their own lives.

It was time for Wendy to make hers. She wasn't just making her own life for herself, she was doing it for everyone in her life. She wanted to make something of herself so she could have something to offer them in return.

She remembered standing at Leanne's doorway that day more than five months before, and she had the same feeling she had now, that if she walked in the door she wouldn't be the same anymore, everything was about to change. But back then she had nothing to lose; back then, if everything hadn't changed, she would have died.

She remembered this feeling of sweaty palms and the gulp in her throat, and the lead deadness in her body. This was called the crossroad, this was the moment of choice. To go backwards or go forward was always our choice, and if Wendy had learned anything, we could never go back. Backwards would burn us, and forward would evolve and liberate us.

Without any warning, the wind picked up, and the sky darkened, just like the swift and sudden change of a mood, and the air came rushing from behind her, sweeping toward the farms, rolling through the hills and rippling through the grass like the hair on a cat's back.

And that was when she felt something like a push at her back, right under her shoulder blades, and it pushed her body forward so deeply that it pressed her foot right down onto the gas pedal. She felt herself driving toward the cabins, as she did so, the methodical banging got louder and louder.

She found herself parked right at the door of the big main cabin, right under the swinging sign that said *Guest Check-In*. She looked at her face one more time in the rear-view mirror, saw behind the mask of the grown woman, into the eyes of the little girl who used to look in the mirror and dream of a big, full, happy healthy life.

This was one more chance to give that to her. So she took it. She took one more chance. She stepped out of the Jeep, took a big breath as the first few drops of rain fell from the gathering clouds.

The hammering vibrated through her body and she looked up, and saw a young man, younger than her by a few years at least, on a roof of a cabin to the right of the main building. He looked down at her and he stopped work for a moment. He had a guarded look, almost mean. Either mean, or cool. She didn't know. She often got them confused.

He had sandy blond hair that was being tussled by the wind, falling in his eyes that were shielded by dark black sunglasses.

"Hi," Wendy said.

He adjusted his work belt and tugged at a leather glove with his teeth.

"I knew I felt a storm coming," he said. Then he turned back to the roof and began to hammer again, deeply immersed in his own world in the air up there, even as the rain started to pour and soaked his broad back through his black t-shirt.

Well, okay then, Wendy mumbled beneath her breath. Then she looked back toward the Main Cottage. A medium-sized black and brown dog that looked like a miniature wolf sat on the front stoop, growling at the thunder that cracked across the sky. The sign on the front door said, "Welcome. We Are All Rescues Here."

She smiled, and stooped to pet the dog and rub the soft dent between its eyes. The dog looked up at her, right into her eyes, in that unabashedly intimate way animals and infants have.

Wendy looked right back into the depths of the brown eyes, and then she walked through the door, the chimes above her head ecstatically screaming out in the wind, and the dog following her in, right at her heels, like a graceful, protective shadow.

27.

Louis and Alba ran the center.

Louis, a sturdy bald man in a green fisherman's sweater and paint-splattered khakis, was manning the check-in desk when Wendy walked in with the wolf dog at her feet.

He told her Alba was out in the pasture feeding the animals.

Louis was a recovered coke addict who used to run the meat-packing district, and by that he meant he supplied all the coke to the clubs, half of which he owned before going broke, losing everything, and hitting rock bottom. He met Alba when Healing Moon Bay was just her small horse therapy farm. He had come after rehab and fell in love and never left.

"Alba healed me," he said.

"You're lucky," Wendy said.

"Don't think luck had anything to do with it," Louis shook his head.

"This place just has a way of doing that," he said.

"It's its dharma."

"Doing what?" Wendy asked.

"Matchmakin'. People who are drawn here tend to be drawn to each other."

"Well," Wendy straightened her back and lifted her head, looking at Louis, "those days are behind me. I'm not looking for that anymore."

Louis sized her up. "That's probably a good temporary plan, but certainly not a long-term one," he said.

Wendy felt warm pressure on her feet. She looked down to see that the dog had made a pillow of her moccasins.

She reached down to stroke its head, while asking Louis, "Why not? Why do people say that to me, when love has caused me so much trouble?"

"Maybe it caused the Old You so much trouble, but the more we heal, the more we attract healed people. Just like the more wounded you are, the more you attract the wounded type."

Wendy thought about that. It made sense. She nodded.

"I can see that," she said. She stood back up and readjusted her pony tail.

"But when are we healed?" she asked.

"When we're self- sourced," he said, "when we're of no harm to ourselves or others."

"I like that," she said, "I'm just here to work and heal."

"And we are happy to help you do both," said Louis. He handed her a gold key affixed to small golden horse.

"You're Cabin Twelve. Still early in the season, so you got it all to yourself."

"Thanks," Wendy said, taking the key chain. Then the dog stood back up on all fours and downward dogged. It stretched its neck and front paws out and pushed its rump up, its tail like a fur flag sticking straight in the air. She smiled, the animal reminded her of the mischievous wolf from *Sword in the Stone*. Then it sat back on its hind legs and watched Wendy and waited, looking to her for her next move.

"Well, looks like you're taking Sadie too," Louis laughed.

Wendy looked back into Sadie's deep brown eyes.

"I've always wanted a dog," she said.

"Well, I think Sadie's always wanted you. She's never taken such a liking," he laughed. "They choose us."

"Where'd you find her?" Wendy asked.

"Just out there on the highway," he said, pointing out toward the road, "someone must have just dumped her off."

Wendy nodded in empathy. "Sounds familiar," she said.

She rubbed behind the dog's ears. "I know your pain, girl."

"She was a hungry, scared little thing," said Louis, "she's done some real good healing, haven't you, Sade?" Sadie looked up at Louis knowingly.

"She hears and knows all," said Louis, "God is Dog and Dog is God."

Wendy tilted her head toward the door. "I'll go get my bags," she said.

"Need any help?" he asked.

"No," Wendy shook her head, "I can do it myself." After having been so weakly dependent on Peter, then a winter of mummified dependence on Leanne, Wendy relished doing everything herself.

"Alright," Louis said, "might want to take a hot bath and get a fire going, this rain doesn't look like it's letting up any time soon. We won't need you till the morning."

She turned to leave, with Sadie clicking her nails on the wood alongside her. She pressed open the door, and looked out at the deluge falling in thick sheets. The man's hammer continued to bang through the rain. She looked back once more at Louis.

"Louis?"

"Yep."

"What's his name? The man with the hammer."

Louis didn't look up, but chuckled as he shuffled a stack of paperwork.

"I'll give you a hint," he said, "it rhymes with God."

28.

Sadie was pressed into Wendy's belly under the soft white sheets of the bottom bunk bed, which was right in front of the wood stove in Cabin Twelve. The dog was curled up like a Cinnabon fur ball, and Wendy hugged her tighter because the fire had gone out over night and the cabin was freezing at 6:30 in the morning. She spooned the soft wolf dog into her body, synched up with her deeply present breathing and tried to fall back asleep.

Louis had asked to meet Alba at eight a.m. at the Stables. She thought she'd lie there until then, until the sun warmed up the little room through the windows, but then the banging began again. Sadie jumped up and off the bed, and began to howl at the door.

Wendy pulled the pillow over her head but it merely muffled the pervasive knocking and Sadie's cries. Finally, naked but for her socked feet, she slipped out and onto the cold wood floor, and rose, taking the patchwork quilt with her.

She flung open the cabin door to a rush of frosty morning air, and looked up to see the blond man again, this time banging shingles onto the side of the cabin next door. Sadie rushed across the grass toward where his ladder perched and put her paws on the bottom rung, as if she could crawl up to him. Wendy hoped to scoot inside before he saw her, but she stood there a second too long and he looked down at her in her socks and quilt cocoon on the porch.

"Hey," he called across the lawn. He was wearing a black sweater and tan Carhartts, with his tool belt around his waist.

"Hey," Wendy said, raising her hand from underneath the blanket.

"New girl," he smiled, raising his hammer in greeting. He was friendlier than he'd been in the storm.

"I'm Wendy," she smiled back.

"What?" he asked, cupping a hand to his ear.

"*Wendy*," she said louder.

"I can't hear you," he shook his head, and beckoned her closer.

Wendy walked in her socks across the wet morning grass. She stood directly beneath him on the side of the ladder, and Sadie settled down at her feet.

She looked up into his eyes. "Wendy," she said.

He nodded, taking her in.

"What's your name?" she asked.

"Todd," he told her. He pulled a nail from his belt and poised the hammer.

"Wait," Wendy said.

Todd looked down.

"Do you mind, holding off on that a bit? It's... it's still pretty early."

"You going back to sleep?" he asked.

"I don't know," she said. "Maybe."

"Well, I can't. Once I'm up, I'm up."

She thought about it and realized she'd never fall back asleep either. "Me too," she nodded.

"Anyway," he said, looking around. "You don't want to miss a minute of it here. It's the good life. I'm sure going to miss it."

"Where are you going?" Wendy asked, surprising herself by asking.

He didn't answer that, but said, "There's coffee in the main cabin. It's good. I made it. Have some and you'll be rearing to go."

She looked up at him through sleepy eyes. She realized she would normally be fretting about how she looked, talking to a man when she just woke up, standing in a bed sheet, but now that she had checked out of the dating game, it didn't matter. Now that her life wasn't programed to please men, or under the belief that only a man would make her happy and complete. She felt comfortable, as if who she was right at that moment, not who she could be, was enough. And while he was attractive, he wasn't one of those devastating men who had a waiting list of women. Beneath his cool guardedness was a warm humanity. He felt familiar, almost like this wasn't their first conversation.

Wendy narrowed her eyes. "Do we know each other?" she asked.

He looked back at her closely. He cocked his head. "I think I'd remember," he said. "Where ya from?"

"Kind of all over," Wendy said. "You?"

"Upstate New York," he said, fidgeting with the nails in his hand.

"Where?" Wendy asked.

"New Paltz," he said.

"What you do? I mean, for a living?"

He paused. "No offense, but I really don't feel like getting into my story. It's kinda why I came here. To leave it behind."

Wendy smiled. "Me too. I just forgot for a second. I don't feel like getting into my story either. Sorry, I was being polite... you know, small talk."

Todd smiled back but shook his head, his dark blond hair falling over his eyes. "You don't have to do that with me," he said,

"Got it," she said. Then she looked up and squinted into the sun. "I know this is weird, but I'm kind of sorry you're leaving."

Todd smiled. "It's for the best. I have a life to attend to back home. Had to come here to make sense of it."

"Did you?" she asked.

Todd sighed and looked down at the nails in his hands. "I don't know," he said. "I just know it's time to go back."

He looked at her again. "You know," he said, "to real life."

"What is that?" she asked.

He laughed at her. "Go get your coffee." He had a wry mischievous smile. He was so confident, but he wasn't cocky, just at ease with himself.

Wendy laughed back.

"I just don't think I've ever had one," she said, "so I'm curious."

"Coffee," he said. "Clothes first, maybe. Or not."

She laughed. She was so comfortable she had forgotten she was basically naked. "Okay," she said. "But...when are you leaving?"

"Don't worry," he said, "I'll see you. There's a dance tonight, the locals come and we host them in the barn. Lou's jazz band plays. You don't want to miss that."

"I'll check my schedule," Wendy said.

"That's a joke, right?"

She shrugged. "I tried."

He shook his head. "Again, you don't have to try with me," he said.

That relaxed Wendy more, she felt her shoulders drop. "Okay, I'm getting coffee," she said, even though she didn't really feel like leaving him. "And clothes."

"It's liquid cocaine," he said, turning back to his shingles, "you'll love it."

Wendy was quiet, and as if he could feel her hesitation, he swiveled back around. He gestured at her with his hammer.

"Not that I'm assuming you love, or even, did or do coke."

He cares what I think, Wendy registered. It felt nice.

"It's okay," she said, "I sure did once."

"Okay, maybe I could tell," he said.

"I was really wild once," she told him.

"And I hope you'll be again," he said, "just the good kind of wild. There's a difference."

"What is it?" she asked, "the good kind of wild?"

He paused, and then surveyed the land again.

"These animals will teach you," he said, "they're present. At one with their instincts. Un-self-conscious. Free. They're just, alive. So totally themselves. We forget there's no one else to be."

She nodded.

"I think you're going to like it here, Wendy."

She looked up at Todd, the morning sun shining around his head like a halo.

"I already do," she said, and then headed back to her cabin to throw on her jeans and sweater. She felt like for the first time in her life, she was in the right place in the right time, and she could just stop seeking and relax into it.

She and Sadie were half way across the lawn when she heard Todd call out.

"Hey Wendy," he said.

She looked back over her shoulder. And he stared at her, almost like he recognized her too.

Then he said, "Bring me one too, please."

Wendy turned back around and smiled to herself. He made her feel less alone.

"You got it," she told him.

29.

In the application process to work at Healing Moon Bay, Wendy had told Alba and Louis of her story, and her fall in the fall. So Alba let Wendy know she had no intention of placing her on a horse right away, even if they were a stable full of therapy horses.

"I will tell ya," Alba said, handing her a shovel, "these horses are better than any therapist you'll ever see."

Alba squinted at her in the early light. "Ever been to a shrink?"

"On and off since I was 12," Wendy said.

"Lie to them, secretly hate them, and count the seconds till they'd refill your pills?" she asked Wendy.

"Something like that," Wendy conceded. "Or," she smiled up at Alba, "a lot like that."

"I was always too good with words to tell the truth," Alba shook her head and laughed at herself. "A real silver tongue. You could say my charm harmed. But you can't lie to these animals, and these animals never lie. Trying to be someone we're not makes us sick, but you can't pull that with these horses. They ask for authenticity and presence. You have to be in your truth with them, and being in your truth heals you."

"You liked pills too?" Wendy asked.

"Well, I didn't just like pills, I got so hooked on them they damn near killed me. Pills and wine. The Housewife Special. It was Valium and Klonopin; these days it's cat's claw and turmeric, chugged down with herbal tea."

"I miss wine," Wendy said.

"What do you miss about it?"

"I guess just not having to be stuck with myself, all the time. Getting to feel something else."

"You miss escaping."

"Aren't we allowed?"

"The thing is, you think you want out, but you actually want in." She looked over at Wendy.

"Keep going," she said.

Wendy thought maybe Alba was offering her some sort of esoteric wisdom to heal her wounds, but Alba just nodded at the piles of horse manure that filled the stable.

"Oh," she said, scooping a pile and lifting it into the old blue wheelbarrow.

"Substance is the band aid. But sobriety is the sustainable surgery. You think wine's the trip? Nah, that always leads to the same dark place. This life, this experience, is the never-ending, always expanding, wild mysterious trip, woman."

Wendy nodded. She was still suddenly thirsting hard for a glass of wine.

Alba paused and rested her foot on her shovel and slugged from her portable coffee mug. "You're coming to the dance tonight right? You'll only know me and Lou. 'Less of course you've met Todd too."

"Um, I did," Wendy cleared her throat, "it's too bad he's leaving, he seems pretty great." Wendy couldn't stop thinking about him, even as she reminded herself she had sworn off men. It was definitely an addiction, to focus on men and not her own evolution and well being. She shook it off and returned to shoveling manure with meditative scoops.

Alba didn't look up from her stall but said, "He certainly is great. His wife's great too."

Wendy bristled. There it was. *Good*, she thought, that was over before it began. There'd be no boy distraction on her healing journey. The last thing she wanted to bring into her new life was man drama. Drinking drama, or man drama. That aside, her curiosity got the best of her.

"He's married?" she asked. She hadn't seen a ring because of those big carpentry gloves he wore.

"Well, it's not perfect, but no marriage is."

"He didn't say anything about that."

"He's pretty private. A good man like that."

"Hey," Alba said, walking into Wendy's stall and taking the shovel from her, "How about you go brush Gina?" She cocked her head in the direction of a massive caramel-colored horse with eyes like wet brown saucers. "She could use a little love."

Alba handed Wendy a dark brown bristled grooming brush.

"Go gentle when you brush her, she's been through it."

"Got it," Wendy said. She approached the horse who stared her directly in her eyes, as if to say, "OK, but I'm watching you," and she began to brush Gina, gently, and suddenly, she imagined she was brushing her mother's hair, even back in her mother's sick bed, the one she'd abandoned. As if she could have stayed and not run. What if she'd *gone in, and not out.*

And she grew even more tender with the horse, imagining she could touch her mother just one more time, and show her, with care, how much she desperately loved her. Back then, she was too young to know about the sands in the hourglass. She just brushed Gina's neck and mane like that, as softly and lovingly as she could.

And then it was as if she could almost hear her mother, whispering to her, "Treat yourself with this tenderness, treat you with the tenderness you would treat me, with your own little girl." Wendy breathed in sharply. She hoped she'd have a little girl someday. She'd wanted one with James but thought they would have all the time in the world to do that. Now she didn't know if or how that would ever happen, or if she truly felt worthy or capable of being a Mother. She was only just learning to care for herself. She recognized that the word Mother held the word "other," and that to be a mother meant caring for the other. She wondered if she was capable of that. She so wanted to be. She fell against the horse and let Gina's sturdy strength hold her up. Gina craned her neck around and pressed her massive felt nose flat against Wendy's forehead.

At first Wendy lurched back, startled.

"She's kissing you," Alba said, "let her."

Wendy sucked in some cold air and leaned back in toward Gina, who went for the kind kiss again, and as she did so, she stared at Wendy with those eyes like planets, almost emotionless, but with the same unflinching, unapologetic intimacy as Sadie.

Wendy's eyes darted over to Alba, waiting for her next cue.

"She won't bite, I promise," Alba said.

"Okay," Wendy whispered, looking back into Gina's eyes.

"Just borrow from her strength. Bet she's giving you some of that."

Gina removed her nose from Wendy's brow, and then Wendy threw her arms around the horse's neck and burrowed into her so tight she couldn't see anything, she just rose and fell with the massive animal's warm breath. Now it felt like Gina was mothering her, and it was strong, nurturing, protective energy.

"Looks like true love to me," Alba said.

"I never want to let her go," replied Wendy.

"You don't have to," Alba said.

"Everything goes," Wendy heard herself say, her voice muffled in Gina's thick neck, "everyone eventually leaves."

"If you think that, then that will be true for you. But some people stay, Wendy. Some things really do last."

Wendy couldn't remember that ever being the case. Then Alba lifted the wheelbarrow, which was now filled to the brim with hay and manure, and maneuvered the heavy load away from the stalls. "See you at the dance, Miss Wendy."

Wendy wasn't so sure. She didn't feel like dealing with the complicated feeling in her sternum about Todd, the one that made her a little excited and sick and self conscious at once. It was like how she avoided bars now. If you didn't go in you didn't have to deal with the temptation. She still didn't know what she'd do if she were actually offered a glass of wine.

"Todd's last night, if you want to say goodbye."

Wendy waved but tried to look blank, as if his name barely registered in her body.

30.

It was 7 o'clock, and Wendy and Sadie had been lying in bed listening to Lou's jazz band echo across the field from the main hall for over an hour.

Wendy was scrolling through her phone with an adamant feeling that she was missing real life to look at others' lives on Instagram. She remembered an Anthropology course senior year where the teacher had told her how eventually technology would become a mode of keeping us all separate and asleep. And Wendy felt separate, and asleep. She'd lit a fire but kept the windows open to hear the dance, and she tapped her bare feet on the comforter impatiently to the music that drifted in through the screens. Sadie swished her tail along with Wendy's impatient feet, then she pawed at Wendy's belly. Wendy absentmindedly reached over and petted Sadie's head, her eyes still locked into the Instagram scroll. Then Sadie whined, low and deep.

Wendy looked over at her.

"What, girl?" she asked. But she knew, Sadie wanted out. And so did Wendy.

Wendy slid off the bed and plunked her slippered feet on the floor.

"Fine," she said. She went to the mirror and pulled back her hair. She cat-eyed her eyes with black liner and painted her lips red. She guessed she looked alright, although she still barely recognized herself. Still, she remembered to be kind to herself, she remembered to acknowledge the insides over the outsides. *"Hi,"* she said sweetly to herself in the mirror. Her whole body sighed and her face softened. It was her own kindness she had always been looking for.

She pulled a big black V-neck cashmere sweater over her head and slipped into tight jeans, and then she walked through a cloud of her mother's *Tresor* perfume.

"We'll just go for a second," she told Sadie, pulling suede black moccasins on. "But we are not," and she shook a finger at the pup, and then she did that thing where she pointed into her eyes with two fingers and then Sadie's eyes with two fingers, "do you hear me, not making this about Todd. We're going to be polite."

Sadie slinked to the door and scratched at it with her long black nails. Wendy opened the door and stepped through it with her head high as Sadie lurched out and bounded across the moonlit fields. But she found her step became less and less confident as she approached the big wooden building, with its gooey golden light gleaming from its windows, and the sound of chatter and saxophone and strings spilling out its doors.

By the time she reached it she was positively shaking, like a wallflower showing up stag to a high school dance. Sadie shot up across the porch and in through the open door.

"Sadie," Wendy hissed.

"Sadie!!!" she yell-whispered. Wendy put one trepidatious moccasin on the porch. She craned her neck through the doors to look for her, but Sadie was gone, she'd disappeared into the bodies of the dance. With one quick peek, Wendy didn't recognize anyone she knew, meaning Alba, Louis, or Todd. She stepped back into the darkness.

She'd lost all confidence, and as she waited for it to return, she lurked outside of the hall like Michael Myers, before completely giving up and then turning to head back to her cabin. She walked alongside the hall in the grass, stealing glances through the windows, pretending to herself she didn't know what she was looking for, when he caught her eye.

He was dancing in the center of the room with Alba to Louis's sax solo of "Moonlight in Vermont," swirling Alba round and round as she laughed like a child. Wendy smiled at sight of the two of them.

He caught Alba, in her black dress and big goddessy crystal pendant, as she fell back into his strong arms. He was clad in a plaid shirt with a cotton tan tie. Alba was right. He was a good man. And dammit, a good dancer. And anyway, it wasn't any of Wendy's business whether he was married or not. They had just met. She caught those temptressy, dramatic feelings and relaxed, *nice try, Old Me,* she thought.

She stepped a little closer to the barn to watch the dance. Maybe she'd go in now, and practice social sobriety. Todd and Alba swirled away through the crowd and she suddenly lost sight of them. Or, maybe in ten minutes.

She needed a better view, so she climbed up on a pile of old wooden crates that sat beneath the window. She rested her elbows on the sill, outside with the crickets and the breeze in the trees. Inside they were gleeful and warm, their cheeks glowed and the air was thick with laughter.

Wendy felt this was all too familiar, to be outside looking in, to be waiting at windows while others lived, and she was ready to get up, to go in or go home, but she was transfixed, under a spell, watching Todd and Alba dance. She was lost in the way Todd moved, with the grace he held Alba, with that glint of both sweetness and mischief in his eyes. Alba's head rested dreamily on his shoulder as he glided her around the floor.

It was then that Todd looked up and caught sight of Wendy, perched on the crate, staring in. She ducked fast. At first she thought it was possible he hadn't really seen her, just something out of the window, but when she peeked up to check, he was still looking at her.

She rose her hand sheepishly and then he took his hand off Alba's back and raised his in return. And for a moment it was just the two of them staring at each other as she sat there on that old crate, waiting until she knew what to do.

But then he smiled at her and she smiled back, and that made it all normal and friendly. She relaxed back into her perch on the crate and that's when she felt it crash beneath her.

31.

"Wendy," Todd said. "Wendy," he pressed. He shook her body alive in his arms.

She fluttered her eyes open, sprawled out in his plaid-covered arms, her head back heavy and loose like in the Pieta.

Todd's, Alba's and Sadie's concerned faces came into focus above her.

"Oh God," Wendy said.

"Just me," Todd quipped.

Sadie licked her anxiously and Wendy scrunched her face under the kisses. "Thank you, Sadie," she said.

"Are you okay?" Todd asked.

Alba pulled Sadie back by her leather collar and asked her to sit, and then she kissed her dark brown head. "Good job taking care of your Mommy, Sadie," Alba told her, giving her another reaffirming pat, even though Sadie still looked on with wild, worried eyes. Wendy reached out and softly stroked Sadie's leg, and then looked up at Todd.

"I'm totally fine. Just totally embarrassed."

"You could have used the door," Todd said. Wendy rolled her eyes. Alba cleared her throat and stood up. "Well, I'll let you two kids… sort this out. Glad you're alright, Wendy. But he's right. Next time, why don't you just come on in?"

"Thank you, Alba, I will. Still a little scared of being social. Last time I was out at night I blacked out in front of Drew Barrymore. Last thing I remember was her rolling her eyes at something I said as I stumbled across the backstage room. That sucked, I grew up wanting to be her best friend. "

"Yikes," Alba said. "You don't need anymore of those nights in your life. Won't have 'em here neither, you can count on it. Drug free zone for a reason. Alright, now I'm really off. Come on in if you feel like it," she nodded back toward the barn.

"Thanks Alba," Wendy said, and Todd gave her a nod as she walked away.

"Do you know what happened?" Todd asked. "How you fell, can you remember?"

She thought a minute. She looked back up at the mess of white stars in the sky. She once heard a story where when you got to heaven, you could choose your favorite memory to live in for eternity. She didn't know why she thought of that just then, as his fingers dug deep into her back and he breathed more heavily, she could feel it on her face. And, he could have put her down by now, she realized. She looked back into his eyes, and she smiled, she was so comfortable she could fall asleep.

"I do remember," she answered, "I mean, I wish I could black it out-"

"No you don't," he said. "Stop it with the self degrading jokes. You don't want to black out any moments of your life anymore. Trust me, you don't want to miss your life. At the end of it you'll be really bummed out if you did. My dad was a drunk. Worst way to waste a life."

"OK," Amy agreed, it was an old pattern, to speak poorly of herself like that, and she was grateful for the reminder.

"I remember. I was standing on this crate…" She stopped for a minute. "Watching you dance, I mean *the* dance. Like, everyone, all of it. And then the crate just shattered."

He nodded, but it felt a little like what really wanted to be said was just under the surface, like the truth was a person coming up for air from the water, and they she just pressed its head back under.

He looked over his shoulder at the wooden wreckage. "It was kind of a long fall," he said, "I'm just glad you're okay. I was saving you a dance."

The fall had knocked her filter free. "Why would you do that?" she asked. "You're married."

"Did you Google me or something?" he shot back.

"No," she said. "You Google me?"

He shrugged, but it was a yes shrug, "It's not a big deal. I Google everyone. You... you know, in case you were a serial killer. or something."

"Ah," Wendy said. "But what if I had just killed one person. Like, not *serial*. Like a one-time whoops." She was hoping to deflect him from thinking about what he actually might have found.

He laughed in spite of himself. "Shut up, Wendy," he said, a little shy now.

He paused, then seemed to take a chance. "Why not Google me?"

She smiled. "No wifi password."

"Ah," he nodded.

Then the truth came back up for air, and this time she let it breathe.

"And I didn't want to know anymore about you after..."

"After what?"

"Well, after I found out that you were married."

"Oh," he said.

She bit her lip. They were quiet for a moment.

"Can you let me go?" she asked, looking down at his arms that held her. "I'm pretty sure I'm ok."

"Oh, sure," he said. He cleared his throat and gently placed her on the ground.

"This..." she started to say *is not why I'm here and not something I want to involve myself in- married man drama-* but she didn't want to be presumptuous about the chemistry she felt. It was very possible it was one sided, even though someone had once told her chemistry was never one sided. Crushes, yes, but the electric volleyball feeling of tossing energy back and forth, lighting each other up as you went, was a two person game. "I should go back to my cabin," she said instead, "and ice my butt."

He laughed.

"Guess you're too beat up for that dance," he said.

"As friends?" she raised an eyebrow then she shook her head.

"It does work," he said.

"No it doesn't, not in my life, anyway. It always gets weird with men and women. No matter what."

"Let's just unweird it," he said. He dusted off his hands and held them in the air. "Done. It's not weird."

"Can we un-do the part where I fell off a crate?"

"No," he said, "I want to keep that part."

"Fine," she brushed the dirt off the back of her jeans, "can I just hobble back to my cabin alone like a wounded animal now?" she asked.

"Lemme walk you."

"No, it's okay," she told him, trying her best to put an energetic wall between them, even though, it felt like the opposite of things falling apart as they had with James. It felt like things rapidly coming together. The only chance to stop it was to get away from him. "Come on, Sadie." She made a half-assed attempt at a whistle, but it just sounded like "*pfffft*."

"You suck at whistling," Todd smiled.

She stifled a smile. It was true.

"Please let me walk you," he said.

"No," she said firmly.

He crossed his arms in defiance. She watched a muscle flex beneath the plaid and was mad at herself for noticing.

"You sure quit a lot of things before they quit you," he said. Her face flushed hot, wondering what else he might know. "That's not fair," she said, "I didn't Google you."

He shrugged. "Nothing to Google really. I'm a carpenter from upstate New York. Work for a green company. I just got lost. Wasn't a good husband or even person anymore. A friend had been here and seemed, a little closer to happier when he came back. So I took some time here too."

Wendy nodded. "A carpenter, like Jesus."

"Well I've made a lot more mistakes than him."

"And I'm not going to be another one."

"Who says it would be one?" Todd asked. "I meant to just hang out."

He scuffed some dirt with his foot. "Anyway, do you really believe in mistakes?"

Wendy reeled through her mind's film of all her drunken nights. She sure did. "I'm going back to my cabin now," she said.

"It's pre-season. We're the only people here under sixty. We have the whole night," he looked at his watch. "It's seven thirty. Young. The night's barely a teenager. Come on."

She wanted to, but she still felt her inner pause, which always meant not to move forward. She felt it like the yellow warning of traffic lights, *slow down*.

"No," she said. Then she took off running despite the pain across the field toward her cabin.

But he was fast, and she soon realized he had caught up with her, and he was running alongside her in his construction boots.

"High school track," he said out of the corner of his mouth.

She was so surprised she started to laugh, and it echoed across the fields. She was laughing so hard, those big full-body laughs, that she didn't see the branch that tripped her, and she fell down in the grass.

"Oh my God, I give up," she said.

Todd fell down next to her laughing, and Sadie joined them, flopping beside them, panting heavily. It seemed like they were directly under the moon, she was flooding them with light so bright Wendy had to squint to look over at him.

"You're relentless," she said.

"Yep," he said proudly.

Then he pulled a silver flask out of his jean pocket and held it, glinting, in the moon's light.

"What should we toast to," he asked. She sighed, heavily. She hadn't told him she and drinking weren't a healthy combination. She hadn't told him she seemed to do a hell of a lot better without it, that it turned her into someone she wasn't proud of. She hadn't told him in the morning it made her want to die. But even so, she had been pining for it, just one drink. One goodbye drink, before he left for his life, before they never saw each other again, couldn't hurt.

"A brand new life," she said.

He raised the flask. "To a brand new life," he said.

He took a hearty swig of Bourbon, then passed it to her. Her heart thudded, she saw warning signs within, of the yellow, orange, then red spinning lights, but she drank it anyway. And the first sip made her whole body warm and relaxed, and she thought maybe this time it wouldn't be so bad.

Then they laid there, under the stars, passing the flask and talking and laughing like old friends reunited. And then, then she got really, really, really drunk.

And the last thing she remembered was staring up at the stars, and him asking her, "Why were you really in the window of the barn?"

Her eyes were trying to fix on just one specific star, she chose a tiny twinkling one, not a big glaring show off. She liked under dogs. "I guess I just wanted to watch you," she said, the liquid honesty coursing through her veins.

"You just had to ask," he said. And then he was quiet, she could literally only hear crickets. When Wendy turned and looked at him, he was staring straight at her.

"I'll watch you, and you can watch me," he said.

"Ok," she'd said, as his eyes looked into hers, and she unselfconsciously took in his handsome, familiar face.

32.

Wendy woke with Sadie huddled along her naked body under the sheets. She kissed Sadie's snoot and rubbed her belly before she felt the anxiety of the hangover flood her system. Her hand stopped petting Sadie mid stroke. She peered over the side of the bed, where her clothes lay in a messy pool. She racked her mind for a memory of what happened with Todd. She looked down at Sadie, who looked back at her with big worried brown eyes.

"It's ok, girl. I'm ok. But what the hell happened last night?"

Sadie was silent. She nuzzled back down into the sheets. Wendy lay her heavy head back down on the pillow, feeling the sickness of the alcohol rise in her stomach. The birds chirped outside and a cold refreshing wind blew through the window. She wished she had the energy to make a fire. Sadie probably needed to go out. So much for a brand new start. So much for commitment to health. She hoped she hadn't seen anyone but Todd. She hoped Alba or Lou didn't know she'd gotten drunk on her first night. She wanted to run away, but she knew she couldn't, there wasn't anywhere left to go. She fell back asleep for another hour before Sadie woke her up, scratching at the door to go out. Wendy got up naked and crossed over to the door. She hid behind it as she opened it for the dog to slink outside. She stood there for what felt like ten minutes, waiting for Sadie to come back.

She peered her head around the door, careful to keep her body behind it. Out on the lawn, Todd was massaging Sadie's head, and the dog looked deeply content to stay there all morning. He was in his worn flannel and Carhartt's and was working his strong fingers behind Sadie's ears. Wendy sighed. He was the last person she wanted to see, usually after she blacked out she would avoid whoever she had been with, if she had been with anyone, for as long as she could. She could never face what she had done wasted or who she had done it with. She always through the baby out with the bathwater, or, the person out with the alcohol.

"Sadie," Wendy croaked. Todd looked up.

"Morning, Wendy." He said, warmly.

She mustered together her dignity, despite being naked behind the door with a pounding headache and a blank page from the night before.

"I thought you'd have left by now," she said.

"I'm on my way out," he said. "Glad I saw you before I did."

"Well, bye," she said. "Have a nice life."

He smiled at her, laughing at her feigned toughness.

"OK, then, you too." He saluted her for affect.

"Good luck with your wife," she quipped.

He stood up and crossed his arms. "Thanks. I guess we'll see." Then he cocked his head and looked more closely at her. Suddenly she flashed back to them on the grass, staring at each other in starlight.

She blanched. *"Sadie,"* she said, firmly.

"You ok, Wendy?" he asked.

"Yes, I'm fine. Just.. .tired."

What more was there to say to a man you liked who had a wife? If you were a good woman, nothing.

"Sadie. In the house."

"Well," he said. "You have an email, or something?" he asked.

"Yes," Wendy said. "But it's... sort of complicated." This was getting more awkward by the moment. Of course *he* wasn't hungover. He'd probably cleared his head with one cup of coffee. Meanwhile her head was on fire and stomach felt full of acidic soup. She needed to lie back down. She'd need the whole day to recover, she would suffer the consequences for days.

"Well mine's not," he said. "Toddmiles@yahoo."

I should have guessed he still had a yahoo address, she thought. Next he'll say he never really checks it.

"I don't really check it, but—"

Wendy rolled her eyes, but laughed in spite of herself. He was comfortably predictable. She looked down at Sadie and patted her thigh. "Come on girl," she said to the dog, who had started to trot back over to the cabin. Wendy began to close the door. She looked up once more at Todd and gave him a small smile. "Drive safe."

He gave her a weird look. "Will do. Thanks Wendy. Hope everything works out for you."

"I'll be fine."

"You already are."

She also knew he was going to say that.

"Bye," she said.

"Bye." He looked a little hurt, like he didn't want to end it that way, but he was following Wendy's lead. She watched him settle into his truck through the window and drive slowly toward the main road. Then she spent the whole day in bed wanting to die with the taste of whiskey in her mouth, remembering why she had sworn off men and alcohol for good.

And then the next day, she started over.

APRIL.

A month later Wendy was out for a ride on Gina.

She was calm and content, even confident. She had been learning how to stay in her serene center, not let every little thing knock her over. She carried her body like a Queen's carriage, her back was straight, her head was high, her lungs were open to the April air and she moved like water with Gina, the strong mare beneath her legs. She was reflecting on how it had been the best month and a half of her life. She was practicing response over reaction, and it kept her out of drama. She was focused on her inner beauty, not outer, but she found the more beautiful she felt inside, the more beautiful she felt on the outside. She was moved by her inner voice, not the outer voices. And every time she listened to it, the inner voice grew louder and clearer. She could self Mother herself, check in on her own needs and feelings and not make them someone else's problem. She wasn't dependent on others or substance, she was autonomous, self-reliant. She had begun to feel like a safe person, like she was safe for herself and others. She used to feel like the storm, now she was the port in the storm. The better care she learned to take of herself, the better she could care for others.

Every day since Todd had left had been about service to others, and after a self indulgent, gluttonous life, that was healing her. She thought about how healthy Danny was, and it was this, this endless service and movement kept you out of your own swamp head. She had learned to care for herself through a healthy routine of good food and good sleep and good exercise through the animal chores. Her body was growing strong and lithe, her head clear. She woke up with the sun and fed the pigs, sheep, cows and horses. She shoveled manure and hay and learned to love the smell and the methodic movement. Alba had asked her to lead women's moon circles when the summer came, and she was studying the Summer Moons' meanings and writing blueprints for the circles. She took Sadie on long leash-less walks through the woods, where they would sit and connect to the earth. And Sadie, she had given her even more purpose, and the dog loved her with the endless gratitude of a rescue, and Wendy loved the feeling of reliability, which caring for Sadie fostered.

And being rarely on the internet, that was helping her sanity. Except suddenly she had an inner tug- she should check her email. It had been too long and it felt like there was something she needed to see.

"Remind me to check email," she said to Gina, who flicked an ear carelessly.

Normally she didn't have any interest whatsoever to be online. Instead she found herself reading books, meditating, and writing in her journal at night by the fire, if she wasn't having tea and dessert with Lou and Alba. She'd set up a little altar to the Goddess in one corner of the room and spent five minutes before the sun rose and chores began to center, ask to be guided and protected, and offer gratitude. The consistency of devotion worked. She felt fulfilled, she felt like she might have found her way into the doorway of her life. She didn't want to be anyone, or anywhere else. She no longer felt outside looking in. *She was in.*

Except, today she felt a little off.

"Hold up, girl," she she pulled Gina's reins in gently. She felt sick to her stomach. She knew what it was, she thought. Those eggs at breakfast had been pretty runny, and the milk in her coffee had looked a little spoiled.

That had to be it. She felt herself lurch off of the side of the mare and throw up her breakfast. Gina looked back at her, eyebrows raised, a concerned look with big brown eyes.

"I'm fine. I feel fine. Just, queasy." They turned around anyway, and headed back to the stables. She returned Gina to her field and headed off to lunch, where she sat down next to Alba, who told her she looked pale.

"I do? I was just out riding Gina."

Alba placed the back of her hand to Wendy's head. "You don't have a temperature."

"Honestly I feel fine. I am a little queasy. I think it was the eggs this morning. They were weird."

"You're all that's weird around here, those eggs were same as they've always been."

The smell of lunch wafted in from over the counter. Normally, Wendy would have been excited about fish tacos. Not today. The smell punched her right in the empty gut.

"Um, Alba, I'm gonna skip lunch. Just, got a lot on my mind."

Alba sat there with her *nothing gets past me* look. But she said, "Do your thing, woman. I'll happily eat yours."

Wendy rushed out into the open air. What was wrong with her? She took big gasps with her lungs and fished a couple quarters from her jeans pocket on her way to the vending machine on the side of the lodge. She slid the quarters in the slot and out plunked a gingerale, which she downed in greedy gulps. She was exhausted, in a way she hadn't felt since her month of healthy living at the lodge. She saw Sadie sleeping under a tree in the sun near the stables and thought she had the right idea.

"Sadie," she called. The wolf mix lifted her head at her mother's voice.

"Wanna nap with me?" she asked. Sadie followed her into the cabin where all the windows were open and the bed was still unmade from when Wendy had risen for her chores at 6 am. She slid under the sheets in her jeans and t-shirt and Sadie spooned into her belly like a fur covered hot water bottle.

"Mmm, thank you Sadie," Wendy murmured. She was dozing off to sleep when she remembered to check her email. She retrieved her laptop from underneath the bed and found the wifi connection. She saw she had almost a hundred unread emails and she balked. She didn't have the energy to deal with them. But two stood out. The first was from Danny. "OPEN IMMEDIATELY," said the subject.

"Hey Girlfriend," Danny wrote. *"So I'm a big fat liar. I did steal your diaries. And I sent them to a bunch of publishers because I knew you never would. This little press*

called Blue Feather, in Taos, New Mexico loved them! Now they need to talk to you. Call them. Don't forget me when you're famous...for the right reasons. Love, D."

Wendy didn't know how to process that. Embarrassment? Excitement. Nerves. Disbelief, gratitude for Danny certainly, for she certainly hadn't thought the diaries were worth...and there was that nausea again. She managed to gulp it back down. She scrolled down to the other email that caught her eye- from Todd. She took a breath, holding her stomach to calm it, and clicked the message open.

"Hi Wendy, I hope you're doing well. I just wanted you to know I am thinking about you and hoping all is well with you. And despite the complicated nature of our situation, I will never regret what we shared that night. Give Sadie a rub for me, Todd."

Wendy deleted it, she wasn't starting a correspondence with a married man. Her karma had only begun to clear from her old life.

She flopped back down in the sheets and tried to fall back asleep. *What we shared?* She pulled Sadie in tighter to her belly. *All we shared was a flirtation and a flask,* she thought.

But then she lurched back up. Suddenly, her body remembered what had been blacked out. She saw herself and Todd in that starlit field. Then she remembered how he had rolled over to face her, and his arm fell around her waist and he had pulled her closer. And all she could really remember was the fusion of their bodies, natural, like stars colliding on an inevitable, destined path.

"Oh, God," she moaned. She leapt up, and Sadie flew off the bed, startled, skittering across the floor. Wendy ran to the toilet and threw up once more. She heard Sadie's long nails tap across the wood, and Wendy looked up to see her wolfish head, her neck craned around the bathroom door, looking in at her mother on her knees. Wendy fumbled under the sink for her make up bag. Deep in the blush and foundation caked depths was an old pregnancy test from her days with Peter- they'd bought it in a British pharmacy in Manchester. She read the side of the package. It would read *True* for Pregnant, and *False* for Not.

Five minutes later, a result revealed itself in blue ink.

"Oh, Sadie," she said.

"*I'm ... True.*"

And then she started to cry, tears of fear and joy.

52058413R00182

Made in the USA
San Bernardino, CA
09 August 2017